HUSBAND AND WIVES

Husbands and wives, secrets and lies ...
The brilliant new Milt Kovak mystery

When Mary Hudson is discovered on her kitchen floor, bludgeoned to death with a meat tenderizer, Sheriff Milt Kovak of Prophesy County, Oklahoma, and his psychiatrist wife Dr Jean McDonnell are drawn into a murder investigation that is as intriguing as it is chilling. It soon emerges that Mary's husband, Jerry, is a polygamist, and the family belong to a church called the New Saints Tabernacle. As Milt and Jean delve deeper into the church and its customs, they soon become embroiled in a murky and mysterious world.

A Selection of Recent Titles by
Susan Rogers Cooper

The Milt Kovak Series
DEAD MOON ON THE RISE
DOCTORS AND LAWYERS AND SUCH
LYING WONDERS
VEGAS NERVE
SHOTGUN WEDDING *
RUDE AWAKENING *
HUSBAND AND WIVES *

The E J Pugh Mysteries
HOME AGAIN, HOME AGAIN
THERE WAS A LITTLE GIRL
A CROOKED LITTLE HOUSE
NOT IN MY BACK YARD
DON'T DRINK THE WATER
ROMANCED TO DEATH *
FULL CIRCLE *

The Kimmey Kruse Series
FUNNY AS A DEAD COMIC
FUNNY AS A DEAD RELATIVE

*available from Severn House

HUSBAND AND WIVES

Susan Rogers Cooper

Severn House Large Print
London & New York

This first large print edition published 2013
in Great Britain and the USA by
SEVERN HOUSE PUBLISHERS LTD of
19 Cedar Road, Sutton, Surrey, England, SM2 5DA.
First world regular print edition published 2012 by
Severn House Publishers Ltd., London and New York.

British Library Cataloguing in Publication Data

Cooper, Susan Rogers. author.
  Husband and wives. -- Large print edition. -- (A Milt Kovak
  mystery ; 11)
  1. Kovak, Milton (Fictitious character)--Fiction.
  2. Sheriffs--Oklahoma--Fiction. 3. Detective and mystery
  stories. 4. Large type books.
  I. Title II. Series
  813.6-dc23

  ISBN-13: 978-0-7278-9622-3

Severn House Publishers support the Forest Stewardship Council™
[FSC™], the leading international forest certification organisation. All
our titles that are printed on FSC certified paper carry the FSC logo.

Printed and bound in Great Britain by
TJ International Ltd, Padstow, Cornwall.

To my daughter, Evin, for her love and support, and without whom E.J.'s books would never have a plot. But mostly, I want to thank her sincerely for giving me grandchildren.

ACKNOWLEDGMENTS

I would like to thank the usual suspects: my friend, writer, and reader, Jan Grape, for her critique; and my agent, Vicky Bijur, for her help and support.

ONE

Milt Kovak – Monday

You'd think my life would have gotten easier, what with me having a second-in-command and four deputies, and a new civilian aid answering the phones instead of Gladys who had finally, thank God, retired, and God bless her all to hell and back.

In case you're not familiar with Prophesy County, Oklahoma, and the way the sheriff's department does business, let me set you straight. I'm Milt Kovak, sheriff of Prophesy County, and my second-in-command is Emmett Hopkins who, besides being my BFF, used to be police chief of Longbranch, the county seat of Prophesy County, before some political mess screwed that up for him. And my four deputies are Jasmine Bodine Hopkins, my long-time deputy and Emmett's new wife; Anthony Dobbins, Prophesy County's first African-American deputy sheriff; Anthony's cousin, Nita Dobbins Skitteridge, not only our second African-American deputy but our second female deputy as well (got a two-fer there!); and my long-time

9

deputy (can't get rid of him) Dalton Pettigrew, who is a really nice fella but stupid as a bag of rocks. Dalton's mama is the former sheriff's first cousin, so nepotism got him in, and guilt on my part keeps him here. But, like I said, he's a real nice fella.

Our civilian aid mans the phones and the radios and acts as sort of a receptionist/ secretary. Gladys had been doing that job since before my time, and my time started back in the late seventies, so God only knows how long she'd been there. All I know is once our old sheriff left she got the notion that she was boss of everything and treated me – duly appointed sheriff in charge and finally duly *elected* sheriff of Prophesy County – like I was the skinny one on her football team and she'd changed her name to Bob Stoops (in case you don't know, that's the coach of the finest football team in America – The University of Oklahoma Sooners). But finally she got so old that she'd be making more money with social security and her pension than she made working and her husband, bless him, begged her to retire. We gave her a big old party, and the next day I hired a young gal who'd gotten to Longbranch in a very strange way. Her name is Holly Humphries and for some reason she seems smitten with my deputy Dalton, which somehow makes him seem a little less stupid.

Now on this particular day, a Monday (isn't that always when the shit hits the fan?), Holly came into my office and said, 'Sheriff, we've got a problem.' I don't like little Miss Holly just because she's not Gladys. There's a lot to like. She's pretty, she's smart, and she calls me 'Sheriff,' unlike Gladys who just called me Milt.

The problem was that it was three thirty in the afternoon and Emmett was in Oklahoma City at a seminar, Jasmine was just finishing up giving a safety assembly at a high school in the far south side of the county, Anthony and his cousin Nita were both out in the north of the county at a tractor-trailer/four-car pile-up, and Dalton was off duty and taking his mother to a specialist in Tulsa. That's why Holly said what she did, which was, 'Sheriff, we've got a problem.'

'What's that?' I asked, looking up from the paperwork on my desk.

'I've got a girl on the phone and she sounds hysterical. I can't make any sense of what she's saying, and there's nobody here to help me,' Holly said. Then she got a stricken look on her face. 'Except you, of course.'

I looked at my phone and saw the line that was blinking. 'I'll take it,' I said, and heard Holly breathe a sigh of relief.

I picked up the phone and said, 'This is Sheriff Kovak. To whom am I speaking?'

'Oh my God oh my God oh my God ...'

'Calm down now, honey,' I said in the soothing tones I'd learned at a seminar in Dallas. It was a child's voice, and endearments are OK when talking to a child. 'Take a deep breath, now breathe with me, honey ...' And I started doing deep breathing, finally hearing her copying me on the other end of the line. 'Good girl,' I said in that soothing tone. 'You're doing great. Take a couple more deep breaths, sweetheart.' I listened. 'That's good,' I said. 'Real good. Now, can you tell me what happened? Start at the beginning, honey.'

'I ... I came home ... with my brothers and sisters ... I had Mama's car, I picked everybody up ... I came in and ... oh my God ... oh my God...'

'Take another deep breath,' I said, soothing-like. 'In, one-two-three, out, one-two-three ... Now, what happened when you came in?'

'Mama ... Mama's on the floor in the kitchen ... she's here now, just lying here ... And there's blood...'

'Now, sweetie, I need to get an ambulance over there. What's your name, honey, and your address?'

I heard a sob over the phone. 'She's dead. Her eyes are open and she's dead!'

'I'm so sorry, darlin'. What's your name and your address so we can get someone over there for you and your brothers and sisters?'

'Lyn ... Lynnie Hudson. 1803 Magnolia Way, in The Branches.'

Now, The Branches (and yes, that *is* a capital 'T' in 'the') is the newest and ritziest subdivision in the town of Bishop, which is Prophesy County's answer to Beverly Hills.

'OK, Lynnie, honey,' I said, 'you've done real good. I'm on my way over there right now, and I'm sending an ambulance too. Now I want you and your brothers and sisters to step outside the house and wait for us out front. OK, darlin'?'

'Just ... just leave her here?'

'That way the crime scene...' I heard her sob '. . . if it is a crime scene, won't get messed up, you understand, honey?'

'Yes, sir.'

'Is this a cell phone you're on?'

'Yes, sir.'

'Then you take it out with you and stay on the line. I'm gonna have you talk to my friend Holly until I get there. OK, Lynnie?'

Another sob. 'Yes, sir,' she said. Then she screamed.

'What?' I yelled. 'What happened?'

'Little Mark! I forgot all about him!'

'Who's Little Mark?' I asked.

'My baby brother! Where is he? Oh my God oh my God!'

'Lynnie, now just hold on—'

'I've got to go find him!'

'No!' I said emphatically. 'Absolutely not! If you haven't heard him by now, he's probably asleep. Let him be and go outside like I said. Now, Lynnie, I hate to say it, but that's an order, honey.'

Just the thought of her finding her baby

13

brother dead was doing things to my head – none of 'em good.

Still talking to her on the phone, I grabbed up my paraphernalia and said, 'I'm gonna hafta put you on hold, Lynnie, while I go get Holly. Just hold on a second, sweetie. We'll be right back.' I headed quickly to the front office and picked up Holly's phone, pushing the button for Lynnie. 'OK, honey, I'm back. You're gonna talk to Holly now. You and the kids outside yet?'

'Yes, sir, but Little Mark—'

'I'm on my way, y'all just stay outside, honey. Now I'm giving the phone to my friend Holly. She's real good people and I'll be right there, OK?'

'Yes, sir,' she said, but I could hear the tears in her voice.

Putting my hand over the mouthpiece of the phone, I said to Holly, 'Her name's Lynnie. Her mama's dead in the kitchen. There's a baby in the house someplace. Girl's near hysterics. Talk to her in a calm voice, keep her and the other kids – don't know how many – out of the house until we get there, got it?'

Holly said, 'Yes, sir,' took the phone from my hand and in a soft voice said, 'Lynnie? Hi, it's Holly...'

That's all I heard as I radioed for an ambulance and headed out to my squad car.

Bishop's like twenty minutes away from Long-

14

branch in miles, but about $200,000 per annum away in terms of income. That's where all the doctors, lawyers and accountants live. And probably a few drug dealers I'm not yet aware of. The little township itself has boutiques and natural food stores and a store that sells kitchen crap, where I found a potato peeler they were selling for $65. Hand to God. They've got massage parlors that women go to (not like the trailers outside of Longbranch with the Asian girls). And they've got children's stores with baby dresses that cost more than my wife's wedding dress. I kid you not. Needless to say, I don't go to Bishop a lot, other than command performances at my sister's mini-mansion. Her husband owns used-car parts stores. Ten of 'em.

Now, The Branches was new and totally concealed by a six-foot-high rock fence surrounding the entire subdivision and, if I was pushed, I'd say the place was at least a couple of hundred acres. There was a manned front gate (in this instance, womanned) and heavy iron gates that didn't open without the permission of the uniformed and armed guard. (The armed part was on the up-and-up because they had to come to me to get their carry licenses and take shooting lessons at our range.) I showed the lady guard on duty my badge, told her the problem, and said, 'Who's your security chief out here?'

'Maynard Ritchie, Sheriff. Want me to call him?' she said.

'Yeah, have him meet me at the house,' I said,

and squealed tires getting through the gate.

1803 Magnolia Way was the tip end of a cul-de-sac with only three houses, each of which appeared to sit upon at least a half acre. The house in question was pretty dang big, but looking at the crew of kids hanging out in front of the house, I figured any property that housed this bunch would have to be big. I counted seven kids as I walked up.

'Lynnie?' I asked, moving through the obviously upset children.

'Sheriff?' she cried, then ran up to me and grabbed my hand. 'Mark! You've got to find Little Mark!'

She was a pretty girl, sixteen or seventeen years old, blonde hair that reached her butt, big blue eyes, on the short side, a little thick through the middle, wearing a long dress that looked like the material my mama used to make curtains out of, and thick-soled black shoes.

I looked around the bunch of kids. Four of them were girls, all wearing long dresses made out of similar material. The boys wore blue jeans and shirts made of the same sort of material, with the top button buttoned up tight. 'Everybody all right?' I asked.

Stepping closer to me she whispered, 'The little ones didn't see her. They know something's wrong, but they don't know what.'

'Have you contacted your father?' I asked her.

She shook her head. 'He works at Telecom International. I left a message on his voicemail to call me on my cell phone immediately, but he's an engineer and he's in meetings all the time.'

'Let me go in and get Little Mark, OK, Lynnie? I'll be right back. Y'all stay right here.'

I headed for the front door. The house was two and a half stories of white rock with a double front door made of hand-carved oak with inlays of beveled glass. I opened it gingerly and went inside. Beautifully crafted hardwood floors gleamed in the foyer and off to the right where there appeared to be a living room. At a glance it was sparkling clean and neat as a pin. Hard to believe seven – no, make that eight – children lived here. To the left was a large dining room with an enormous oak table with ten oak chairs arranged around it. Each corner of the room had an oak corner cabinet built in, displaying children's crafts. I could see the kitchen to the back of the dining room. I headed in that direction. Mama laid on the floor my side of an island that held the stove top and a rack above, showing off sparkling copper pots and pans. I know I've probably said 'sparkling' or 'shiny' a hundred and eleven times, but with reason. The whole house shone like a Christmas tree.

The lady in question was on her back, her head being the source of all the blood. Her hair had to be as long as her daughter's, spread out all over the place – blood-soaked blonde hair. Squatting down, I could see a gash on the right

17

side of her head. There was a dishrag clutched in her left hand and a wooden spoon in her right. She was wearing a larger version of the dresses the girls outside were wearing, but her feet were shod in pink fuzzy slippers. I put in a call to the ME, who was already on her way and slightly miffed that I would question her ETA.

Just as I was hanging up from having my butt chewed out, I heard a squeal from further back in the house. Then a yell and some more squealing. Having a six-year-old myself, I knew the sound of a baby up from his nap. I followed the sound only a few feet, beyond a bar that separated the kitchen from the family room, which was furnished in beanbag chairs, plastic slides, a small see-saw, bouncy toys, and shelves crammed with books and toys. Little Mark was standing up in a playpen, cotton-blond hair sticking up all over his head, and his coveralls showing wet stains all down the front. He looked to be about a year to eighteen months. Hard to tell with some babies.

I picked him up, cooing at him, and used my cell phone to call my wife. Jean's a psychiatrist and she's on the county roll to call in such cases. Not finding her, I called Holly at the shop and told her to try to get in touch with Jean and why, then I grabbed a diaper and the box of wipes and headed outside with my new pal.

I'd barely gotten out the front door before a minivan pulled up and was abandoned behind The Branches' official security car, wherein still

18

sat Maynard Ritchie, I presumed. Two women jumped out of the front of the minivan, and a mass of children came out of the back. They all ran to Lynnie and her siblings, one of the women snatching Little Mark out of my arms.

'What's going on?' demanded the woman who snatched the baby out of my arms. Four boys, pre- to mid-teens, were following along behind her like ducklings. She was somewhere in her mid-thirties, reddish-blonde hair, slim, but wearing the same long dress, long hair hanging down her back.

The other woman was much younger, maybe in her early twenties, very long brown hair, a long, shapeless dress, a baby in her arms and one clinging to her leg. Something clued me in that these people were family.

'Ma'am, may I speak to you privately?' I asked the older one.

She nodded and pointed at the four young boys. 'Stay with Mama Rene,' she said, and moved to the side with me.

'Sorry to say the lady in that house,' I used my head to point in the direction of Lynnie Hudson's house, 'is dead.'

'Oh, sweet Lord Jesus!' the woman said. 'Mary's dead?' The woman began to shake, and I grabbed her by the elbow to steady her. She thrust Little Mark into my arms. 'No, oh, Lord, no.'

'Ma'am, I'm so sorry,' I said, trying to hold her up while holding the baby. 'Lynnie!' I called out. She came to me. 'Take Mark,' I said, which she did. I moved the woman carefully to my car so she could sit down.

'I'm sorry, ma'am,' I said, once I'd gotten her settled. 'But I've got to ask you some questions.'

'Are you sure?' she said. 'That it's Mary? That she's dead?'

'Yes, ma'am. I'm real sorry.'

She shook her head and began to sob. I let her go for a couple of minutes, waving off the security chief as he walked towards my car. Finally I said, 'Lynnie said she tried to call her daddy but she's only been able to leave messages—'

She rolled down the window and called out, 'Rene, call Jerry! On his cell!' She turned to me. 'The children aren't supposed to call him on his cell,' she said, pulling a small pack of tissues out of her purse and blowing her nose.

'Could you tell me the name of the lady of that house? And her husband's name as well?' I asked.

'Mary Hudson, and her husband is Jerry Hudson. We all just moved here from the west coast. Well, two years ago, but still...'

I smiled. 'I got the felling y'all are family,' I said.

She nodded, tears pooling in her eyes.

'And you are?' I asked.

'Oh, sorry. Carol Anne.'

'Carol Anne...?'

'Carol Anne Hudson.'

I wrote the name down. 'Your husband and Mary's husband are brothers?'

'My husband will explain it to you when he gets home,' she said. 'I need to be with the children.' She got out of my Jeep and walked over to Mary Hudson's children, pulling as many as possible to her side.

At that point, I got out of the Jeep myself and found Maynard Ritchie, the head of security for The Branches. He was maybe a couple inches shy of my five feet ten, and maybe a few pounds heavier. His hair was that weird color red turns when it wants to go gray, kinda pink. He had on a brown uniform with a jacket that had real live epaulets, I swear to God. When he introduced himself, he said he preferred to be called 'Captain,' which I was disinclined to do.

I filled him in on the tragedy at 1803 Magnolia Way, and asked him what he knew about Mr and Mrs Jerry Hudson.

'Not much,' he said. Then he waved his arms, encompassing the cul-de-sac. 'See these three houses?' I nodded. 'Mr Hudson bought all three. Well, I guess you can't say bought,' Maynard Ritchie said. 'Stole would be a better word.'

'Pardon?' I asked, and if I could raise just one eyebrow like my wife, I woulda done it for sure.

'The builder who bought this little section here, and that one over there,' he said, pointing to the cul-de-sac one over, 'went belly-up last year after he built all six houses. Total bank-ruptcy. Mr Hudson got these three houses, and those over there were bought by individual buyers.' He snorted. 'Until that happened, this was a real nice place.'

'You saying you had some trouble with the Hudsons?' I asked.

He scratched his head. 'No, not really. Although they got some teenaged boys, and usually that means trouble, but these kids are pretty quiet. Some kind of weird church thing, I think. Now on the other side over there,' he said, pointing to the other cul-de-sac and, lean-ing in, he half-whispered, 'Mexicans.'

I pulled back from him. 'You don't say?' I said.

'Hell, man, I *do* say!'

'Trouble?' I asked.

'Any day now,' he answered.

The ME, the ambulance, my wife, and the victim's husband all arrived at the same time, or pretty close to it. The husband was the first one to get out of his car, and everybody, and I mean *everybody* – kids and neighbor ladies – all ran up to him and it was the group hug to end all group hugs. He was a tall, thin man with light brown hair turning gray. He wore polyester slacks and a polyester short-sleeved shirt, no tie. His shoes were well-worn loafers. The ducklings – the four boys who'd been following Carol Anne – were all yelling 'Daddy' at the top

22

of their lungs. This confused me, but that's not an uncommon occurrence for me, so I let it slide.

'Mr Hudson?' I said, breaking up the huddle.

'Sheriff! My wife?' he said, face blanched white, hair disheveled, eyes red.

'Inside, sir,' I said, and led him and the ME into the house.

Once in the kitchen I held up my hand to stop the ME and the ambulance guys, while the husband knelt next to his wife. 'Try not to touch anything, sir,' I said.

He nodded his head, and put his hands behind his back, like a little kid. Finally he looked up at me, tears streaming down his face. 'Who did this?' he asked, his voice choked.

'We're not sure yet, sir,' I said. 'Can we go in the living room while I ask you some questions?'

He nodded and stood up, leading me into the sparkling living room. There was a cross over the mantel and nicely framed prints of Norman Rockwell paintings in a grouping over the couch. The outside wall of the room held double windows with professional portraits of all eight children, four on one side of the windows, four on the other. The room was furnished in old-fashioned 'early American' furniture covered in the kinds of prints I haven't seen since my mama passed away and I gave her furniture to Good Will. Which was a good thirty years ago.

Jerry Hudson took the large armchair with the

ottoman (obviously his) while I sat on the couch. 'Sir, I'm sorry to bother you at a time like this, but it's important that I get as much information as possible as soon as possible if we're going to find whoever is responsible for this,' I told him.

He nodded, leaning his elbows on his knees, his hands clasped together as if in prayer. 'Whatever you need, Sheriff,' he said.

'Do you or your wife have any enemies?' I asked.

'No. Not at all. Mary was well loved by everyone who knew her. And I – well, as far as I know I don't. There's a guy at work who does not like me, but that's because I got a project he wanted. I doubt he'd kill my wife for revenge.'

'Sir, you just never know,' I said. 'Why don't you give me his name and number?'

He jumped up from his chair, his hands in his hair as he moved around. 'This is ridiculous! No one would kill Mary! Everybody loved her! This *could not* have happened!'

'Mr Hudson, I need you to sit down. This did happen, and sir, your children witnessed the carnage.'

Hudson fell back into his chair, a sob escaping him. 'Oh my God! My poor Lynnie.'

'Your neighbor said y'all moved here from the west coast a while back. Do you think some trouble there may have followed you?'

He shook his head. 'No. Everything was fine there. I just got this job with Telecom Inter-

24

national, offering twice as much as I was making in Oregon, so we decided to move.' Again, he jumped up. 'Oh my God, if I hadn't taken this job, Mary would be alive right now!'

I got him settled back down in his chair and decided to ask some easier questions. 'Who all lives in this house?'

'My wife ... Mary did, with eight of my children.'

'Sir?'

He looked up, his formerly white face taking on color fast. 'Ah, Sheriff, I might as well tell you upfront, my family is breaking the law here, or at least I am. We're a plural family.'

I nodded my head. 'OK,' I said. 'What's a plural family?'

Jerry Hudson halfway smiled at me. 'The two ladies out front are also my wives. All the children out front are mine.'

I nodded my head. Who'd a thought this guy was a glutton for punishment?

Jean McDonnell – Monday
There is a list used by both the county sheriff's department and the Longbranch police department of psychiatrists on call. There are two names on it. Mine has been on top since Dr Leonard got fed up and refused to take any more cases about six months ago. I've been called by the police department four times in that six months. I've never been called by the sheriff's department. Trying to be honest with

my feelings on this subject, I do believe it has more to do with the fact that Milt doesn't want to overwork me than the fact that he feels I'm incompetent. Any feelings of incompetence, I'm sure, belong to me alone. I have told my husband repeatedly that my caseload at the hospital is slim and I'd welcome a call from him if the occasion ever arose. In six months it has not.

So color me surprised when I received a call Monday afternoon from Holly, the new dispatcher at the sheriff's department, asking me to meet Milt at a house in Bishop for a consult. As I had no one in my office and my time was being consumed by hospital busy-work, I dropped everything and headed to my car.

Due to early childhood polio, I don't move at a rapid pace on my crutches, but once I'm in my car I can, excuse the expression, haul ass. And since I got my name on that list, the police department gave me one of those light/siren things that adhere to the top of the car. I turned it on and put the pedal to the metal.

I made the twenty-minute drive to Bishop in ten. It's the little victories that keep us sane. I got to the cul-de-sac the same time as the ME and the ambulance, and one other car. The cul-de-sac itself looked like a scene from Dante's *Inferno*, the level of hell he didn't write, about wailing children – what seemed like thousands of them – all blond-headed, all wearing almost the same thing. The boys in jeans and printed shirts, the girls in long, shapeless printed dresses, hair streaming long down their backs. Or it could have been the set of a movie about cults in the nineteenth century.

The man who drove in the same time as me jumped out of his car first and ran into the gang of children and babies, which I finally saw included two adult women. As I got out of my car and adjusted my crutches, I saw my husband neatly divide the man from the herd and lead him into the house. The wailing resumed with the two women ineffectually trying to calm the children. All I knew at this point was what Holly had told me: a woman, a mother of several children, had been murdered and one child – presumably a baby – was still in the house. But since two of the women were holding babies, with a third older baby attached to one's leg, and Milt had just led what I assumed to be the father into the house, I could only deduce that the baby was now safely in the arms of one of the women.

My cell phone rang and I saw that it was Milt. I said, 'Yes, Sheriff?'

'Hey, babe, glad you could make it.'

'What do you need me to do?' I asked.

'You know what a plural family is?' he asked me.

'Yes, a polygamist – usually, almost always male – with multiple wives.'

'Yep. Well, that's what we got here,' he said. 'The two women out there on the street are the two surviving wives, and all the children are this man's kids. Can you take them into one of the other houses and get what you can out of 'em?'

'No problem,' I said, although I'd rather have a go at the husband. I knew very little about plural families, but had my own feelings on the subject. Subservient women, domineering men, and children raised to continue the tradition, if one wanted to call such behavior a 'tradition.'

I walked up to the group, working my way up to the two women holding babies. 'Excuse me, ladies,' I said. 'I'm Dr McDonnell, a consultant with the sheriff's department. The sheriff has asked me to talk to the two of you. Would it be possible for all of us, including the children, to move into one of the other houses?'

'Of course,' the older of the two women said. She held out the hand that wasn't holding a baby. 'I'm Carol Anne Hudson, and this,' she said, indicating the younger woman, 'is Rene Hudson. These,' she said, spreading her arm to indicate all the children, 'are our children.'

At that declaration, the oldest of the girls ran up to her and latched on, hugging her tight. Carol Anne pulled the girl to her. 'It's all right, Lynnie. It's all right.' She turned to the younger wife. 'Rene, why don't we take everybody into my house?'

Rene nodded. Of the two, Carol Anne stood out. She was tall and slender, her strawberry-blonde hair shining in the sunlight of an autumn day. Her face, devoid of make-up, was lovely and so pale you could actually see blue veins beneath the skin of her throat. Her eyes were a piercing blue and her mouth wide with generous lips. And even in the shapeless housedress she was wearing, you could almost see a perfect body beneath.

Rene, on the other hand, appeared to be lacking in all categories while standing beside her fellow wife. She had mousy brown hair and was short and somewhat pudgy. Nothing stood out about Rene. She was just there. Theirs would be an interesting dichotomy.

The house Carol Anne led us to – the one she declared to be hers – was on the right as you entered the cul-de-sac. It was a large, two-story house, all gray-blue with white trim and shutters and a bright red front door. The driveway that led to a detached garage was littered with bikes, skateboards, scooters, and other boy-stuff, including a basketball hoop attached to the front of the garage.

The red door led us into a home as outstanding as Carol Anne. The foyer was tiled in white ceramic, the walls painted a dark blue, and the stair rails and doorframes were a brilliant white. A great deal of the dark blue wall space was taken up with exquisite black and white close-up photos of the four boys. On the right of the foyer was a large dining room with a table that sat ten. The table was old and trestle style, while each ladder-back chair was individually painted in bright primary colors to depict different scenes. The walls were painted a bright red and covered in colorful tropical-looking paintings. On the left of the foyer was the living room. It housed the largest flat-screen TV I've ever seen, and the furniture consisted of several old and slightly decrepit recliners and futons, all covered with bright-colored throws. The walls, painted a bright yellow, were filled with photos and paintings and *objets d'art*.

'Ben,' Carol Anne said to one of the boys, 'please take everyone upstairs, OK?'

Three of the older girls grabbed the babies and trudged up the stairs behind the others.

'You have a lovely home, Mrs Hudson,' I said as I took a seat on a futon.

'Please, call me Carol Anne.' She grinned. 'There are too many Mrs Hudsons.' Her face fell and tears sprang to her eyes. 'Oh, dear Lord, I don't believe I said that.'

Rene came over and sat next to Carol Anne on the other futon. The women hugged, holding on to each other for what seemed an inordinate length of time.

Finally they broke apart and Carol Anne said, 'What can we tell you, Dr McDonnell?'

I had an overwhelming urge to tell her to call me Jean, but didn't give in to it. I needed to control the situation as much as I could, and keeping myself in the role of authority figure would help me do that. 'To start with, I don't know a lot about plural families. Could you tell me the origin of yours?'

'The origin? Well, it goes back to the origins of the Church of the Latter Day Saints. Monogamy is new to the Church. Rene and I were both raised in plural families. My mother was my father's second wife out of three, and Rene, your mom...?'

'She was Daddy's fourth, and last,' she said with pride, 'wife. But this was after his first wife had died, and her children, my brothers and sisters, were all adults by then.'

'And your husband and Mary?' I asked.

'Jerry's mom was a second wife, but it didn't work out and there was a divorce. She raised Jerry all by herself, but in a plural community, so he saw how well it *could* work,' Carol Anne said. 'Mary was from a single family with several siblings. She and Jerry met in high school and were married right after graduation. They both went on to college. Mary got her teaching degree, and Jerry got his masters in electrical engineering.'

'And Mary had three of her babies while she was still in college!' Rene said proudly, then welled up, realizing she was talking about her deceased friend, or whatever you'd call that relationship.

'At what point did you join their family, Carol Anne?' I asked.

'When I was seventeen. Right after I graduated high school. I knew them both quite well from church, and Jerry had been quite attentive

31

to me, and he and Mary came together to ask my parents, since I was technically underage, but they agreed. It was right after Jerry and Mary both graduated from college. Mary worked for several years as a teacher while Jerry was getting his masters, and I was the homemaker, taking care of Mary's three and then having three of my own pretty quickly,' she said with a smile. 'It was a very good time. We all lived in one house, and then when Jerry got his masters we were going to continue with the two incomes, but then Mary got pregnant with Nathaniel...'

Rene laughed. 'And then you got pregnant with Oscar...'

Carol Anne laughed back. 'My fourth son. And then Mary got pregnant with Candice, and then Nell and then Margaret, so it just seemed better for both Mary and me to stay at home with our children. There were too many children for just one house, so Jerry built Mary a really nice house on the same property as the original house back in Oregon, and then the eight of them – Mary and her seven children, moved into that house, and my four boys and I stayed in the older house. Which, believe me, was plenty big enough!'

'I take it Little Mark wasn't born until you moved here?'

'Right. He's only fourteen months,' Carol Anne said.

'Didn't you resent Mary getting the new

house?' I asked.

For a second Carol Anne looked genuinely confused. Then she smiled. 'Oh! I guess some people would,' she said, 'but that's not how we work.' She smiled at me and, to my amazement, I believed her. Was it just because of the beautiful smile, the lilting voice? Was I getting a girl-crush on beautiful Carol Anne?

Rene spoke up. 'Jerry told both of us – Carol Anne and me – that Mary was his soulmate. She would always come first, but that they both had love enough in their hearts for more.'

'And the children!' Carol Anne spoke up, her face beaming. 'I couldn't love Mary's children more if they came from my womb. And Rene's, too.' She shook her head. 'It must be difficult if you're not from a plural community, or know plural families, to understand the...' she tilted her head and said, 'dynamic? Is that the word you use?' I nodded. 'OK, the dynamic of our lifestyle. God, family, country. In a lot of Christian homes, it's God, country, family. But when you're in a plural family...' She looked to Rene and they spoke in unison, both smiling. 'Family *is* country!' And they laughed.

'Gross!' came loud and proud from the stairway as two boys bounded down the stairs and into the living room.

One, with reddish-blond hair and freckles on his nose, said, 'Michael just did a number two so bad we'll have to fumigate, Mom!'

'Oscar!' Carol Anne said, as the other boy

interrupted. 'Yeah, Mama Carol Anne. It was ripe!'

Standing and taking both boys by the nape of the neck, Carol Anne said, 'Dr McDonnell, this,' she said, shaking the smiling boy with the reddish-blond hair, 'is my son, Oscar, and this,' she said, indicating the other boy, 'is my son by Mary, Nathaniel. They are both very rude.' The way she said 'my son by Mary' came out as almost one word.

Rene stood up. 'I do believe that's my cue to go change a diaper,' she said and headed up the stairs.

Both boys tried to hide their smiles. 'Sorry,' they said in unison.

'Say hello to Dr McDonnell,' Carol Anne said.

They both did.

'Now if you're so sure you're going to vomit, why don't you go outside and play?' she said.

'Yes, ma'am,' they said in faux-rejection, then both ran screaming for the front door.

After the door closed, I asked Carol Anne, 'Nathaniel is Mary's son, right?'

'Yes,' she said, pulling her arms across her chest, as if suddenly cold.

'Does he know?' I asked.

She shrugged. 'That's up to his father,' she said. At which point the front door opened and a disheveled and beaten-down Jerry Hudson walked in the door. I took that opportunity to leave.

TWO

Milt Kovak – Monday

'I just think it's another way of subjugating women,' she said as we came in the front door.

'What is, Mama?' Johnny Mac, our six-year-old son, asked.

'Sorry, honey,' Jean said, ruffling his hair. 'Work talk. Promise – no more.'

'What's subgating?' he asked.

'Sub-ju-gating,' Jean supplied. 'Look it up in the dictionary.'

'I don't care that much!' Johnny Mac muttered under his breath as he turned and headed for the living room.

I laughed and Jean threw her purse on the kitchen table and leaned her crutches against the wall.

'Oh, you think that's funny, do you?' she said. 'At that age, I would have looked up the word then been in the encyclopedias looking up proof!'

'Yeah, kinda neat having a normal kid, huh?' I said, smiling.

'He is *not* normal!' Jean replied.

I got behind her where she stood at the sink

and kissed her neck. 'Sorry, sweetie. I don't think our Johnny Mac is gonna skip three grades and be a freshman in college at fourteen.'

'He could!' she said, a little whine in her voice as she brutalized a potato.

'I'm gonna change clothes,' I said, heading to our bedroom, which was on the other side of the kitchen.

'I'll be there in just a minute. I want to get these potatoes on first.'

It had been a rough day, for me and Jean both. Although she appeared to disapprove of a plural family, she seemed somewhat fascinated by the idea. And to tell the truth, so was I. Where the man, Jerry Hudson, got the nads to try to support three women and three households of kids was beyond me. Where he got the funds was another matter. Would that be enough to make a man want to kill his wife? His oldest wife. Running out of money, gotta get rid of one, why not the oldest? The other two – whoa. The redhead was hot, but that little brunette – she had one of those round little butts that you just wanna . . .

Anyway, that was one theory. Jerry came home, killed his wife, while his kid was asleep in the next room? Cold, man. Really cold. I couldn't see the man I met doing that. But I've read up in Jean's books about sociopaths, who mimic the behavior of others, as they have no indicators in themselves to real feelings and stuff. Jerry Hudson could be one of those. But somehow I doubted it. What about the wives? Gotta be some jealousy going on. How could there not be? Three women, one man? Shit. Have you ever tried just dating two women? A man could get killed that way.

We had some dinner and Jean got Johnny Mac bathed and dressed for bed. I took him upstairs to his bathroom to brush his teeth. Then we hit the bed, said our prayers, and I got him tucked in.

'Daddy?' he said as I started to leave the room.

'Yeah, tiger?'

'When did you know you loved Mommy?' he asked.

Hum. 'Well,' I said, 'just about the minute I saw her.'

'No, really.'

'It was pretty fast, big guy. Why do you ask?'

He rolled over, his back to me. 'Oh, no reason. I just think I love somebody.'

I sat down on the side of his bed. 'Who's that?' I asked.

'Miss Crenshaw.'

'Miss Crenshaw your teacher?'

'Yeah,' he said. 'She's beautiful.'

'You're right, son. She's a real pretty lady.'

''Night, Daddy,' he said.

I kissed his ear. ''Night, son.'

I left the room, heading back down the stairs. When I was in first grade, my teacher was a mean old bag named Mrs Van Nubbins. She had tightly curled gray hair, thick glasses, and a big ass. She also carried a ruler around and would always swat your knuckles for no good reason. Nowadays teachers are always young, pretty, actually talk to the kids, and they don't hit. There's something to be said, every once in a while, for progress.

Later, when Jean and I crawled into bed, I told her about Johnny Mac's crush on Miss Crenshaw.

'OK,' she said putting down her medical journal and taking off her reading glasses. 'The general therapy for this—'

'Whoa now!' I said. 'I didn't tell you this as a psychiatrist, I told you this as his mama, for God's sake.'

'I'm both,' she said.

'I know that, and you know that, but Johnny Mac doesn't know that. He's in love with his teacher. OK. Let him have it. It's barely October. By Christmas, he'll have a crush on some little girl.'

'You're right,' she said.

I faked a heart attack. 'Lord, I'm coming!' I said to the ceiling. 'Take me now! She actually said it!'

My wife hit me with her journal. 'Ha, ha,' she said, in her usual deadpan way.

I leaned over and started nibbling her neck. 'You think I'm funny,' I whispered. 'And sexy.'

She giggled. 'It's funny that *you* think you're

sexy!' she said.

I headed for her fun spots.

Milt Kovak – Tuesday

I had Holly run the Hudsons on the computer, see what she could find out. The only discrepancy we found was that Jerry Hudson named nineteen dependents on his 1040 tax form. I started counting up: Carol Anne said that Mary had had eight children, Carol Anne had four children, and Rene had two. Add the kids and the wives all together that made seventeen dependents, not nineteen.

So I called the number for Carol Anne's house and a woman answered the phone.

'Mrs Hudson?' I said.

'Are you looking for Carol Anne?' the woman asked. I could tell when she said more than 'hello' that this voice belonged to an older woman.

'Yes, ma'am. And you are?'

'This is Carol Anne's mother. She's over at Mary's house right now dealing with the children. Do you know what happened over there?'

'Yes, ma'am. This is Sheriff Kovak calling. I'll just call her at Mary's house.'

'Have you found out yet who did this terrible thing?' she asked.

'No, ma'am, not yet. I'll just call her at Mary's house—'

'Well, truthfully, I never really trusted that Mary,' Carol Anne's mother said. 'She was a sly one.'

'Oh?' I said. 'How's that?'

'Well, just look how many babies she had, for goodness' sake! My Carol Anne has her four babies then Mary just goes and pops out one after the other like she's showing who's boss! I don't think how many babies you can have proves a darn thing!' she said.

'Yes, ma'am,' I said, not sure how to answer her comments. 'I'll just call Carol Anne—'

'And then he goes and marries that mousy Rene! *That* was Mary's doing, you can count on that!'

'Thanks for the information—'

'I told my son, Dennis. I said, "Dennis, that Jerry is up to no good marrying that Rene!" And Dennis agreed with me. He said, "Mama, you are right!" Now don't you think that's true?'

'Ma'am...'

'That Mary was in her forties when she had her last baby. It's just God's sweet love that managed to make that child normal!'

'I gotta go!' I said quickly and hung up.

I was afraid I was gonna have to actually meet that woman, 'cause the venom spewing out of her mouth sounded like motive to me.

I called Mary's house and got hold of Carol Anne. 'How's everybody?' I asked.

She sighed heavily. 'Not well,' she said. 'Jerry's got the older children upstairs praying, and I've got the little ones down here, trying to keep them relatively busy.'

'He still hasn't told all of 'em?' I asked.

'He and Rene and I were up all night talking about it, and we decided the cut-off point was five. Six and up we tell, five and below ... not for a while.'

'Won't the older kids tell them about it?' I asked.

'Probably. We're just trying to keep it quiet for a couple of days. When will Mary's body be released?' she asked.

'I'll check with the ME, find out when the autopsy will be,' I told her. 'Ah, ma'am, I spoke with your mother—'

'Oh, Lord!' she cried. 'I'm so sorry! Did she talk your ear off?'

I laughed. 'Little bit,' I said. 'I also noted that Jerry lists nineteen dependents on his 1040 tax return, but there are only seventeen of y'all, to my count.'

'Bet you didn't count Mama!' Carol Anne said. 'Or my brother, Dennis.'

'You're right, I didn't. Well, I just spoke to your mama, but I didn't know about your brother. How are they dependents of Jerry's?' I'd sorta spaced out when the old lady was talking to me – she might have mentioned Carol Anne's brother, but really, who cared?

'Well, they're both on disability and they live with me and the boys in my house. They are totally dependent on Jerry and their social security.'

41

'I'm sorry to hear that – that they're both disabled. What's wrong with your brother?'

'He was in a car wreck and hurt his back. Mama was in the car with him and she lost a leg and hurt her back, too, and then my daddy died, and they came to live with us.'

I was beginning to feel real sorry for Jerry Hudson. It's a wonder he didn't kill the lot of 'em. 'It was nice of Jerry to do that,' I said, unable to come up with anything else to say.

'Jerry is God's original,' Carol Anne said proudly. 'The Good Lord broke the mold after he made Jerry.'

'Yes, ma'am,' I said. 'I'm gonna need to talk to your mama and your brother sometime today, if possible, Mrs Hudson.'

'Please call me Carol Anne, Sheriff,' she said. 'I'll set that up for you. Mama should be no problem, but I'm not sure about Dennis. I'll see if I can track him down.'

'I thought you said he was living with you?' I asked.

'Yes, he is, but he's out a lot. I'll call you,' she said, and hung up quickly.

I sat there in my office, looking at the phone and thinking, how does old Dennis get around so much with a back so bad he can't work? Then I thought it would be a sorry job if the only thing I got these people on was a little bitty fraud against old Uncle Sam.

Around noon I took Nita Skitteridge with me to talk to Carol Anne's mama, and hopefully her

42

brother, Dennis. We stopped on our way out of Longbranch and picked up a couple of Big Macs and some fries and drinks for the trip. We just got a McDonalds a couple of years ago, and I'm afraid it's done a job on the diner at the Longbranch Inn. I'm still a devout customer, but there are days when it's just easier to pick up a Big Mac or some Chicken McNuggets and be on your way. But truthfully, there's still nothing better than a sit-down lunch at the Longbranch with yeast rolls, cornbread, sweet butter, chicken fried steak and cream gravy, and three sides off the board. It's just a little bit of heaven. And if it comes to it, I'd give up Mc-Donalds in a heartbeat.

This was my first time to work on a case with Nita. She was a pretty lady, with beautiful dark skin and huge brown eyes. She wore her hair as short as her cousin's, but somehow it just made her look more feminine. She had a nice chest and a cute butt and what more can a man ask for, tell me that? She was also smart as a whip and nice and polite, although the polite may have had more to do with my rank than any real feelings on her part.

When we got to The Branches, Nita let out a slow whistle. 'Wow, would you look at this?' she said.

'Yeah,' I said, showing my badge to the gate-keeper and driving through. 'It's pretty upscale, huh?'

'Yes, sir,' she said, letting me know she hadn't

really thought about the whistle before she did it.

'But these people, the Hudsons?' I said, thinking out loud. 'I don't think they're rich like these other people. Lord, how could they be? You look in their houses, well, I've seen the insides of two of 'em, and while they look great the furniture is old, I mean really old. And there's not much of it. They got these three houses at a tax auction, so I'm wondering if they didn't get 'em for a song, all together like they are, and just lucked out?'

'Yes, sir, sounds likely,' Nita said.

'Now, the house we're going to belongs to the second wife, Carol Anne. She's the artistic type. Lots of paintings and pictures and geegaws on the walls and such – all the walls painted bright colors. But the furniture's still old. See if you don't notice that.'

'Yes, sir,' Nita said.

'If the mama and the brother are both there, you take the mama and I'll take the brother. Got that?' I asked.

'Yes, sir,' Nita said.

I parked the car in Carol Anne's driveway and we went together to the front door. Before I could knock, we were accosted by the largest, ugliest dog I'd ever seen. His fur was blond with a greenish tinge, his tongue hung about down to his knees (if dogs have knees), he had one ear that pointed up and the other that – well, wasn't much there. His eyes were covered with

44

a ruff of fur like the bushy eyebrows of an old man. And he stank to high heaven. But he seemed friendly enough. The door opened before I had a chance to knock. The lady who answered the door was tall like her daughter with red hair that didn't look quite as ... well, natural as her daughter's. The mama had 'I Love Lucy'-red hair, was wearing black slacks and a black and gold skintight T-shirt that showed gigantic hooters and what my wife would call an unnaturally large muffin-top.

'Scat, you filthy beast!' she yelled, and I finally figured out she was talking about the dog. 'Get!' She shook a magazine at him and he backed away and yipped at her a couple of times, more like he wanted her to throw the magazine than anything dangerous.

'Get!' she shouted again, and the dog finally ran off.

'Ma'am,' I said, holding out my hand to shake, 'I'm Sheriff Milt Kovak, and this here is my deputy, Nita Skitteridge. I'm sorry, I never did get your name.'

'Denise Rigsby.' She looked at Nita slantwise and didn't offer her hand. I wondered if I should let Anthony's cousin interview this woman after all. 'Excuse the dog! Well, there *is* no excuse for that dog! Jerry told the boys they could keep her if they put up one of those doggie fences where it shocks them?' We both nodded our agreement that there was such a thing. 'So they put it at the entrance to the cul-de-sac so the darned thing has the run of all three houses! Little devils,' she said.

'Miz Rigsby,' I said, letting my voice get country-like (that kind of thing works a lot with women of a certain age), 'I was wondering if your son might be around?'

'Dennis!' she screamed over her shoulder.

'Ma'am,' I said, all smiles, 'may we come in?'

She stood her ground. 'I'm not sure how my son-in-law feels about letting mud people into his houses.'

I could feel Nita stiffen next to me. Mud people. Never heard that one, but it sounded just as nasty as most of the words ignorant people call any people different from them.

I used my bulk to get into the house. The lady had pissed me off. Once inside, with Nita beside me, I said, 'Now, ma'am, exactly who you calling mud people? Me, 'cause I'm an old man, my deputy here because she's an African-American, or both of us 'cause we're police officers?'

Denise Rigsby stiffened. 'We're not used to coloreds,' she said.

A man came in from the back of the house. He was shorter than his mother and sister both, slightly bent at the shoulders, had receding reddish-blond hair, a mustache that couldn't make its mind up if it wanted to be or not to be, and watery blue eyes.

'Mama, behave,' he said, coming up to us and

46

holding out his hand to Nita. 'I'm Dennis Rigsby, and you are...?'

She shook his hand and said, 'Deputy Nita Skitteridge, and this is Sheriff Milt Kovak,' she said, indicating me.

He let go of her hand and gave me his. It was damp and the grip was weak. I decided to give him the benefit of the doubt on being disabled. Having already talked to Mrs Rigsby on the phone, I figured if there was anything new to get out of her, Nita would be getting it.

'Miz Rigsby,' I said, smiling bright, 'my deputy here, Deputy Skitteridge, is gonna take you in the living room to talk, while your son and I go in the dining room. That all right with everybody?'

When I got no verbal objections, I pointed to the dining room and followed Dennis Rigsby in there. After we both picked out a brightly painted ladder-back chair and sat, I said to the brother, 'Now, what can you tell me about the relationship everybody – or anybody, for that matter – had with Mary Hudson?'

He shrugged. 'Seemed fine,' he said. 'Carol Anne seemed to like her a lot.'

'Your mama thought there was some tension,' I said.

'Only tension going on around here is Mama's. Look, Sheriff,' he said, leaning toward me and lowering his voice, 'my mother had a hard time in her marriage, being the second wife. The first wife was pretty mean to her. And

I think she was afraid Mary was going to do the same to Carol Anne, but I never saw it.'

'Any tension with the third wife, Rene?' I asked.

He shook his head. 'Not that I ever saw. Jerry seemed to have found the right fit. Everybody seemed very happy.' He leaned back and smiled at me. And that's when I decided that something wasn't kosher in this happy plural family.

On the way back to Longbranch, I quizzed Nita about the mama, Denise Rigsby. 'You get anything out of her?' I asked.

Nita shrugged. 'She didn't like Mary. Of course, she doesn't like Rene either. And she made it a point to tell me she doesn't like Obama.' She looked at me out of the corner of her eye. 'Me being a mud person and all, I guess she thought I should know that.'

'What *is* a mud person?' I asked her.

Again, the shrug. 'You got me. Whatever it is, she doesn't like them either.'

'She have any ideas about Mary's murder?' I asked.

'Other than the fact that Mary either did it herself or Rene did it?'

'Yeah,' I said. 'Other than that.'

'Not much. Tell you the truth, Sheriff, mostly she talked about how uncomfortable she was around me, as a mud person and all, and how bad a person Mary was. But for facts on Mary's "badness"' (and here Nita used air quotes) 'she didn't have much. She had too many babies.

Carol Anne lost a baby after her son, Oscar, and they had to do a hysterectomy. As far as Denise Rigsby is concerned, Mary should have had a hysterectomy, too, in sympathy for Carol Anne. She was incensed that Mary went on and had more babies.'

'OK, that's just weird,' I said.

'No shi— I mean, I agree, Sheriff.'

'Nita, honey, you gotta get hold of yourself. It's OK if you cuss when you feel like it – within reason, of course – and please, please call me Milt. All this formality makes my stomach hurt.'

That got me a little smile. 'Yes, sir,' she said.

I sighed. 'Think Denise did it?'

Another shrug. 'Who knows? She's a mean and crazy lady, Milt, but a murderer? I don't know. If Mary up and told her in private that she was having another baby, maybe, but I doubt Mary was.'

That made me think. 'I think I'll call the ME's office and see about that autopsy.'

Jean McDonnell – Tuesday

I'd made an appointment the day before with Rene Hudson to come to my office. She showed up a half-hour late with both her babies in tow. I asked my secretary to watch them, then brought Rene into the office.

'Wow, you have really pretty furniture!' she said on entering my office. 'Where did you get this?' she said, moving to an old rocker that

49

used to be my grandmother's.

'An heirloom,' I said, steering her toward the sofa. 'Please have a seat. I'm afraid your being late will mean I'll have to shorten our session.'

'Oh, that's OK,' she said.

I was sitting at my desk with my pad and pen at my elbow. I picked up the pen and wrote 'inappropriate affect,' on the pad. 'Rene, I want to make sure you understand that since this is a police investigation, that this session is not confidential. Anything you tell me I will repeat to the sheriff.'

'Okie-doke!' she said, smiling wide.

'Let's take care of some business here first. I have your address. How about your birthdate?' I asked.

She rattled off a date that put her age, not in her mid- or even early twenties, as I'd previously thought, but rather nineteen.

'You're nineteen?' I said to confirm.

'Yeah,' she said.

'If your daughter is two, can I assume you married Jerry when you were sixteen or seventeen?'

'Sixteen,' she said and grinned. 'The first girl in my class to get married!'

I sighed inwardly. 'Tell me, Rene, how you came to be part of the Hudson family.'

'Oh, I dunno,' she said, at which point I noted she was chewing gum. I wrote that down, and added that she'd brought her children to the session. 'It's kinda private,' she said, pulling part of her gum out of her mouth with her fingers and letting it pop back in.

I took a Kleenex and handed it to her. 'Please put your gum in this tissue. I find it distracting.'

'Really?' she said, grabbing the tissue. 'That's weird,' she added, although she did, thankfully, put the gum in the tissue and threw it away in the trash can.

'I will be asking you some personal questions, Mrs Hudson, and they won't be private because this is a police investigation. But if the answers don't concern Mary's death, then they won't go any further than the sheriff and me.'

'He's like your husband, right? The sheriff?' she asked.

'Yes, he is.'

'Cool. I'd like to marry a policeman,' she said.

'But you're married to Jerry Hudson,' I reminded her.

'Huh?' Then her eyes got wide and she actually turned red in the face. 'Oh, right!' She laughed. 'Stupid me!'

I was getting a funny feeling. I'm fairly good at catching lies, and somehow I had the feeling I was catching a whole bucketful.

Dalton Pettigrew – Tuesday
Dalton came in the front door of the sheriff's department, as he'd begun to do since Holly came to work at the station. He used to use the employee entrance that went by the sheriff's

51

office, but he liked to come in the front now, because he could look at Holly from outside the door all the way into the room without her thinking he was staring at her, which he was. He liked to see what she'd be wearing each day – that sweater thing with the hoody and the tight jeans, or one of those short skirts with the tights and a T-shirt, or maybe a dress. And how she'd wear her hair – down like he liked it, or up in a scruffy bun or a ponytail. And he liked to see how many earrings she'd be wearing and which ones. He thought he knew most of her earrings, and he thought, some day, when she got to know him better, maybe he'd buy her a pair. He'd seen some at Miss Julia's on the square that he thought she'd like – butterflies with jade wings. Really pretty.

He couldn't see her that good this day because Milt was standing at the counter talking on Holly's phone. When he turned and saw Dalton, he said into the phone, 'I'll have someone out there in a jiffy,' and hung up. To Dalton, the sheriff said, 'Glad you finally made it. Get a squad car and go over to Vern's Auto Repair on Stillwater. They got a DB behind the dumpster.'

'Yes, sir,' Dalton said and followed Milt as he went back to his office. Sticking his head in the sheriff's doorway, Dalton asked, 'Ah, Milt, a DB, that's like a dead body, right?'

Milt sighed. 'Yes, Dalton, a dead body.'

'And you want me on this all alone?' Dalton asked.

Milt looked Dalton square in the eye. 'You can do it, boy. See who it is, get the ME out to see if it's natural, notify next of kin. You know the drill, son.'

'Yes, sir,' Dalton said and headed out the side door for his squad car.

Milt Kovak – Tuesday

I was sitting in my office when the back door of the sheriff's department (the one that went to the parking lot and was usually kept locked) burst open and, being that my office was closest to the door, I got the full presence of Brother Bob Nathanson, pastor of the United Brethren of the Holy Church of Jesus Christ in His Almighty Goodness. Brother Bob and the Brethren weren't my cup of tea, but mostly they were an OK lot, just a bit zealous, I guess you could say.

He stood in my doorway, the wrath of God in his eyes. Brother Bob is six foot eight inches tall, weighs in at somewhere, I'd say, over 300 pounds, had more shiny black wavy hair than the Lord should allow one man, and dressed like a lumberjack, even at the pulpit, or so I hear.

'Sheriff!' he boomed.

'Well, hey there, Brother Bob,' I said, standing. I held my hand out to shake and, although he hesitated just a fraction, he *did* take my hand. 'Have a seat and tell me what I can do for you. Other than showing you where the front

53

door is, of course.' I laughed when I said that last part. Although I was serious. I'm learning how to be a political animal.

'What do you know about this despicable mess up in Bishop? A bigamist with a bunch of wives and bastard children all running around murdering people!' He stood up in his excitement. 'It's blasphemy! It's sacrilege!' A Bible appeared as if out of nowhere. 'The Good Lord does not condone such heathen behavior! And to think that it's going on right here in Prophesy County! In Oklahoma, for God's sake! In God's country!'

Tears were now running down his cheeks. I had a feeling this Sunday's sermon was gonna be a doozy.

'Please have a seat, Brother Bob,' I said, hoping he would because I sure couldn't see myself trying to seat him. I'd have to jump on his head and pound him with a ball-peen hammer.

He sat. 'Sheriff, we cannot have this libertine, humanistic behavior in our county. Now I know the township of Bishop pays a lot of taxes, but that don't mean they can start breaking laws! Next thing you know there will be homosexuals walking the streets! Kissing!' He made a face like he'd tasted something bad.

'Brother Bob, ain't nothing illegal about homosexuality.'

'Not yet!' he said, raising his fisted hand. 'But there will be! Just you wait! The righteous will rise up and take over this country and then you'll see—'

I stood up. 'Brother Bob, you talking sedition? 'Cause I'd be happy to call the FBI right now, or would that be Homeland Security? I'll have to check. You wanna wait here while I do that?'

Brother Bob stood up too. 'Sheriff, I think you're taking this lightly. This is not a laughing matter. A woman, a wanton woman, no doubt, but still a living, breathing woman, was murdered by someone in her heathen family. I want to know what you're going to do about it?'

'I'm running an investigation, Brother Bob, and toward that end, sir, you wanna tell me where you were yesterday from, say, eight in the morning to three in the afternoon?' I said, mentioning the hours when the kids left for school and when they came home, which was as narrow a field as we could get.

He straightened himself and almost hit the doorjamb of my office. 'I will not dignify that question with an answer, sir. Good day!'

He turned and was out the back door as quickly as he'd come in. And then I had to wonder: what *was* Brother Bob, not to mention his few but feisty congregants, doing yesterday?

THREE

Milt Kovak – Tuesday

Me and Jean met for lunch that day at the Long-branch Inn. I'd rather not go there with Jean because she's had me on a diet since the day we met, practically. And I can't get the usual when I'm with her. So I ordered a chef's salad. It comes with yeast rolls and cornbread too. When the bread basket came, I slipped a couple of each in my pockets when Jean wasn't looking.

'There's something not right about Rene Hudson,' Jean said as she buttered a yeast roll (or margarined, I guess you'd say, since Jean always insists they bring her margarine instead of the real sweet butter they usually bring with the bread basket).

'What's that?' I asked.

'Her affect is off,' my wife said, like I knew what she meant by affect. The way she said it made the word sound different.

'What do you mean?' I asked. Sometimes when I say that, I can actually find out what the hell she's talking about without her knowing I got no idea.

'When she was with Carol Anne, she seemed genuinely upset by Mary's death, but when we

56

were alone together in my office, she seemed, um, I don't know, almost cavalier,' Jean said.

'You mean like she was having fun?' I asked.

'I guess you could say that. She certainly didn't seem to be taking anything very seriously. Even her marriage.'

'Huh?' I said. 'What do you mean?'

'Well, for one thing, when she realized I was married to you, she said, and I quote, "I'd sure like to be married to a policeman."'

At first I was flattered, then it hit me. 'Oh. But she's married to Jerry!'

'Exactly,' my wife said. 'I don't think she's terribly bright, which is odd.'

'How so?' I asked.

'Well, look at Carol Anne and Mary. Both bright women! Carol Anne didn't go to college, but she's a smart woman, you can tell that just by talking to her. And Mary had a degree. So why would Jerry Hudson marry two bright women, then dumb and dowdy little Rene?'

'Dowdy?' I said, my eyebrows raised. 'Is that a new word for hot? 'Cause if it still means what it used to, that chick is not dowdy.'

My darlin' wife raised that one infamous eyebrow at me. 'You think *Rene* is hot?'

'No, well, I mean, no.'

She laughed. 'I'm not challenging you as your wife; I'm challenging you as a woman. I see her as very plain and, yes, dowdy. But you see what?'

I looked deep into her eyes to make sure I

wasn't being set up. You never can tell with women. They say one thing when they mean another, and tell you they're 'just fine' when they really mean they're mad as hell. It's hard dealing with women. But usually Jean's worth it. I decided that her eyes were telling me I'd be OK if I answered truthfully. OK, maybe semi-truthfully.

'Well, she's got that little overbite. That's sexy. And *some* men find short women attractive because they can feel all manly around them. But mainly, it's her ass. Honey, she's got a great ass. Like a little basketball just riding along in the back there.'

Jean nodded her head. 'That's interesting. I've been considering Carol Anne the "hot" one. Her hair, her wonderful complexion, her lithe body, the generous mouth...'

'Whoa now!' I said. 'And I thought you were the one who was gonna get jealous!'

'Are you jealous?' she asked me.

'Well, now, the more I think about it, the more I'm not exactly jealous.'

'Then what are you?' she asked.

'Horny,' was the only answer I could come up with.

That afternoon I called the ME's office and, thank God, got her assistant, Terry Blanchard. He's a nice kid, son of a guy I played ball with in high school, and he looks like and is built like his father, Marvin. Marvin was a good guy.

He died about five years ago and me and the other eight surviving members of our football team showed up at his funeral. His wife, Molly, one of the prettier girls in school, was real glad to see us all there together. Terry was in his early thirties but he wasn't a doctor. He was a certified medical examiner's assistant, or something like that.

'Hey, Terry, boy, it's me, Milt Kovak,' I said when he answered the phone.

'Hey, Sheriff! We've got that murdered lady's body here,' he said.

'Doc do the autopsy yet?'

'Yes, sir. She hasn't called you with the results?' he asked.

'No, and I know you can't legally read 'em to me, but just answer me this, Terr...'

'Yes, sir?'

'Was she pregnant?' I asked.

'No, sir. No fetus. And Sheriff?'

'Yeah, Terr?'

'Lady was healthy as a horse.' His voice got very quiet. 'Somebody hit her over the head with a sharp, heavy object. The skin was cut but her death was caused by the blow.'

'Thanks, kid. We never talked,' I said.

'Now who were you calling?' he asked and I hung up.

And I sat there thinking. The Longbranch police department had trained one of their guys in crime scene investigation and I'd called him to come out. Hadn't gotten a report back. So I

59

picked up the phone and rang.

Clive Macabee answered the phone. 'Crime Lab,' he said, just like he was on one of those *CSI* shows.

'Clive, hey, this is Sheriff Kovak. Got anything for me?'

'I'm telling you, Sheriff, never seen a cleaner house. We've got next to nothing.'

'Then tell me what the next is.'

'There was a lot of blood on the floor, all consistent with Mrs Hudson's blood type. The few strands of hair we found all seemed consistent with the lady's own hair.'

'I hear from the ME that COD was blunt force trauma. You find anything around there that coulda done the deed?'

'Well, she had all those copper-bottomed pots and pans hanging over the stove, but not a one of 'em had a bit of anything on it. There was absolutely nothing out of place. My conclusion on this is whatever killed her was either taken from the scene or the guy brought it with him and took it with him.'

'Clive, you're not one bit of help,' I said.

He laughed. 'We aim to please, Sheriff.'

I said goodbye and hung up. Then thought: anything missing? If it was a crime of passion, a heat of the moment thing, then they woulda used whatever was handy. But if he (and I mean that in a generic sense – coulda been a she) brought the weapon with him, then that's premeditated and that's not good. I needed to talk to Jerry Hudson and find out if anything was missing from the scene.

Dalton Pettigrew – Tuesday
Dalton looked at the dead body. He couldn't help it – every time he looked at one, he thought about his daddy laid up in his casket. Although Dalton's daddy had died over twenty years before, it had been a traumatic event that had colored Dalton's life forever. Sometimes he thought maybe being a sheriff's deputy had not been such a good idea. But then it hadn't really been his idea at all. His mama and the old sheriff, the one before Milt, Elberry Blankenship, were cousins and when Dalton couldn't pass the test to get into the Navy, his mama had suggested to Cousin Elberry that maybe Dalton could work at the sheriff's department. He'd started out as the former clerk Glady's assistant, but got promoted to deputy after one of the deputies quit, leaving just one working. Although Dalton was only nineteen at the time, he did fairly well. But he still hadn't gotten used to dead bodies.

This dead body was that of an old man, like, in his fifties, Dalton decided, not anybody he knew, and he wondered if maybe he should have been a medical examiner because just by looking, Dalton was pretty sure this wasn't a natural death. The guy's eyes were open and kinda popped out, like, and his lips were blue and his tongue was sorta swollen-looking. Like

61

he'd been strangled or something. Dalton donned a pair of gloves and was just about to look for ID when he remembered he wasn't supposed to touch the body until the ME's people got there. So he stood up from his crouched position and asked Vern Casselton, owner of Vern's Auto Repair, how he happened to find the DB, or dead body, as Dalton preferred to call it.

'I got these tires here,' Vern said, pointing at two tires leaning against the front of the dumpster, 'and I was gonna throw 'em away – now don't you get started on me about how I'm supposed to *re*cycle the rubber and all that shit – anyways, that's when I saw his foot sticking out from behind the dumpster. Thought it was one of those homeless people they's always talkin' about on the TV, so I pulled on his leg and yelled at him to get the fuck offa my property, but he didn't move none, so I looked, and sure enough, he was dead as a doornail.'

'You ever seen him before, Vern?' Dalton asked.

Vern shook his head. 'Naw. Don't know him from shit.'

'So, OK,' Dalton said as the medical examiner's van pulled into the back of Vern's Auto. 'That'll be it for now.'

Vern went back into his garage as Terry Blanchard, the ME's assistant, got out of the van.

'What'ya got, Dalton?' Terry asked.

'Dead body,' Dalton said.

'Hell, I figured that, me being the ME's assistant and all. Y'all don't call us out for jaywalking.'

Dalton thought about that for a minute, then laughed sheepishly. 'Naw, I guess not.'

Terry patted Dalton on the shoulder. 'I was just kidding. That him?' he asked, pointing at the foot sticking out from behind the dumpster.

'Yeah. I didn't touch him yet. Vern said he grabbed his foot and pulled 'cause he thought it was a homeless person, but that's all the touching I know about.'

Dalton helped Terry pull the body out from behind the dumpster, then Terry squatted down next to the body, gloves on, and began to do his thing, moving the body this way and that.

'Y'all been busy,' Terry said, his eyes on his work.

'Huh?' Dalton said.

Terry looked up. 'Second body in two days that might be a homicide. I'd call that busy.'

Dalton slowly nodded his head. 'Yeah,' he said, 'you're right. That is busy.'

Terry kept working and after about twenty minutes, he got up, stretched, and said, 'He's all yours, Dalton.'

'Anything interesting?' Dalton asked.

'It'll all be in the ME's report to the sheriff,' Terry said. 'You wanna check for ID or whatever so I can take the body?'

'Sure thing,' Dalton said, squatting down next to it. 'Cause of death seems pretty obvious?' he said, looking up at Terry. 'Like, maybe he's been strangled or something?'

'I never comment until the ME's written it down on paper,' Terry said. 'She'd skin me alive if I did.'

Dalton checked all the man's pockets. There was some change in one side pocket of his polyester pants and a Swiss army knife in the other; the back pockets were empty.

'Got nothing,' Dalton said, standing.

'Give me a hand getting him on the gurney?' Terry asked.

Dalton nodded and Terry went to the van and brought back the gurney, locked it in place, then he and Dalton began the not-so-pleasant task of moving the dead body to the gurney.

After Terry drove off, Dalton noticed he had dirt and grease all over his uniform shirt.

'Well, dang,' he said. Did he go home and hope he had another shirt ironed and ready (his mama usually had one or two hanging up in his closet for him) or did he go back to the station, sneak in the back door and try to make it to his locker, where he had a sheriff's department T-shirt, without being seen by Holly? He didn't want her to see him dirty.

Milt Kovak – Tuesday
I got Nita and we headed back to Bishop. It was getting on to five o'clock and there was some traffic. It was almost five thirty when we got to Mary Hudson's house. I noticed Jerry's car in

the driveway, along with Mary's minivan and another car, a Cadillac Escalade, parked slant-wise behind the two of them. I parked on the street and we headed up the slight incline to Mary's house. When I rang the bell, Carol Anne answered. Her long, reddish-blonde hair was pulled back in a ponytail and her dress, although still loose and baggy, was a solid, dark color: navy or black, I couldn't tell.

'Sheriff,' she said. 'What can I do for you?'

'I need to talk to Jerry,' I said.

'He's with one of the deacons from our church,' she said.

'That's fine. I won't keep him.'

Noticing Nita behind me, she reached out her hand and touched Nita's arm. 'I'm so sorry about my mother – Dennis told me,' she said. 'Mud people is an old, old term used for Native and African-Americans. The church is now inclusive and takes all races.' She shook her head while still holding on to Nita's arm. 'My mother is ... well...'

Nita smiled at her. 'Is your mother. You can't help what she says or does. And you can't correct her. She's your mother.'

Carol Anne sighed. 'I'm so glad you under-stand!'

'Yeah, well, she's not my mother and if she calls me a mud person again we'll see how understanding I'm gonna be,' Nita said, giving Carol Anne a look.

Carol Anne sighed but opened the door wider

65

to let us enter. We followed her to the living room, the one with the early American furniture and the Norman Rockwell prints.

Jerry and the man with him stood when we entered.

Carol Anne said, 'Jerry, the sheriff and Deputy...' She looked at Nita to fill in the blank.

'Nita Skitteridge,' she said, holding out her hand.

Jerry took it and shook and the older man, although hesitant, took her hand, too, saying his name was Andrew Schmidt. Then all us men did our manly shakes and we finally got to sit down with Carol Anne standing in the doorway.

'Can I get you anything?' she asked us. 'Jerry and Andrew are having lemonade. Can I get you some?'

'Why thank you, ma'am, that'd be great,' I said for both me and Nita.

'How goes the investigation, Sheriff?' Andrew Schmidt asked.

'Slow, Mr Schmidt. Lots of things to do.' I turned toward Jerry. 'Mr Hudson, I got a preliminary look at the autopsy report, enough to know that your wife Mary died from blunt force trauma. She was hit with something that broke the skin, which caused all the blood, but death was caused by the force of the blow. Our crime lab didn't find anything at the scene that showed any signs of being that object. Have you noticed anything missing?'

Jerry looked at me with wide eyes. 'I ... I

66

don't...' He turned when Carol Anne came in with the lemonades and some cookies on a small tray.

'These are homemade,' she said. 'Macaroons. Mary made them. These are the last of them,' she said, her eyes welling up.

'Ah, that's OK, we don't wanna eat the last of 'em...' I started.

'No, no, that's OK. The kids won't eat them because ... Well, just because. And we don't waste in this family.'

I nodded my head and picked up a cookie. So did Nita.

Standing up, Jerry said, 'Carol Anne, have you noticed anything missing from the kitchen? Something that could cause...' He looked at me.

'Something that could be used to hit Mary,' I said. I told her the information I'd gotten from both the ME's office and the crime lab.

She sank down into a chair. 'Oh my Lord,' she said. 'You think she was killed with something from her own kitchen?'

'Not necessarily,' I said. 'Either the person who did this did it on the spur of the moment and just grabbed something, or it was planned and that person brought something with him or her,' I finished, trying to cover all the bases.

'Oh.' She turned to look at Jerry. 'I don't know,' she said to him. 'I haven't really inventoried the kitchen.' Turning to me, she said, 'But Mary kept a very orderly house. If there's something missing in the kitchen, I should be able to tell you.'

She jumped up from her chair and rushed out of the room. I nodded at Nita and she stood up, saying to the room, 'I think I'll go help,' and she was out of there, following Carol Anne.

I turned back to the two men. 'So, Mr Schmidt, I understand you're from the Hudsons' church?'

'Yes, sir, I'm one of the deacons of the New Saints Tabernacle. We're a relatively small group.'

'And y'all are all into plural marriage?' I asked.

Andrew Schmidt stood up, ignoring my inquiry. Turning to Jerry, he said, 'Again, Jerry, I'm sorry for your loss. Please let me know when you hear from the ME's office and we'll make the arrangements.'

Jerry took the offered hand and said, 'Thanks, Andrew. Let me see you to the door.'

I stood as the two men left the room, then sat down and waited for Jerry. When he came back in the room, he was grinning from ear to ear. 'You got old Andrew on the run. He's one of the most seriously paranoid polygamists I've ever known.'

I laughed. 'Probably not a lifestyle he should have chosen.'

Jerry shook his head. 'I don't ever want to speak ill of the true Church, but the LDS believed totally in plural marriage until the late 1800s, when there were threats by the government to take away church land if LDS didn't give up the practice. So, of course, it was banned. Now you can get excommunicated. That's why there are so many small sects around. They take the Mormon teachings of John Smith, including polygamy. In a lot of ways, well, in most ways, actually, we're much closer to the teachings of John Smith than the modern LDS.'

'Well, you know,' I said, staring hard at Jerry, 'there's more than just excommunication from the Church. It *is* against the law. You could be arrested.'

He held his hands out to me, wrists together. 'At your leisure, Sheriff.'

Nita Skitteridge – Tuesday
I followed the blonde into the kitchen. I've got to say this was one of the cleanest houses I'd ever seen. But then Carol Anne began opening cabinets. If the dead one, Mary, hadn't been OCD, then something else was wrong with her. On the backside of each door was a sort of floor plan of the interior of that cabinet. I guess in case anyone else put up dishes. The dead woman was obviously a strict believer in 'a place for everything and everything in its place.' Even her Tupperware cabinet was neat, with a rack for lids and a special place (as indicated on the floor plan on the back of the door) for every size of container.

Carol Anne and I discussed what could have been used as a murder weapon. What could slice her skin while bashing her head in? That was the question to be answered.

'Does she have anything heavy with a sharp edge?' I asked.

Carol Anne looked at me blankly. 'Like what?' she finally asked.

Pointing at the copper-bottomed pots on the rack above the stove, I asked, 'Are these just for show? Are there more pots and pans somewhere?'

'She used these all the time, but of course she had more,' Carol Anne said, going to the cabinets below the stove.

There were more pots, pans, lids, roasting pans, stew pots, you name it, but nothing with a sharp edge. Then I opened one of the drawers above the cabinets, right below the stove-top.

'Anything in here missing?' I asked.

Carol Anne came over and looked. Then frowned and began to open the other drawers. There were four of them, and none of them took the frown off her face. She shut the last drawer and looked at me, tears stinging her eyes.

'The tenderizer,' she said.

'Excuse me?' I said.

'The meat tenderizer. She had one of the really big ones because she saved money by buying large pieces of meat that often could be tough.'

At the look of confusion on my face (I'm not one to cook a lot – or ever. If I don't get take-out, my husband does), she said, 'It's a big metal tool, long handle with a big square head that has divots cut on two sides: one side small divots, the other large. It's for pounding meat.'

'Could this thing do what was done to Mary?' I asked.

Carol Anne nodded her head, both hands over her mouth, tears falling down.

I couldn't help it; I reached out and touched her arm. 'I'm so sorry, Carol Anne.'

Again, she nodded, then quickly fled the room.

Milt Kovak – Tuesday

Alone with Jerry Hudson, I asked him, 'You done any thinking on who might've done this?'

He was sitting on the couch, his elbows on his knees, arms out, hands clasped, head bowed. 'I haven't been doing much of anything else,' he said. Looking up, he said to me, 'Sheriff, I can't imagine in my worst nightmare who could have done this. We knew so few people here. Mary was a homebody. I'm sure she and Carol Anne knew some of the other mothers at the kids' schools, and some of the women at church.'

I noticed someone missing, so I said, 'What about Rene?'

He looked up again and laughed slightly, a laugh without humor. 'Oh, her too. I'm so sorry and please don't tell her I did that! I've been with just Mary and Carol Anne for so long that sometimes I leave Rene out when I'm talking about my family. But don't you think this was probably some vagrant? Maybe a burglar?' he asked.

I shrugged. 'Could be. You notice anything missing?'

He shook his head. 'We don't have the kind of things people would want to steal. No high-end electronics, no jewelry, nothing like that. I mean, we have three TVs, but the newest one is ten years old!'

'Well, with you saying that, and the fact that The Branches seems pretty well sealed—'

'The rock walls are not electrified, Sheriff. Anyone could climb over.'

I nodded. 'OK. Good point. I'll do some more talking with the security chief,' I said. Then added, 'You know, one of these days, we're gonna have to have a long talk about how you manage this lifestyle – both financially and, well, you know, just handle it.'

Jerry turned red. 'Maybe one of these days,' he said, his head down again.

My deputy Nita came back in the living room. 'Think we found out what the murder weapon was,' she said, perking me up and bringing Jerry's head back up.

'What's that?' I asked.

'You ever heard of a meat tenderizer?' she asked.

'I suspect you're not talking about the power-ed kind,' I said.

She said, 'Huh?' and I just shook my head for her to go on. 'No, it's a metal object—'

'Sorry, Deputy, I know what it is. So one's missing?'

'Yes, sir, and Carol— Mrs Hudson said it was a large one...'

Jerry spoke up. 'Yes, I remember it! I've seen Mary use it often! The handle was about a foot long and the head was a large square, maybe four by four. I used to laugh about her being able to use it – it was so heavy. Our oldest son had a hard time picking it up.' The light that had come to his eyes when he spoke of this reminder of a whole and happy family, died. He looked down at his hands again.

I stood up. 'That's great, Nita. Let's get the Boy Scouts out here tomorrow to search the cul-de-sac and the whole damn neighborhood if need be.' My eyes landed on the huge cross on top of the mantel. I turned to Jerry. 'Ah, sorry about the cussing.'

Milt Kovak – Tuesday

I got home close to seven, and Jean already had supper on the stove. Me and Jean have different views on food, which is why we switch off nights cooking. Tonight was supposed to be my night and I'd been soaking red beans since yesterday and had some collards and pork chops waiting in the fridge. When I said Jean already had supper on the stove, I meant that figuratively. There was a big salad on the table with arugula greens (you ever tasted them? Bitter and they got stems! I hate stems), hearts of palm (which are tasteless hunks of something, I'm not sure what), a few things not so bad, like tomatoes and radishes and celery, and some chicken that looked like it had been boiled. Which it mighta been. All dressed with totally tasteless oil and vinegar. Jean was taking homemade bread (and by that I mean her bread-machine bread) out of the oven and I thanked God for that. At least I'd have one thing solid to eat.

I greeted my family and sat down to the big old salad and we all pretended to have a grand old time eating it. Well, maybe just me.

I was real glad that Jean was officially on this case. I always discussed cases with her, but felt guilty. With her officially on this one, I didn't have to feel guilty when I discussed it with her.

'So they're not Mormons, not officially anyway,' I told her, explaining what Jerry Hudson had told me about his church. 'So wherever they were raised, in Oregon it was an off-shoot, too, I suppose, since Carol Anne and Rene told me their families were plural. But there is a church here, which means we got more plural families in Prophesy County than I ever thought.' I stopped for a moment, then added, 'Course, I never thought about having even one plural family here. I thought all that happened in Utah and Texas.'

'How many do you think there are?' Jean asked me.

I shrugged. 'The guy from the church that I

met, that Andrew Schmidt, Mr Paranoid, said it was a "small congregation,"' I told her. 'What constitutes a small congregation, I don't know.'

'What's the name of the church?' Jean asked.

'New Saints Tabernacle,' I said.

'I'll check into it tomorrow,' she said.

'Think it'll be on the Internet?' I asked, because that's what Jean meant when she said she'd 'check into it.'

She nodded. 'If not, I'll find another way,' she said, and by the look on her face, I think she meant it.

Jean McDonnell – Wednesday
I checked the Internet the next day, Googling my brains out – nothing at all on a New Saints Tabernacle anywhere in Oklahoma. There was one in Utah, so I looked that up. There were no names associated with the website, since polygamy is against the law, but there was some information. New Saints Tabernacle was started in the late 1950s in a valley in Utah where there was no electricity and the only water was a creek that ran through the valley. Wells were dug and homes sprang up and a small church house was built for the nine families (forty-two men, women, and children) that now lived in the small village they named New Saints. New Saints, Utah was never recorded with the post office, it being a plural community, so whoever made this website had to be a citizen or former citizen of the small town.

By 2007, the date of the last entry on this website, the community now had seventy-five families, totaling almost 900 people, including children. According to the website, New Saints was still 'off the grid,' with the only electricity supplied by generators that were used sparingly, the water by wells. The children were taught in a communal school with various parents teaching them, mostly lessons they would need to live in their own community, such as sewing, cooking, making and using cleaning agents, how to plant a house garden, and child-rearing for the girls, and carpentry, mechanics, animal husbandry, and soil retention and farming for the boys. According to the author of the website, some children did go off to college, but the 'majority' came back to New Saints afterwards to offer what they learned to the community and to raise their own families.

I couldn't help but wonder what any of these people would say if someone were to mention to them how close their community was to the original idea of communism? It tickled me to think of it.

All of this Googled information was fine, but it still didn't answer the question of how many families in Prophesy County were plural. So I got off the computer and picked up the telephone off my desk. My next client wasn't due for another half hour, and this was official business, even if I was enjoying myself. Research has always been my secret love.

There was no listing in any of the small towns in our area code for New Saints Tabernacle, and the only listing I got from directory assistance for Andrew Schmidt, the man from the church Milt had met the night before, was unlisted. Milt did mention he was a little paranoid. I wondered about the straight-ahead approach, looked at my notes and called Rene Hudson. She seemed to be the one most likely to blab.

'Hello?' she said in a sing-song voice when she picked up the phone.

'Rene? Hi, it's Jean McDonnell,' I said.

'Who?' she asked.

'Dr McDonnell? The sheriff's wife?' I tried.

'Oh, yeah! Hey, how you doing?' she asked.

'I'm just fine, Rene, how are you?' I asked.

'Oh, OK, I guess. Me and Carol Anne have to get everything ready for the funeral and it's a real bummer,' she said.

'Have they released the body yet?' I asked, surprised.

'No, I don't think so,' she said. 'Carol Anne just said we need to be ready when they do.'

'That makes sense,' I said. 'The reason I'm calling, Rene, is about your church.'

'The New Saints Tabernacle?' she asked.

'Yes,' I answered. 'How many people go to your church?'

'I dunno. I never counted,' she said.

'Approximately,' I encouraged.

'Well, there's maybe ten on the men's side – bunch more on the women's side, of course.'

'So men and women are separated during the service?' I asked.

'Of course,' she said. 'How else would the men be able to concentrate?'

'Right,' I said. 'So maybe about ten families all together?'

'I guess,' she answered, 'although some of the men might not come to service all the time. So there might be more than that.'

'Can you give me some of the names of the families? I need to talk to them,' I told her.

Taking my request quite casually, Rene said, 'Well, there's the Schmidts, Andrew and his wives...'

'Someone other than Andrew,' I suggested.

'Ah, David Bollinger and his wives. You need their address?' she asked.

I said, 'Yes,' and she read it out to me.

'Oh, and here's another. Sarie Whitman. She's the second wife of Thomas Whitman. She's got two little girls. Here's their address.'

And she read that one off, along with three others. Altogether, including the Schmidts and the Hudsons, that was seven out of maybe ten plural families in Prophesy and Tejas Counties.

'Well, thanks so much, Rene,' I said to her, and really meant it.

'Hey, you're welcome! You should come see the burial dress we're making for Mary. It's gorgeous!'

'Thanks. Maybe I'll come by,' I said and hung up.

FOUR

Dalton Pettigrew – Wednesday

'Milt?' Dalton said timidly, not wanting to disturb the sheriff right now, since he already seemed disturbed enough.

Milt slammed some papers down on his desk and said, real testy-like, 'What is it, Dalton?'

'Ah, you wanted me to tell you about that dead body?'

'What about it?' Milt said, looking back at his desk.

'Ah, I don't have a cause of death yet—'

'Then why are you bothering me with it?' Milt demanded.

'Well, he looked like he'd been strangled...'

Milt's shoulders drooped and he hung his head for a minute, then looked up and sighed. 'Sorry, Dalton. I'm worrying about this other case and being ornery. The ME'll let us know if you're right. You ID him?'

'No sir, nothing on him but some change and a Swiss army knife.'

'Get his prints from the ME's office and have Holly help you get on the right stuff with the computer.' Milt waved him away. 'Just talk to Holly. She knows all about that shit.'

79

'Yes, sir,' Dalton said and headed for the bull-pen. Before disturbing Holly, however, he needed to get the prints. He called the ME's office and Terry answered the phone. 'Hey, Terry, it's Dalton Pettigrew from the sheriff's office?'

'Hey, Dalton. How are you?'

'I'm just fine, Terry. Thanks for asking. Ah, I need to get the fingerprints on that dead body you picked up yesterday?'

'Sure, we already took 'em. Want me to fax 'em over or would you rather we email 'em?'

Dalton thought about it. 'Ah, hold on.' He put Terry on hold and got up slowly, checking out Holly as he did. He'd noticed this morning that she had on something new – at least, new to him. It was a dress, like a sundress, mostly pink but with big yellow flowers on it, with those skinny shoulder straps and all, but with it being late fall she had a long-sleeved yellow T-shirt underneath it. The dress was real short, but she had on black tights without feet, the ones that look like really tight stretch pants – he didn't know what they called them – and yellow shoes with lots of straps. He thought she looked really pretty, especially since her hair was down. He walked to her desk and waited until she was off the phone.

'Hey, Holly?' he said quietly behind her.

Holly jumped and turned around. She laughed nervously. 'Oh, Dalton! I didn't hear you come up. Can I help you?'

'Ah, yeah. I need to check out some fingerprints and Milt said you knew how to do that.'

'Sure! Let me see the prints,' Holly said, smiling at him.

'Ah, I've got Terry from the ME's office on the phone and he's got the prints. He wants to know if we want them faxed over here or email-ed?' he said, letting out a breath. He'd rehearsed that speech all the way over to her desk, and he was glad it was over with.

'Have him email them to me, OK? Then come over here and I'll show you how it's done!' she said, all smiles.

Dalton tried to smile back but was afraid it came out as more of a sneer. He went back to his desk to talk to Terry, but he'd hung up. So Dalton called the ME's office again, got Terry and asked him to email the prints. 'What's the addy?' Terry asked.

Dalton hung his head. This was getting way too complicated. What in the world was an addy? He took a chance and called out to Holly, 'Terry wants to know the addy!'

'I'll take it! Which line?' Holly asked. Dalton gratefully told her then sat back and tried to breathe calmly. If he didn't watch it, his asthma was going to come back, that's what his mama was always telling him.

Holly hung up the phone and called out to Dalton. 'Come on over and I'll show you what to do,' she said.

Dalton levered himself to an upright position – he still worked out enough that his line-back-er's body hadn't turned to fat, but he'd strained his back last weekend helping his mama move furniture – and moved to Holly's desk.

She pulled up a nearby chair next to hers. 'Have a seat,' she said.

Dalton sat down, fully aware of how close he was to Holly. He could smell her, and it was nice. Kind of fruity, a little flowery, but mostly just real nice. He was aware of her voice, telling him this or that as she hit keys on the key pad of her computer, changing the screen from this to that. He saw the fingerprints up on the screen and then something else happened, but he wasn't really listening to the words. He didn't really like computers, afraid they were smarter than him. He just liked listening to Holly's voice. It was a pretty voice, almost musical.

'Sorry,' Holly said. 'He's not in any of the databases.'

Finally realizing she was speaking directly to him, Dalton said, 'Huh?'

'Your guy's not in any of the regular databases,' she repeated. 'I'll keep looking in the not so regular ones, but it doesn't look hopeful.'

'OK then, thanks,' Dalton said, reluctantly standing up.

'You're welcome,' Holly said, again smiling at him. 'Any time.'

He nodded his head and moved on. He sorta wondered if his dead body had anything to do with the sheriff's dead body, but he figured Milt would know more about that than him. It wasn't like they had a whole lot of dead bodies in the county, but they'd been known to have a few. As close as Vern's shop was to the highway, it could have been just a dump job, as far as Dalton knew.

Milt Kovak – Wednesday
The next morning I told Anthony to go to Bishop with Nita and talk to the troop leaders about setting up the Boy Scouts. We'd still have almost three hours of sunlight once they got out of school. We got a lot of Boy Scouts in Prophesy County: two troops in Longbranch, another two in Bishop, and one in Harrellville, which always surprises me 'cause it's a small place, but the boys are all brothers or cousins, or related in some way, so we had plenty of kids to comb the whole cul-de-sac for the suspected murder weapon.

Jean called me around ten and gave me the addresses of five other plural families in Prophesy County. I was flabbergasted.

'There are at least ten families in the church, according to Rene,' Jean said. Then added, 'But of course, you'll have to take that with a grain of salt.'

'Why are you so hard on poor little Rene?' I asked.

'Maybe because you call her "poor little Rene,"' she answered. Then laughed. 'No, dear, I'm not jealous.' There was a silence, then she said, 'There's just something about her. She's so different from the other two—'

'You never met Mary,' I reminded her.

'Not in person, but have you been around her children? Have you heard the way they talk about her? The kids, Jerry, Carol Anne, hell, even Rene? She was a saint. Carol Anne is—'

'Your secret crush,' I said.

'Stop it. She's a stand-up woman. She's trust-worthy. Rene ... isn't.'

'You know, honey, I've never seen you go this much on instinct with patients—'

'These people aren't patients.'

'Well, yeah they are. You had Rene in your office.'

'Interviewing her for the case. Not as a patient,' my wife said.

'Still. You seem to be going more by the seat of your pants than usual. That's my territory, honey.'

Jean sighed. 'I don't know, babe,' she said. 'These people are getting under my skin. Part of it is I have strong opinions on this lifestyle, and these people...'

Her voice drifted off. I said into the silence, 'These people are changing your opinions?'

Again, she sighed. 'I don't know. But they are certainly putting a strain on my certainty.'

With that she said goodbye and hung up, and I looked at the list set before me. The church house, according to what I'd found out, was in Tejas County, which was the next county over, where my amigo Bill Williams was sheriff.

84

Checking out the six names given to me, all except Andrew Schmidt were in Prophesy County. Schmidt was in Tejas County. I wasn't sure how this church worked, if it was like a lot of Protestant sects, where there was a preacher and a board of elders or whatever that oversaw paying him and the bills of the church, or what. But if I had to guess, I'd guess that the other person who lived in Tejas County, where the church house was, would be the person in charge.

I called Bill Williams, found him at his desk like he should be, and told him what had been going on over here with our plural family.

'Ah, hell, I've been keeping quiet about old Earl Mayhew and his wives and kids,' Bill said. 'He's a nice enough old bird and his wives seem happy enough. Kids keep out of trouble. But yeah, he's the preacher or whatever it is at that church. It's way back in the piney woods and I try not to disturb 'em or let anybody else do so. I think to each his own, ya know?'

'Yeah, I know,' I said. 'I haven't arrested the husband over here either. Figure he's got enough trouble. How many wives the preacher got?' I asked.

'Only two that I know of. Ha!' Bill said, letting out a laugh. 'Who'da thought I'd ever say that about wives, huh?'

I laughed back. 'Know what you mean. This kinda thing gets your thoughts all twisted up.'

'Yeah, I know. When I first met Earl, I came

home, looked at my wife, and thought, "now what would she think about us bringing in a cute little twenty-two-year-old?"'

'Whoo, don't I know it. Had the same kinda thought myself. But seriously, Bill, I need to talk to this Earl fella. Find out what I can about Hudson and his three wives.'

'Woodoggies,' Bill said, 'three of 'em. Don't that beat all?'

'I'm tellin' ya,' I said.

'Well, you come on over here and I'll take you out yonder where the church is. He's got a trailer set up right next to it. Church is one of them metal buildings you see, but it's got a big ol' cross on top of it.'

'I'll be there in about twenty,' I told him, and hung up.

It takes about thirty minutes to get to the county seat of Tejas County where Bill Williams' office is, but I drive fast. Me and Bill chewed the fat for a while then he headed out to a four- wheel-drive vehicle.

'Seriously?' I said.

'Hey, wouldn't you go where no one could see you, if you were breaking the law?' Bill asked.

'Never thought about it much, but I guess you're right. Of course, I rarely, if ever, contemplate things criminal,' I said.

Bill hooted with laughter. 'Yeah, just things immoral, anti-social, and bad for the complexion.'

'Drive,' I suggested.

86

Now we don't have a lot of piny woods in Oklahoma, but there's a little hidden dab of 'em on the east side of Tejas County – Tejas County is just to the west of us, so this was close. The trees reached the sky, all skinny and tall, not the Christmas tree kind at all. And they had big ol' pine cones falling off of 'em. Just getting out of the car I spied half a dozen pristine cones, the middle of 'em bigger than my two hands cupped together. I picked up a bunch and threw them in the back of Bill's car.

'What?' he whined on seeing me do it.

'My wife'll do something creative with these come Christmas. Just wait and see.'

'I'd rather not,' he said.

I could spy the church through the trees, and it was exactly what Bill had said it was: a manufactured metal building with a cross on top. There was another building to the right of it, I think for Sunday school, or whatever it is these Mormon offshoots liked to call their in-doctrination of children. We Baptists call it Sunday school. To the left of the church build-ing was a double-wide trailer, what we Baptists would call a parsonage. Getting closer, I could see a single-wide one scrunched up to the back of it.

Pointing, I asked Bill, 'What's that?'

He shrugged. 'Dunno.'

He walked up the aluminum steps of the dou-ble-wide and rapped sharply on the door. In less than a minute a woman opened it. Even from where I was standing at the bottom of the steps, I could tell she was short, maybe five feet even, with graying brown hair pulled back and clipped at the nape of her neck. She was wearing a long skirt that touched the tops of her sensible-looking shoes and a blouse that started at her throat with sleeves that went to her wrists. This whole ensemble was covered with a handmade apron displaying Noah and his animals.

The woman's smile barely lifted her lips and never reached her eyes. 'Hello, Sheriff,' she said to Bill. 'How may we help you?'

'Earl around?' Bill asked.

'He's in the church house.'

'Be OK if I go over there?' he asked.

She stared at him for a long moment, then said, 'If you don't mind interrupting a man at prayer.' With that said, she shut the door. She didn't slam it. Just shut it firmly.

Bill looked down at me. 'OK, so one wife's not exactly happy,' he said as he came down the steps.

'I'd say she's pretty surly, but that's just me.'

It was about a hundred feet from the door of the double-wide to the door of the metal church building. Bill rapped on the church double doors then opened one. 'Hey, Brother Earl, mind if we come in?' he called into the room.

We both stepped in and I saw a vast room, devoid of anything – pews, chairs, whatever. There was a podium at the back and a man was standing there. He was a short, thin man with wiry gray hair shooting out every which way, a beak of a nose, and small, squinty eyes, color hard to tell.

'Hey there, Sheriff!' the man called back, coming down from the raised dais to meet us. He shook hands with Bill and then got introduced to me.

'I take it you're here about Sister Mary Hudson?' he asked.

I nodded and he shook his head.

'The Lord works in mysterious ways,' he said. 'I'm still praying on this one, though. I don't think this was God's will. Somebody murdered that poor woman and took a good mother away from her children. I am at your beck and call, Sheriff Kovak. Anything you want or need, I will help you receive.'

'Thank you, Brother Earl,' I said. 'If we could sit for a spell so I could ask you a few questions?'

'Absolutely! We got about a couple hundred folding chairs back in that closet,' he said, pointing to the right of the podium. 'Sheriff Bill, why don't you round us up a few?'

Before Bill could even think about protesting, the two of us were knee-deep in the closet pulling out beige folding chairs. 'How come we ended up doing this?' he said in a half whisper.

'Beats the hell out of me,' I whispered back, before I remembered I was in a house of God and therefore shouldn't be cussing out loud, or even to myself, really.

We took the chairs back to where Brother Earl waited for us. Once the three of us were seated, I said, 'Brother Earl, I thank you for taking the time. I just wanted to know if you had any idea who might have done such a thing? If Mary or her husband Jerry Hudson had any enemies that you knew of?'

'Well, now,' he said, looking off, 'I don't know the Hudsons really well; they've only been with us two years, and though I did get to know Jerry some through our men's group, I didn't know Mary that well. My ladies tell me she was a wonderful mother and a gifted homemaker.'

'Any troubles that might have reached your ears? Rumors about trouble in the family, some other lady mad at Mary about something? Any gossip at all?'

Brother Earl frowned. 'I don't hold with gossip, Sheriff,' he said in a stiff tone. 'As a group, we do not condone gossip and I'm sure no one would tell tales to either myself or my wives.' At this point he sighed heavily. 'But, and this is a big but, gentlemen, I have been known to hear things through ... um ... the grapevine, shall we say?' He leaned forward to impart his wisdom. 'Sister Carol Anne Hudson's brother seemed to be a bother to Sister Mary.' Straightening up, he added, 'Now I can't say what it was about, just that there appeared to be a ... um ... dispute amongst the two.'

'That'd be Dennis Rigsby?' I said.

'Um-hum. He and his mama come to our church with the Hudson family. I just noticed the two of 'em having words after Sunday service a couple of weeks ago. And one of our congregation mentioned the two of them having at it after a Thursday social supper, last week I think it was.'

'You remember which member of your congregation mentioned this to you, Brother Earl?' I asked.

'That would be confidential, Sheriff,' he said. 'I would not be at liberty to divulge that information.'

I looked at Bill Williams and he shrugged. I took a minute to think about it. I knew Catholic confession was confidential, but I knew that anything told to a priest outside of the confessional, in conversation, wasn't. So, in a Protestant sect, counseling would be like a confession, and a conversation would just be a conversation, right? I hoped so.

'Brother Earl,' I said, 'were you having a formal counseling session with this person?'

'What person?' he countered.

'The one who said they saw Mary Hudson and Carol Anne Hudson's brother Dennis having at it?'

'Now, what do you mean by a formal counseling session?' he asked.

I sighed deep. 'Mr Mayhew, I do believe you know what I'm talking about. If this wasn't a formal counseling session, then it was not confidential and you are required to tell me who it was.'

He sighed right back at me. 'Rachael McKinsey,' he said. 'Brother Michael McKinsey's wife.'

'And where would I find them?' I asked, looking quickly at my list of congregants. I didn't see the McKinseys on there.

'Michael and his family live in Longbranch,' he said. 'I'll get you the address.'

'Before we do that, Brother Earl, is there anything else you can tell me about the Hudsons?'

'Like I said, Jerry's a nice enough fella, his wives seem fine, and their kids – other than being a handful – are good kids. I don't know anybody who'd want to kill Sister Mary. And I want this duly noted: neither I nor Sister Rachael McKinsey have accused Brother Dennis Rigsby of a darned thing, OK?'

I stood up. 'Understood, Brother Earl. Now, about Mrs McKinsey's address?'

On the way back to Longbranch, I called my wife on my cell phone and asked her if she was busy.

'No. I finished with patients this morning. Just busy-work for the hospital this afternoon. What's up?'

'You wanna help me interview another plural family?' I asked.

'Why, yes, Sheriff, I believe I would like that very much,' my wife said. I think she was being flippant.

I picked her up in my Jeep and we headed to the house in town belonging to Michael McKinsey and his family.

The house that matched the address was in an area of houses with acreage. The McKinseys had about five acres, I'd say, and the house that sprawled out on those acres might have taken up at least one all by itself. It was a one-story house that, from the front anyway, appeared to be shaped like an off-center 'U,' with the wings going toward the back.

I'd called ahead to make sure Rachael McKinsey would be there and she'd answered the phone herself. She'd refused to talk to me without her husband present, and I'd asked her to get him to come home because I needed to speak to her within the hour. There was a large Dodge Ram pick-up truck in the circle drive, and I pulled in behind it.

A man answered my knock. He was about six foot two, maybe six foot three inches tall, had to weigh well over 200 pounds, had a blond military haircut and his hands, hanging off meaty, muscled forearms, were fisted. I pulled my wife behind me.

'Mr McKinsey?' I said.

'Sheriff,' he said back. If this had been happening a hundred years earlier, somebody would be pulling a gun right about now.

'I need to speak to your wife Rachael about a police matter, sir,' I said.

'I speak for my wife,' he said.

'Well, no, sir, in this case you don't. I understand Mrs McKinsey has an eyewitness account that might be crucial to my investigation of the murder of Mary Hudson.'

'My wife doesn't know anything about Mary Hudson,' he said, and started to shut the door.

I almost hesitated putting my boot-shod foot in the door, but a man has to do what a man has to do. So I did.

'Ow!' I said.

'Then move your foot, Sheriff,' he said.

'Mr McKinsey, you're gonna make me come back here with a warrant? It's just gonna waste my time and this psychiatrist's time,' I said, pointing at Jean behind me. 'And your time too, if you took time off work. I mean, you'd barely get back to work before we had a deputy out there pulling you into the station so your wife can talk to us. I understand she doesn't speak without you present?'

'Damn right she doesn't. And you know what?' he said.

'What?' I said.

'You're right.' He opened the door wider. 'I don't really give a crap about your time or her time, but I do about my own. So come on in and get this over with.'

Rachael McKinsey was already sitting in the living room, an immaculate room with no personality at all. All the furniture looked generic in shades of brown and beige. The only adornment on the walls was a cross over the mantle, and under foot was a thin beige carpet.

The lady sitting on the brown sofa was the only woman in this sect I'd seen with shortish hair. It was still long by most standards, but not by the standard that seemed to be set by the women I'd seen. Her dress was beige, totally covering her body from head to foot. The only spark of color in the entire room was the bright red shape of a handprint on her right cheek.

I wasn't surprised that Michael McKinsey was a hitter. I made a mental note to check with Charlie Smith, police chief of Longbranch, when I got back to the sheriff's department. See if there'd been domestics called on this house. With all the land around it, and the stifled demeanor of the woman sitting on the sofa, it was a good bet she didn't make much noise when he abused her.

'Mrs McKinsey,' I said, addressing the woman on the sofa who still hadn't looked up from her folded hands in her lap, 'I'm Sheriff Milt Kovak, and this is Dr Jean McDonnell, a department consultant. I understand you witnessed a confrontation between Sister Mary Hudson and Dennis Rigsby last Thursday after a social at the church. Is that correct, ma'am?'

She said nothing. Just sat there staring at her hands.

'Ma'am?' I said again.

Still no answer.

I looked at Michael McKinsey. 'Would you

95

ask your wife to answer us, please?'

'I said you could talk to her. I didn't say she'd talk back,' he said, as a smile played across his mouth.

I stood up. 'OK, then, Mrs McKinsey, looks like you're what they call a hostile witness and I'll have to take you into custody until I find out what happened.'

I walked over to her and pulled her up by one arm. She flinched, bit her lip, but stood up. I loosened my grip on her arm. Who knew what kind of bruises that ugly beige dress covered.

'OK, Rachael, we'll be seeing you,' Michael said.

Tears were streaming down her face, but she still said nothing.

'Mommy!' wailed a young voice, and a little girl of about four came running from the back of the house. Her blonde hair was shorn almost to her scalp. She wore a black dress that was too long for her and she tripped as she ran. Her little fists pounded my leg. 'You can't take my mommy! You can't! You can't!'

'Emily!' McKinsey shouted. 'Come get this kid!'

A young woman, whose age I was definitely going to check, came out of the hall and took the child. She didn't look more than fifteen or sixteen, but she wore the same kind of band on her ring finger as Rachael. Her carrot-red hair hung down to her waist and her pale blue dress was cut the same as Rachael's. I was startled to

96

see the look she gave Rachael – a half-hidden smile and a look of triumph. The child beat at the young woman, trying to get away from her. I let go of Rachael's arm.

'Mr McKinsey, who is that young woman?' I asked.

'My sister-in-law,' he said, a smile on his face.

'I'm going to be back in the morning and I want to see her birth certificate and your wife Rachael's birth certificate and, just for the hell of it, birth certificates for every child in this house. Anybody who doesn't have one will be going into custody. And yours too, you big-boned asshole son-of-a-bitchin' mother—'

Jean had my arm by then and was hauling me out the door, which was rude. I had a lot more to say.

She got me outside and I asked her, 'You got a camera in your telephone, right?'

'Yes,' she said, staring hard at me.

'I want you to go back in and take a record of Rachael's bruises. Count 'em if you have to. I just wanna make sure he knows we know and that there better not be any more in the morning!' I said, breathing hard. I was so mad I could've gotten physical with Michael McKinsey, which would probably have gotten me killed; but I gotta say, that first punch of mine woulda felt *so* good.

'There's no way that woman will strip in front of me,' Jean said. 'She doesn't want anyone to know he beats her. And the other one – the, excuse the expression, 'sister-in-law' – she won't help. Milt, we need to just leave here, OK?'

'He's gonna beat her again!' I said.

'Come on, honey,' Jean coaxed, pulling me by the arm. 'There's nothing we can do here. You know that. You have to actually see him assault her, or have someone call—'

'I know, I know!' I snapped, shaking off her arm and going on my own to the Jeep. 'Just pisses me off!' I said, once we were both in the car.

'I know, honey,' she said.

'Sorry,' I said. 'Didn't mean to take it out on you.'

'You didn't. I know how you feel. Impotent.'

The word stopped me. 'You mean like I can't do anything about McKinsey, right?'

Jean smiled and traced my cheek with her index finger. 'Yes, honey. You are definitely not impotent any other way.'

'Damn straight,' I said, as I started the car.

Jean McDonnell – Wednesday

I knew how Milt felt. He dropped me off at the hospital and I stood in the foyer, considering what I could do. One thing was screaming at me loud and clear. Michael McKinsey had another punishment for his women other than beating. The length of Rachael McKinsey's hair, and the shorn state of the rambunctious little girl's hair, reminded me of a documentary I'd seen in med

98

school. A documentary that depicted resistance fighters cutting the hair or shaving the heads of women who had slept with Nazis during World War II. In a sect like the one we were dealing with, this kind of punishment went to the very core of their womanhood. Women in this sect never cut their hair, and even after marriage kept their hair loose, hanging down their backs. To cut their hair showed the other women how 'bad' this one had been, and was a lesson to them all.

The whole thing made me want to puke. I felt like I'd been taken in by Jerry Hudson and his clan. Lured into a false sense of security. The true story lay in the clan of Michael McKinsey. Something had to be done for Rachael and her small daughter. And I decided that I was probably the one to do it.

Milt Kovak – Wednesday

After I dropped Jean off at the hospital, I figured there was nothing to it but to do it. Go to the source. I headed to The Branches to have a serious talk with Dennis Rigsby.

Unfortunately, he wasn't home, but his mother was.

'Dennis is not home at the moment, Sheriff,' she said upon opening the door. 'What can I do for you?'

'Could you tell me where I could find him, Mrs Rigsby?' I asked.

'He's at work, of course. Come in, Sheriff.

Let me get you a glass of lemonade.'

'No, ma'am, I'm afraid I'm in a bit of a hurry. Could you tell me, please, where Dennis works?'

'Oh, no, I can't do that, Sheriff,' she said. 'You can't go disturbing him at work! They're just awful to him there, and a visit by the police would just be the excuse they need to fire him!' She welled up. 'Oh, no, you just can't do that!'

I checked my watch. It was getting close to five o'clock. 'Ma'am, what time does he get off?'

'His shift ends at five,' she said.

'Well, it's almost that now. If it's close, I can run by and catch him as he gets off. Won't have to actually bother him at work at all. Now, where is it he works?'

She sighed. 'Just don't get him fired!' she pleaded.

'I won't,' I assured her.

'At the Jack-in-the-Box on Rancho Road.'

I had to wonder what Dennis Rigsby, whose back was so bad he was on social security disability benefit and relied on Jerry Hudson for the rest of his keep, was doing with a job. And if social security knew about it. I thought I might bring this up when I talked to him – if I thought he didn't kill Mary Hudson. A little social security fraud was nothing compared to murder.

Rancho Road where the Jack-in-the-Box was located was the main strip of Bishop and the

Jack-in-the-Box franchise had to get special permission to put their trademark box up in the air. Most everything on Rancho Road was made of red rock and Mexican tile, save the Jack-in-the-Box and McDonalds.

I found Dennis Rigsby, all dolled up in his Jack-in-the-Box get-up, getting into a navy blue and rust Honda Civic, vintage 1989–90, somewhere around there. I pulled up next to him and motioned for him to get in the passenger seat of my Jeep. He did. He smelled like French fries. Not a bad smell.

'Hey, Sheriff,' he said on sliding in. 'What can I do you for?'

Witty, I thought. 'Got some questions for you, Dennis.'

'Well, I'll check and see if I got answers.'

Jack Benny he wasn't. 'I been hearing some stuff about you and Mary Hudson,' I said.

His hands went up in a defensive gesture. 'I swear I never laid a hand on the woman!' And then he laughed.

'Now why would you say that?' I asked.

'What?' he said, hands now down and a frown on his face.

'That you never laid a hand on her. How about a meat tenderizer?'

'Oh, jeez!' he said, a frightened look on his face. 'Ah, no, Sheriff! Really, I was just teasing! I thought you were insinuating that me and her – that you know, were, like, doing it or something.'

101

'Were you?' I countered.

'Oh, God no! That's why it was a joke, see? Like, I would never, ever touch that woman! Ever,' he said. Then ended with a sincerely spoken, 'Never ever.'

'Wasn't your type?' I said.

He rolled his eyes. 'Hardly!'

'So what were the two of you fighting about after the church social last week?'

That pulled him up short. He just stared at me. Then he said, 'Church social? When was that?'

'The Thursday before she was killed on Monday.'

'Gosh, it must not have been important, Sheriff. I can't even remember talking to her that— Now wait!' he said, and I gotta say, the guy was a lousy actor. 'I believe we did speak for just a moment that evening. About the boys! My oldest nephew Ben and her son Jason. They're both fourteen and they've been acting out. Mostly it's Jason, Ben's just following along, you know, and I wanted her to rein Jason in—'

'Isn't that something the mothers would handle?' I asked, not buying this for a minute.

'Carol Anne didn't know about this incident. And I didn't want her to know. That's why I went to Mary about it and she got defensive. You know,' he said, in a conspiratorial aside to me, 'all mother-hen stuff. It might have looked like we were fighting, but that's all it was.'

'Uh huh,' I said. 'What were the boys doing

that you felt compelled to keep it from your sister and run to Mary about it?'

'I don't think I have the right to tell you, Sheriff. The boys have since owned up to it and taken their licks, and it's not something anyone in the family would want to tell the authorities about.'

'Well, tell you what. Nobody else in the family needs to know about this. Just you, me, and the boys. I'll follow you back to your house, we'll get the boys and go have a talk. How does that sound?'

'The boys have after-school activities...'

'Let me call Carol Anne and check,' I said, getting out my cell phone.

Dennis sighed. 'It wasn't about the boys,' he said.

'Then what was it about?' I asked.

'Why don't you arrest me, Sheriff? 'Cause I'm not telling you. It had nothing to do with her getting murdered. *I* had nothing to do with her getting murdered. I've never harmed anyone in my life! But what Mary and I said to each other was private. And that's all I'm gonna say.'

I stared at the whiny little bastard. I could take him in, make him stew in a jail cell for a couple of days. Doubt if he could take it. But I thought about his mother and her worry that just me talking to him would get him fired. Hell, if he landed in jail for a couple of days they surely would fire him. Even though he was on dis-

103

ability, and living off Jerry Hudson.

'So why you working at Jack-in-the-Box?' I asked. 'I thought if you were on disability, you weren't supposed to have a job.'

'It's part-time. And they let me sit on a stool while I work. Social security says it's OK if it's part-time and I'm paid under a certain amount of money.'

But Jack-in-the-Box? You had to wonder. Well, that was judgmental, I thought. Who am I to decide how a person lives or how much they need to live on? Maybe he had to take lots of meds and it cost a lot. Or maybe he was paying off hospital bills for him and his mama. Hell, I didn't know.

Did I think he killed Mary Hudson? No. I really didn't. But damned if now I didn't want to know what he and Mary were talking about – and I wanted to know real bad.

I sighed. 'Look, Dennis, I don't want to cause you problems with your job or your mama or your sister or anybody, OK? I just want to know what you and Mary were talking about.'

He shook his head, mimed locking his mouth and throwing away the key. Real grown-up, this guy.

'Just go home,' I said, as I started the Jeep. He got out and I burned rubber getting out of there.

Nita Skitteridge – Wednesday
It was getting dark when I let the Boy Scouts go. They'd gotten there at three thirty that after-

104

noon and I'd done a grid for the search, starting half of them at the street level by Rene Hudson's house, the other half at street level by Carol Anne Hudson's house. Since we had eighteen Scouts, that meant nine on each side, walking arm's length from each other, from the fence at the back of each property to the sidewalk in front of each property.

The only excitement of the day was the yellow dog who was very excited about all the activity. I finally had to go to Mary Hudson's house to get Carol Anne to come get the dog. She went inside for some dog biscuits and came out, squatting down and calling, 'Come here, Butch! Good dog, here, Butch!'

'His name's Butch?' I said, laughing.

'No,' she said, '*her* name is Butch. We had the kids vote on what name they wanted, and since there are more boys than girls, we ended up with Butch.'

The yellow dog – Butch – came lumbering up to Carol Anne and almost knocked her over in her excitement. She licked Carol Anne, grabbed a biscuit and then jumped on me, her paws on my shoulders, biscuit in mouth, as if offering it to me.

'No, thanks, Butch,' I said, 'I'll let you have it.'

'Get down, Butch!' Carol Anne scolded. To me she said, as she grabbed Butch's collar, 'I'll put her in the garage until you're through.'

'Thanks,' I said, and headed back to the

105

Scouts. For another hour of nothing.

After the troop leaders had taken the boys home, I again rang Carol Anne's – or Mary's – doorbell. Carol Anne came to the door.

'We're through,' I said. 'You can let Butch out.'

'Thank you,' she said, smiling. 'She'll be thrilled.'

I waved goodbye and headed to my squad car.

My impression: whoever killed Mary Hudson with that foot-long meat tenderizer thing must have taken it home with them, or dumped it in the woods on the way. It was definitely not on the cul-de-sac. And, something I won't admit to my husband who's been trying to get me to agree to buy a Rottweiler for a year now, I found a dog I actually liked. A little.

Dalton Pettigrew – Wednesday
Dalton decided to talk the case over with Anthony Dobbins, another deputy. He didn't want to talk about it with Emmett Hopkins, who was the sheriff's best friend and second in command, or Jasmine, another deputy, because she was Emmett's wife. And he didn't want to talk to Nita Skitteridge about it, because she was brand new and he didn't know her. But, even though Anthony was what was now called African-American, and Dalton had never had a friend who was African-American, or ever really talked to one, he liked Anthony OK, and figured he was a pretty good deputy. And, he

106

had to face it, he needed to talk to someone.

So towards the end of shift on the second day of the case, Dalton walked up to Anthony's desk and stood there. Anthony was on the phone and so he waited. Anthony kept stealing glances at the huge white guy looming over him, and cut short his conversation with his wife.

'Hey, Dalton,' Anthony said, standing up.

'Hey, Anthony,' Dalton said.

They stood there for almost a full minute before Dalton said, 'Ah, can I talk with you after shift?'

Startled, Anthony said, 'Ah, yeah, sure. You want to go get a drink or something?'

'I could use some iced tea,' Dalton said.

Anthony nodded. 'Down on the square? Doris's Diner?'

'OK,' Dalton said and grinned. 'Thanks, Anthony.'

Anthony said, 'You're welcome,' as Dalton walked away.

After shift ended at five o'clock that afternoon, and as both men headed in separate cars toward the square, neither man noticed how good the square was looking on this cool October evening. How mums had been set out in the flowerbeds and how wreaths were on the gas lights surrounding the courthouse. Nor did they notice the fall designs in the windows of the shops that surrounded Doris's Diner. This may have been because they'd both lived in Longbranch their entire lives, but more than likely had more to do with the fact that they were both men.

Once at Doris's, the two men took seats in a booth by the front window, getting many fewer looks than they would have only a few years before.

'So what's up?' Anthony asked, ready to get this, whatever it was, over with.

'You heard about that dead body they found over at Vern's Auto Repair on Stillwater?' Dalton asked.

'Yeah. Sure did. You're handling that, right?' Anthony said.

Dalton sighed. 'Yeah. I guess. I just don't know what to do right now. The guy didn't have any ID on him, and his fingerprints didn't show up in any of the...' he tried to remember the word and finally came up with 'databases that Holly tried.' His face turned red when he mentioned her name. This did not go unnoticed by Anthony. 'And I wonder if this could be connected to the sheriff's case, you know, that lady over at The Branches with all the kids?'

'Yeah, I know,' Anthony said.

'You think it's connected?' Dalton asked.

'What does the sheriff say?' Anthony countered.

'Nothing. I mean, he didn't mention a connection, so I didn't bring it up. Not my place, huh?'

'Well, if you think there is, then, yeah, it's

your place.'

'But I don't think it is,' Dalton said.

Anthony sighed. 'Then no reason to mention it to the sheriff, I guess.'

'So now what?' Dalton asked Anthony, and sat back, waiting for Anthony to tell him what to do.

'You check for missing persons?' Anthony asked.

Dalton shook his head.

'Well, I guess that's the next thing,' Anthony said, trying not to stress how obvious that should be. 'And then follow up on anything that looks promising. And if you don't find anything in the county or state, I guess you'd have to do a wider search, maybe the country.'

'Golly,' Dalton said. 'That would take some time.'

'Holly can help you with that,' Anthony said. 'There are lots more databases for different things, and they have one where you can put in your parameters—'

Seeing the pained look on Dalton's face, Anthony explained, 'Like the guy's approximate age, height, weight, hair color, all that sort of thing. Then the computer will just look for missing men fitting that description. It'll still be a lot, then there's a service we can pay money to use if we have to that'll do facial recognition.' Again, he got the pained look from Dalton. 'What does that sound like, Dalton? Facial recognition?'

Dalton thought about it and Anthony could see on his fellow deputy's face when the light dawned. 'Oh! Something that recognizes faces!'

Anthony smiled and leaned across the table to punch Dalton in the shoulder. 'You got it!' he said, wondering how in the world this big, goofy guy ever got to be a deputy. How did he pass the academy? Then he mentally shook his head and told himself it was none of his business.

He also knew that what he was about to ask was none of his business either, but he decided to risk it. 'So,' he said, after their iced teas had arrived. 'What's up with you and Holly?'

Anthony watched as Dalton's big, usually pale face turned bright red. 'Nothing,' Dalton said.

'You like her, right?' Anthony insisted.

Dalton shrugged.

'Well,' Anthony said, 'I'm pretty sure she likes you.'

Dalton stirred four packets of sugar into his iced tea. 'She seems really happy at work,' he said.

'You must have gotten to know her pretty well, when y'all were lost in the woods that time with your nephew,' Anthony said.

Yes, Dalton thought, he'd gotten to know Holly pretty well out in those woods last summer. In those few hours, OK, bunch of hours, that they were lost with his young nephew, he'd discovered how strong, caring,

110

and giving she was. And he knew that some day she was gonna make a good mom. The thought made him blush anew. Truth be known, he thought about that time a lot, and probably thought way too much about Holly.

Dalton shrugged again and Anthony decided enough was enough. He needed to get home. He downed the rest of his tea and stood up, throwing a couple of ones on the table. 'It was good talking with you, Dalton, but my wife needs me to stop by the store on the way home, so I'd better get my ass in gear.' He grinned when he said it and, after several seconds, Dalton reluctantly grinned back.

Dalton stood and held out his hand. Shaking Anthony's hand, Dalton said, 'Thanks for your help, Anthony. That was real nice of you.'

'Hey, no problem, man. Any time.' He patted Dalton on the shoulder. 'You take care now, hear?'

Dalton nodded as Anthony left the diner.

Milt Kovak – Thursday

The next morning on the way to work, me and Jean dropped by the house of Thomas Whitman and his wife Sarie, another plural family from the New Saints Tabernacle. Their house was a two-story farmhouse on the outskirts of town, on our side of downtown. When we pulled into the long driveway we saw a man at the barn, wearing coveralls and a wide-brimmed hat. He was standing by a tractor, half its hood opened, and he was wiping his hands on a red work cloth.

I turned off the Jeep's engine and rolled down the window. Didn't get out, though. I called through the window, 'Mr Whitman?'

'Yes, sir,' he said, still standing by the tractor.

'Sheriff Kovak, sir. May I get out?'

He nodded his head and Jean and I both got out of the Jeep. Whitman met us halfway and held out his wiped-clean hand. We shook and he said, 'Can I help you, Sheriff?'

Up close he was a lot older than I'd figured, wearing one of those beards that doesn't have a mustache with it – just goes from sideburns down to the chin. The beard was white and the hair I could see under the wide-brimmed hat was salt-and-pepper. His eyes were a washed-out blue and his face was ruddy from the sun and just being a farmer.

'We're interviewing the members of the New Saints Tabernacle concerning the death of Sister Mary Hudson—'

'If you're here because I'm a polygamist, you can just go on home now, Sheriff. My wife Marie died last year and now it's just me and Sarie and the kids. Not breaking any of your laws.'

'No, sir, I'm not concerned right now with the number of your wives. This is about the murder of Mrs Hudson. I just need to interview you and Mrs Whitman, see what y'all know about Mrs Hudson.'

'I didn't know the woman at all. Not my place to. Sarie mighta knowed her,' he said.

I pointed at the farmhouse. 'May I?'

He shrugged his shoulders, sighed, and said, 'Well, come on then,' and led the way to the house.

The house was freshly painted white with no trim color or anything – just all white. But it had a big front porch with white rocking chairs sitting on it. He opened the screen door and hollered, 'Sarie? Got company!'

A young woman came in from the back of the house, drying her hands on a dishtowel. She had gleaming chestnut-brown hair falling below her bottom, a pleasingly plump little body, a pretty face with dimpled cheeks, and wore a gray dress and house slippers.

'Sarie,' Whitman said, 'this is the sheriff. He's got some questions 'bout Mary Hudson. You need to answer him right, you hear?'

'Yes, Thomas,' she said.

'Where's Jane Marie?' he asked.

'Right here, Daddy,' said a voice coming from the room we were in. I swung around to see a woman sitting in a chair by the fireplace. I hadn't seen her on coming in; by their responses, neither had Thomas Whitman or my wife. She stood up and walked toward us. She was seriously tall, tall as me anyway, 'bout five foot ten or so, skinny as a rail, and ugly as a catfish. She wore the same kinda dress as Sarie, but laced up boots covering feet bigger than mine.

113

'You heard?' Whitman asked.

'Yes, Daddy,' Jane Marie answered.

Looking at me, Whitman said, 'Then I'll leave you to it, Sheriff.' With that he walked back out the front door, heading, presumably, back to his tractor.

'Please, Sheriff, ma'am,' Sarie said, looking at Jean with a sweet smile, 'have a seat. Jane Marie, could you go get us all some lemonade?'

'You're playing hostess, Sarie, why don't you do that your own self?' Jane Marie said, sitting down on the couch.

'Because I asked you to do it,' Sarie said, still standing.

'I'm already sittin' down,' Jane Marie said.

'We're fine,' I interjected. 'No need for refreshments. Ma'am,' I said, talking directly to Sarie, 'please have a seat. We just have a few questions.' Once Sarie had finally sat down, I added, 'This is Dr McDonnell. She's a consultant with the sheriff's department.'

'Nice to meet you both,' Sarie said, smiling and nodding at both of us. Jane Marie said nothing.

'We're here about the murder of Sister Mary Hudson,' I said. 'Any information y'all can give me concerning her or her family, the whole bunch of 'em, I'd really appreciate.'

Sarie and Jane Marie looked at each other then quickly looked away. Finally, Sarie said, 'We hardly knew the Hudson family. They're fairly new to the community.'

'That's right,' Jane Marie said, her words almost stumbling over the last of Sarie's statement. Made it all sound a little fishy.

'They've been here two years, I understand,' I said.

Again, the women exchanged looks. 'That's true,' Jane Marie said. 'But we don't have a lot in common.'

'How so?' I pushed.

Sarie sighed and said, 'Mama Marie, Thomas's first wife, was barren after Jane Marie, and Thomas didn't marry me until seven years ago. I have two little girls.' She said all that and stopped talking.

Jane Marie added, 'And they're both retards—'

'They are not!' Sarie said, starring daggers at her ... um, stepdaughter? Who knows.

'Well, they ain't normal!' Jane Marie shot back. 'That's why Daddy won't let her take 'em to church!'

'That's not it at all, Jane Marie, and you better watch your mouth—'

'Or what?' Jane Marie shot back. A smile played at her lips. 'I think I already proved who Daddy stands by, and it ain't you and your retards!'

Sarie stood up and punched Jane Marie in the face with her fist. I was so shocked I couldn't move. Jean was able to pull Sarie away, but Jane Marie came for her and I had to hold her back. I gotta say, these were some interesting families, but really not all that different than the rest of the county, far as I could see.

Jean McDonnell – Thursday
Interesting developments. I was becoming more and more intrigued with the entire plural family dichotomy. Wives who hate each other, wife and older daughter of another wife who hate each other, husbands who either ignored the entire thing or thrived on it. If what I'd seen of the Hudson household were true, then *they* were the exception, not the rule. And I was vastly curious about the 'retarded' daughters of Sarie. I was thinking a little testing might be in order.

'Mrs Whitman?' I said, once Milt and I had the two combatants settled down. 'Would it be possible for me to test your daughters? See if there is a problem? It would be pro bono.' At her puzzled look, I said, 'Free. Because I find it such an interesting case.'

'What kind of testing?' Sarie asked.

Hedging, I said, 'Just some general IQ testing and such.'

'We don't believe in that,' said Jane Marie.

'In what?' I inquired.

'Testing intelligence! That's something you people do. We don't.'

'Sarie?' I said, turning to the mother.

She nodded her head. Turning to Jane Marie, she said, with venom, 'You tell Thomas and I'll smother you while you sleep!'

Surprisingly, there was sudden fear on Jane

116

Marie's face, and I couldn't help thinking, Sarie, you go, girl.

I headed for the door. 'I'll see you at my office at the hospital this afternoon, Sarie. Say around three?' She nodded. To my husband, I said, 'Milt, I think it's time we left.'

'Huh?' he said from the couch. 'Oh, OK.'

Milt stood and joined me. 'Thank you, ladies, for your time.'

And we left. We'd barely gotten in the car before Milt turned on me. 'What was that all about? I barely got a chance to ask 'em anything about Mary Hudson!'

'You wouldn't get any answers with both women in the same room, Milt,' I told him as we pulled back down the long driveway. 'I think when Sarie and her daughters come to my office this afternoon, it might be wise if you sat with her in the waiting room while I talk to the girls.'

Heading to the hospital, I spied Milt's note-book with the addresses of the church members he wanted to interview. I noted that the last one, David Bollinger, lived within blocks of the hospital.

'You want to drop by? We've got an hour before my next patient,' I said.

'Lead on, pretty lady,' my husband said. So I did.

Milt Kovak – Thursday
Bollinger had a neat little ranch in an older

117

subdivision half a mile from the hospital complex. There was a minivan in the driveway, and crowding around it were three women, one man, and a bunch of kids. It was a crowd.

I got out of the car and me and Jean headed into the fray. 'Mr Bollinger?' I called out.

The man turned and headed toward me. He was all smiles. 'Hey, you must be Sheriff Kovak. I hear you're talking to everybody who knew the Hudsons. Hey, girls, come on over,' he said and the three women obliged.

This family appeared to be a little different. For instance, one lady was wearing jeans, another a knee-length skirt, and the third a pair of khakis. One had a short bob kinda haircut, one had shoulder-length hair, and the other had her hair up in a ponytail, but I doubted it would reach anywhere near her waist if it were down. The kids, even the girls, were wearing pants, the boys in jerseys and tees, the girls in varying kinds of tops. In other words, this family looked like the typical family next door. Except for the number of wives, of course.

'Just trying to get any information I can about Mary Hudson – if anyone has any idea who could have done this, or why. If anyone saw anything hinky concerning Mrs Hudson. That sorta thing,' I said.

'Hey, I like Jerry Hudson a lot,' David Bollinger said, shaking my hand. He was a seriously middle-class-looking guy. Medium-brown hair in a businessman's haircut, wearing madras shorts and a blue Izod shirt. He was a little less than six foot, maybe 150–160 pounds, had a cleft chin, as did several of the kids, and a firm handshake. 'He seems like a stand-up guy. Some of our boys play on the same soccer team. And I can tell you this, man, Jerry is dedicated to his family. Seriously. He and Mary are – were – like, solid, you know?' he said, looking at the older of the three women standing by him.

'Mary was a saint,' this woman said. 'But not obnoxiously so. She was just a good woman who happened to have a heck of a sense of humor—'

'Oh, yeah!' said what appeared to be the middle of the three. 'She was hilarious. Remember that time she said that thing—'

'Yeah,' said the older woman, 'about the boy's bathroom—'

'No,' said the middle one, 'the thing about that thing that Jerry found—'

'Oh my gosh,' said the oldest, 'that was hysterical!'

'I know!' said the middle one and all three laughed.

'Did any of you see anything out of the way? Like Mary in an argument with anyone? Or anyone paying more attention to her than they should?'

The oldest wife said, 'Not that I can think of, Sheriff. The family always stayed together, and I know Mary and Carol Anne were like best friends. Poor little Rene was always like a little puppy dog trying to catch up with the other two, but they certainly weren't unkind to her. More like forgetful. I can't say Mary was ever unkind to anyone. As far as seeing her arguing with anyone, I can't recall. I know I saw her and Jerry having words occasionally, but' – and at this point she whacked her husband in the gut – 'what wife doesn't have words with her husband every once in a while?'

'Tell me about it,' said the middle wife.

And, 'You've got that straight,' said the youngest.

The husband put up his hands in a defensive gesture, while a big smile played on his face. 'Guilty as charged!' he said. 'They gotta keep me in my place any way they can.'

The youngest wife looked serious for a moment, but hung her head. Finally, I said, 'Ma'am, something on your mind?'

She looked up, surprised I was talking directly to her. 'Ah.' She looked at her husband.

'Go on, Naomi Ruth, tell him what's on your mind.'

'Well, I did see someone kinda spying on Mary once,' she said, her voice soft.

'Who was that?' I asked.

She lowered her head and I could barely make out the words. 'I don't really want to say.'

David Bollinger put his arm around her and pulled her to him. He leaned down and whispered in her ear. She nodded her head and looked up. And sighed. 'I saw someone peeking in the window of the kindergarten class Mary taught on Sundays. I thought at first he was just checking out the kids, but then I saw them all marching out the door to the sanctuary, and they were with Yancy Lark, Mary's helper. Mary must have still been in the room.' She lifted her head all the way up and said, 'But I'm not even sure Mary was in the room. He mighta just been looking for something, you know? It doesn't mean he was stalking her or anything!'

'Who are we talking about, Mrs Bollinger?' I asked.

She turned to look at her husband. He nodded his head. Again, her head went down. 'My brother,' she said softly.

'How old is he, ma'am?' I asked.

'Twenty-two,' she said.

'And what's his name?' I asked.

'Buddy,' she said.

David Bollinger spoke up. 'Earl Mayhew Jr, Sheriff.'

My head popped up from my notebook where I'd been writing this down. 'The preacher's son?'

Naomi Ruth Mayhew Bollinger burst into tears and turned into the arms of her third of a husband.

FIVE

Jean McDonnell – Thursday

Sarie Whitman showed up at my office at ten minutes to three, a good sign by all accounts. Not so early that she appeared anxious, and not late enough to be challenging. The two little girls with her were adorable. The eldest, who appeared to be about six, had long hair the color of her mother's, but curly. The youngest, about three years old, had blonde hair just as curly as her sister's. I took the eldest, Margaret, into my office.

She was a quiet child, but well-behaved. It took about a quarter of an hour before she would begin to answer the test questions. She didn't appear to be retarded in the least, but her learning skills and general knowledge were nowhere near age-appropriate. I went to the outer room to talk to Sarie and found Milt sitting there with her. I asked to see the second child, Melinda, as well, and was allowed to take both girls into my office, leaving Milt alone with Sarie, which had been the general plan.

Margaret played with the toys in the play area while I chatted with Melinda. She, too, did not appear to be retarded, but was quiet and some-what withdrawn. I could only wonder if the ani-mosity between the two women in the house-hold might be causing problems for these two little girls. And the father's refusal to let them attend church seemed totally wrong. Was Mar-garet home-schooled? I wondered. I had a lot of questions to ask Sarie, but Milt figured the murder came first. I disagreed.

Milt Kovak – Thursday

When I got to Jean's office, Sarie Whitman was already there, sitting in one of Jean's waiting-room chairs with the youngest of her two girls. I said hey and sat down across from her.

'Glad you got a chance to bring your daugh-ters in to see Dr McDonnell,' I said. 'She's really good.'

'Y'all don't have to pretend, Sheriff. I know Dr McDonnell is your wife.' She shook her head. 'Don't see how y'all do it. You must not have children.'

'Well, yes, ma'am, we do,' I said. 'A boy, six. He's in the first grade at Longbranch Elemen-tary.'

She cocked her head, sorta like a bird. 'So your wife only works in the afternoons?'

I was beginning to get her drift. 'No, ma'am. She works a full day, just like me. Johnny Mac stays in the daycare they have here at the hospital. That way Jean's real close if he needs something.'

She slowly shook her head and made a 'tsk, tsk' sound, just like my grandma used to do when me and my best friend Lyn played rock and roll music on the hi-fi. So I knew right off the bat we were being judged. And here I was the one who was supposed to be doing the judging. I was getting pissed. But I'm professional enough to keep it in check.

After Jean took both little girls into her office, I asked Sarie, 'So, I had some questions I wanted to ask you this morning, but you and your – hum, would she be your stepdaughter?'

'She's my daughter,' Sarie said. 'In a plural family, all the children are my children, and all the children are the children of the other wife. When Marie died, nothing changed. Jane Marie stayed on as my daughter.'

'Hum,' I said, 'by looking at her, I'd say she's a mite older than you.'

Sarie sighed and stiffened her shoulders. 'She's thirty-five – ten years older than me.'

'Now that's a bunch.'

'You may think so, but it makes me no never mind. She's my daughter.'

'Yet she treats *you* like a red-headed stepchild,' I countered.

Sarie pursed her lips and shrugged her shoulders.

'One of my questions, Mrs Whitman, is about Sister Mary Hudson, of course. When I asked how well you knew her, seemed about the only time you and Jane Marie agreed on anything.

But somehow, not knowing the Hudsons well seemed like, well, let's call it a falsehood.'

'Lying is a sin,' she said.

I ran through the Ten Commandments quick in my head and couldn't come up with anything on lying. How about the seven deadlies? We Baptists don't harp much on those, so I wasn't real sure.

Deciding on the stern approach, I said, 'Ma'am, how well did you know Mary Hudson?'

She shrugged but didn't say anything.

I sighed big and loud. 'Ma'am, if you don't answer me here, I'm gonna have to take you back to the station to question you. Which means I'll have to call your husband, or your older daughter to come get the little ones. What's it gonna be?'

I felt kinda bad using her kids like that, but I had a murder to solve, and these people were cramping my style.

Sarie sighed and hung her head. 'Mary was upset about Margaret, my oldest daughter. She wanted her to be in her class at Sunday school, but Thomas wouldn't have it. He said she was a disgrace to him, being retarded.' Tears stung her eyes. Looking up at me, she said pleadingly, 'Margaret's not retarded, Sheriff. Neither is Melinda! They're good girls!'

'Did Sister Mary pester your husband about this?' I asked.

'Oh, she never spoke directly to Thomas. It

wouldn't be proper to talk to another woman's husband. She spoke to me about it. I told her how Thomas felt, and she said she'd try to get her husband to talk to Thomas.'

'Did Jerry Hudson ever talk to your husband?' I asked.

Again, she shrugged her shoulders. 'I don't know. If he did, Thomas never told me.'

'You said your family and the Hudson family didn't have a lot in common. What did you mean by that?' I asked.

'Well, they have so many children, and the three wives, and three houses and all that. We're a small family.'

'But Mary wanted to help you do what was best for your daughters, right?' I asked.

She lowered her head. 'I guess she did.'

Jean came out of the room with the two little girls. 'You've got two bright little girls here, Mrs Whitman,' she said.

Both girls ran up to their mother and hugged her. Sarie kissed the tops of their heads and beamed at Jean. 'They're my angels,' she said.

'Would you mind letting Milt watch them for just a moment while you and I speak?' Jean said.

My head popped up, my eyes wide, looking at my wife. A great big 'no' stuck right inside my mouth.

'It wouldn't be proper,' Sarie said, hands folded in her lap.

Jean looked at me, and I thought, Well, shit. I

sighed real deep, and said, 'Mrs Whitman, it would be my pleasure to watch your little girls, and since I have a child of my own, I know what I'm doing. Y'all can keep the door open so you can keep an eye on 'em.'

'Men don't take care of children,' Sarie said, looking at me with a confused look. And all the while I'm thinking, has this girl ever watched TV? A movie? Looked at a magazine? Jeez.

'In many families outside your church men do,' Jean said. 'And I agree with the sheriff. We'll leave the door open.'

'OK,' Sarie said tentatively as she stood. 'Girls, you mind the sheriff. I'll be right in here. The door will be open, OK?'

Both girls were knee-deep in Jean's waiting-room toy box and just nodded their heads. Sarie looked at me and then followed Jean into the office.

I looked at both little girls in their long dresses and pretty hair and thought, Sweet Jesus, don't make me have to *do* anything!

Jean McDonnell – Thursday

I maneuvered our chairs so that Sarie could look out the door at her daughters. After we sat down, I told her, 'Mrs Whitman ... May I call you Sarie?'

'Oh, yes! I'd like that.'

I smiled at her. 'Good. Sarie, I ran some pre-liminary tests, and talked to both girls, and I can see no signs of mental retardation. Who told

127

you they were retarded?'

'Thomas,' she said.

'Your husband?' I asked for clarification.

'Yes, ma'am.'

'Did he take them to a doctor?'

'Oh, no, ma'am. Thomas never takes them nowhere, and we don't believe in doctors.'

'But you're here,' I said.

That stopped her for a moment. 'Well, yes'm. I just don't think they're retarded. They're good girls.'

This wasn't the first time I'd heard her say that – that her daughters weren't retarded because they were good girls. So I said, 'Sarie, being retarded doesn't mean a child is bad. It just means they're slower at learning, or may not be able to learn, and other things. It doesn't mean the child is bad.'

She was shaking her head before I'd finished. 'Oh yes'm, it does. Thomas told me. Being retarded is a sign of the Devil!'

'Why does Thomas think your girls are retarded?' I finally asked.

'Thomas said Margaret was after she started talking. She couldn't say her 's's or her 't's too well, and he said that was a sign of the Devil and that she was mentally retarded.'

'I didn't notice any speech difficulty,' I said.

'Oh, she stopped doing that when she was about four, and when I showed Thomas, he just said it was the Devil's work making us think she was normal.' Tears formed in her eyes. 'My

128

girls are good girls, Doctor.'

'Yes, Sarie. They are good girls. Has anyone been working with them on learning how to read or write?' I asked.

'Yes'm, I have. But not all the time. It's hard work running a farm and Thomas needs me to help him a lot. The girls spend a lot of their days with Jane Marie.'

My first thought was how awful for them. My second was: I wonder what Jane Marie is doing to sabotage her sisters? Because there was no doubt in my mind that she was doing something.

'Listen to me, Sarie. There is nothing wrong with Margaret or Melinda. Margaret should be in school – she's behind in everything she should have been learning for the last two years—'

'Two years?' Sarie said, her voice high.

'Yes. Here in Prophesy County they take children as young as four for pre-K, then kindergarten at five. At six, she should be in first grade.'

Sarie shook her head. 'I don't know a lot about schooling. I was taught at home by my mama, then I married Thomas when I turned eighteen. So I guess I haven't been doing what I should be doing.' Her eyes welled up again. 'But I don't think Thomas will let me send 'em to school. He says boys need schooling, but girls only need to do what their mamas do. They just need to watch me.'

My insides were boiling. I couldn't believe this nineteenth-century bullshit! These two precious little girls were being deprived of an education and called retarded just because they weren't boys. I was trying to think of something concrete I could get Milt to charge Thomas Whitman with so he could be arrested and rot in jail. Then I realized I needed to calm down. I would do Sarie and her daughters no good thinking like this.

'Sarie, there are laws about children getting proper schooling. It's OK to home-school children if you follow the state guidelines and if they're tested by the state every few years to see that they're on task. Otherwise, they need to go to an accredited school. Your best bet would be the local public school for both girls. I think we could get Melinda in the pre-K. She's a little behind in language. And I'd suggest Margaret go into kindergarten. I would be happy to go with you to speak to Mr Whitman about this and let him know that the girls *must* be in school.'

Again, Sarie was shaking her head before I stopped talking. 'Thomas'll just say that me or Jane Marie should home-school 'em.'

'I'm afraid neither of you would be eligible for that. You'd have to pass a test on knowledge and other things.' (I wasn't sure about this, but at this point I didn't care. Neither she nor Jane Marie were competent to teach these girls.) 'I'll tell Thomas that I don't want to have to go to children's services, but if he doesn't enroll these children by the end of the week, I will. Do you think he wants the girls taken into custody?'

Sarie began to cry outright. 'Oh, no! Of course he don't! Oh, please, Doctor, don't do that!'

I touched her hand. 'I don't want to, Sarie. And I'll do everything I can to make sure that doesn't happen. Why don't I follow you home and the two of us talk to Thomas?'

'You know what time it is?' Sarie asked, wiping her eyes with a tissue from the box on the table next to her.

'A little after four,' I said.

'We gotta wait for Thomas. He's gonna pick us back up around six o'clock,' she said.

I smiled. 'Were you planning on having dinner here or in town?'

Sarie shook her head. 'Oh no, ma'am. I don't have any money. Thomas had to go back to the farm and do some work. He said if I was set on coming here, I could just wait until he finished what he was doing and he'd come pick us up.'

My whole body clinched. I so wanted to send Thomas Whitman back to the century where he belonged. I was thinking a swift kick in the ass might do the trick.

'I'll drive you to the farm, Sarie. And we can have that chat with Thomas when we get there.' Maybe, I thought, just maybe, I'll cool down by then. But I kind of doubted it.

Milt Kovak – Thursday

I called Charlie Smith, police chief of Longbranch, when I got back to the office. Charlie
was a good ol' boy, late of Oklahoma City, now
here for about a year. We'd worked a couple of
cases together and I'd say we've become close
to being friends.

When he answered his direct line with a
'Hello,' I said, 'Hey, Charlie, it's me, Milt.'

And he said, 'Well, hey, Milt, how they hanging?'

And we jawed a little like that for a few minutes, then I asked him, 'You ever heard of a guy
named Michael McKinsey?'

'Big ol' boy, blond Marine cut, newish Dodge
Ram?'

'That's the guy,' I said.

'Oh, yeah. Real handy with his fists. Works at
the refinery on Highway Five, on the way to
Tulsa?'

'Yeah, I know the one.'

'Been called on him a couple of times. Likes
to beat up his underlings when they don't do
what he says.' Charlie sighed. 'Wish I could get
away with that.'

'He gets away with it?'

'Nobody ever wants to press charges. I talked
to the powers that be over there and they say
they'll keep an eye on him, but from what I
understand he's got the most productive team
on any shift. They don't wanna mess with a

good thing, know what I mean?'

'Yeah, I hear you. Reason I'm calling, I'm wondering if you ever got a domestic call on him?'

'Domestic? Hum. Let me see. What's the address?' he asked.

I rattled it off to him.

'Don't see anything. But it makes sense. Feels he can rough up people who work under him, wouldn't be a stretch to think he'd be a wife-beater. You get a call?'

'Naw. I went over there...' Now did I tell Charlie we had plural families in our midst? Or not? I finally said, 'I saw his wife. She'd had her face slapped real recent and had bruises on her.'

'Maybe I should have a patrol car cruise by there every once in a while.'

'Couldn't hurt. But he's got a lot of land around him, and his wife doesn't seem like the screaming type. Might be hard to know what's going on inside from the street.'

'Don't worry, Milt,' Charlie said. 'I learned some interesting techniques while on the mean streets of OK City. I've passed 'em on to some of my boys.'

'The mean streets of OK City?' I repeated and laughed. 'Whatever.'

'Hey, it sounded good for a minute there,' Charlie said and hung up.

I was still chuckling about the mean streets of OK City when Holly Humphries came in.

133

'Sheriff?' she said, leaning on the doorjamb.

'Yeah, Holly?' I said.

'You have some visitors. Pastor Earl Mayhew and his son.'

Hum. Now this was interesting. 'Send 'em on back, Holly, and thank you.'

'You're welcome, Sheriff.'

In a minute, Holly was back ushering the two Mayhews into my office. Now see? Gladys never would have done that. She'd just point in the general direction and hope for the best. Well, actually, no, she wouldn't hope for the best. She'd point 'em in the general direction and forget about it.

I stood up as they came in and Holly said, 'Can I get anybody anything to drink?'

Pastor Mayhew, or whatever they called him, and I shook our heads, but Jr said, 'Could I have a Dr Pepper, please?'

Holly smiled. 'Sure. Be right back.'

I shook hands with Pastor Mayhew, Sr. He introduced his son, and I shook hands with him too. By the time that was finished, Holly was back with the Dr Pepper and I asked her to shut the door on her way out. Then we all sat down. Sometimes it seems to take a while to be civil-ized.

'What can I do for you, Pastor Mayhew?' I asked.

'Please, it's not Pastor. Just call me Brother Earl.'

'OK, fine, Brother Earl. What can I do for

you?'

He put a hand on his son's shoulder. 'My daughter, Naomi Ruth? She's married to David Bollinger?'

'Yes, sir. I met them and the rest of the family earlier.'

'Naomi Ruth tells me she mentioned to you that Buddy here – he's Christened Earl Vernon Mayhew Jr, but we just call him Buddy – that he had seemed overly interested in Sister Mary Hudson, and we just came here to straighten all that out.'

'I see,' I said. Then I looked right at Buddy and he spilled a little of the Dr Pepper he'd just put to his mouth. 'Were you overly interested in Sister Mary Hudson?' I asked.

Some of the Dr Pepper dribbled down his chin as he drew the bottle back. 'Oh, no, sir,' he said. 'Not at all.'

'You were seen peeking in the windows of the kindergarten class she taught at the church,' I said.

'Ah...' He looked at his father.

'Go ahead, boy,' Brother Earl said. 'Tell him what you were doing and why!'

Buddy took a deep breath and blurted out the following: 'I was suspicious that some of the teenagers were picking on the little kids and I looked in the window of the kindergarten class to make sure they weren't, just like I checked all the little kid classes, and when I realized they weren't there and I saw Sister Mary all by

135

herself I was worried those boys might come in and bother her so I just watched to make sure they didn't.' And then he took another breath. And yes, it sounded rehearsed.

'Um hum,' I said. I leaned back in my chair, elbows on the arms of the chair, and steepled my fingers. That wasn't rehearsed, but it looked damned impressive. 'Well now, son, I thank you for coming in.' I stood up and reached a hand out to Brother Earl. We shook, then I shook Jr's hand. 'Boy, you work or what?'

'Buddy is my second-in-command at the church,' Brother Earl said. 'I'm training him to take my place in a few years.'

'Well, ain't that nice,' I said. 'I may have to come up y'all's way a couple more times, but I'll try my darnedest not to be intrusive,' I said, ushering them out the door.

They were both smiling when they left. I didn't intend for them to keep those smiles. Earl Jr was lying through his teeth and Daddy Earl knew it, had even probably told the boy what to say. This whole thing was turning out to be more fun than I ever thought it was gonna be.

Jean McDonnell – Thursday
I drove Sarie Whitman and her girls home in my car. She wasn't the world's greatest conversationalist. As a matter of fact, she was quite poor at that particular art. My initial conversational gambits, such as, 'So, Sarie, what do you do for fun?' and 'How do you like living in this

area?' and 'It's fairly warm for October!' were met with one- or two-word answers. Finally she started a conversation of her own.

'Dr McDonnell, how come you wear them braces and walk with them crutches?'

'I had polio as a child,' I told her.

'What's that?' she asked.

So I told her about the plague of polio that had long since been eradicated, and about all the children it had taken for so long. She shuddered thinking about it. 'That's just horrible,' she said.

'I was one of the lucky ones,' I told her.

'But you can't hardly walk!' she said.

I laughed. I knew she wasn't being mean. She was just being earnestly ignorant. 'Actually I walk quite well,' I said. 'The only time in my life I haven't been able to get around on my own was in the last couple of months of my pregnancy with my son. I had to use a wheelchair because my balance was off.'

Sarie laughed. 'I understand that! I coulda used a wheelchair with both my girls. I fell down a lot!'

I pulled into the driveway of the farm and Sarie quieted down. I could see Thomas Whitman on his tractor, turning over a field a few hundred yards to the left of us. I pulled the car into the yard and we all piled out. Jane Marie came out of the house and stood on the porch, looking at us. She wore the same dark dress she'd worn before, and her lusterless hair still hung in strings down her back. She didn't say anything, and the two little girls certainly didn't run to her with open arms.

Thomas appeared to see us, pulled up the equipment on the back of the tractor, and drove the tractor toward us.

I asked Sarie, 'Can Jane Marie take the girls inside?'

Sarie was chewing her lips. Finally she said, 'Girls, go with Jane Marie.'

The girls didn't hesitate, but headed up to the porch. Jane Marie didn't smile at them, but she did touch them both gently on their heads and ushered them inside.

Thomas Whitman stopped the tractor and climbed down. 'Thought you was gonna wait for me in town?' he said to Sarie.

'The doctor wanted to talk to you anyway, Thomas, so she drove us home.'

Not looking at me, he said, 'Do I owe her money?'

'For driving us?' she asked.

He laughed and came closer, taking her hand. 'No, silly. For seeing you and the girls.'

'No,' I said. 'This was on the county.'

The smile left his face. Again, to his wife, he said, 'Tell her we don't take charity, Sarie.'

She turned to look at me, her mouth open to speak. I interrupted. 'This isn't charity, Mr Whitman. It's part of the school board's new policy about enrolling children in school,' I said, making it up as I went along. 'When I realized neither girl was in school, I felt it was my

138

responsibility to see to it that they were set up to enter. I know Melinda's a little young, but she would surely benefit from pre-K, and Margaret is way overdue for schooling. She's a bright young girl who needs to be in a proper setting to reach her potential.'

'Tell that doctor that those girls are retarded and I can't have them—'

'No, sir!' Sarie said, squaring her shoulders. 'I will not say my daughters are retarded! Because they're not! The doctor said so! And I won't be having you calling them retarded either! Because they're not! Do you hear me, Thomas Whitman?'

Whitman scowled at his wife. 'Go in the house now, girl!'

'I will not! I don't know what Jane Marie has been telling you about my girls, but there's nothing wrong with them! They are not possessed by the Devil! Margaret talked funny when she was a baby but...' She turned to look at me, a pleading look on her face.

'A lot of children have early speech problems, but they often just work themselves out, like Margaret's did.'

'And a lot of children are possessed by demons!' Thomas Whitman said, still looking only at his wife.

Sarie put her hands on her hips. 'You listen here, Thomas! I never once defied you in all these seven years I've been married to you. But on this I'm taking a stand! Those girls are going to school. If they don't then I'm gonna have to leave you because the doctor here said the State of Oklahoma will come and take away my children because you won't let them go to school! So I'll leave you and find someplace else to live so that my girls *can* go to school! Do you hear me, Thomas? Do you want me to leave? Because I'll do it! And all you'll have is Jane Marie for company, Thomas! Is that what you want? And while we're on the subject –' Sarie's voice was getting louder – 'it's beyond time for Jane Marie to move on. She's thirty-five years old, Thomas, and I know and you know that there's no man out there gonna marry her, so it's time she moved in with those women over in Tejas County that live in that dorm thingy by the church. Now you agree to all this right here and now or me and the girls will just ride back into town with Dr McDonnell and find us a room to live in.'

I was totally dumbfounded. But I just stood there and waited. As did Sarie. Thomas Whitman worked his jaw some, took off his hat twice and put it back on twice, then looked at his wife. 'OK,' he said.

SIX

Milt Kovak – Thursday

It was still daytime and I figured Michael
McKinsey was at work. So I grabbed Jasmine
Bodine Hopkins, one of my deputies, and headed the couple of miles to the McKinsey house.
I knew Rachael wouldn't talk to *me* without her
husband, but maybe she'd talk to Jasmine. Just
a hunch.

The other wife, Emily if I remembered cor-
rectly, opened the door. She looked directly at
me and said, 'What can I do for you, Sheriff?'

I nudged Jasmine and she said, 'We'd like to
see Mrs McKinsey.' I nudged her again. 'The
other Mrs McKinsey.' I nudged her again, hoping she wouldn't bruise. 'Rachael McKinsey.'

Emily gave Jasmine a smirk. 'I'm afraid
Sister Rachael is not receiving visitors today.'

Excuse my French, but I thought *fuck it*, and
said, 'Let me in now or I come back with a
warrant.'

The little bitch said, 'Come back with a warrant,' and slammed the door in my face.

I gave Jasmine the keys to my Jeep. 'Go see
Judge Lee and get me a goddamned warrant

141

now! Use the siren coming and going!'

Jasmine took off at a trot to the Jeep and burned rubber getting out of the driveway.

I stood in the driveway, placing bets with myself on who would show up first – Jasmine with the warrant or Michael McKinsey and his Dodge Ram pick-up. It was almost a tie: Jasmine came screeching in with the warrant only a minute before Michael McKinsey came Rambo-ing in from the other side of the circular drive. It looked amusing, but actually that was the last thing it was.

I grabbed the warrant from Jasmine and hit the front door the same time as Michael. I handed him the warrant as I banged on the door.

'What are you looking for?' Michael demanded.

'Everything,' I said as I pushed past Emily and headed into the bowels of the house.

I found Rachael in a small room off the kitchen. Inside was a large crib with a top on it that was locked with a padlock. The little girl I'd seen the last time I'd been in the house – the little girl with the shorn head and the black dress – was inside the crib. The stench in the room was unbearable. There was a bare mattress on the floor and Rachael was on that. She was naked and her head had been shaved. As there were no blankets or anything else in the room, Jasmine said, 'Give me your jacket,' then took it and covered Rachael with it. The woman was alive, but not by much. It was hard to see any pink skin on her naked form – most of her body was covered in bruises, in all shades, from the deepest black to purple and yellow, some parts oozing blood.

I used my walkie to call for an ambulance and back-up. Everybody in this house was going in. I went back in the living room. Michael was yelling at Emily, who was yelling back. I went up to the man of the house, stared him in the face and started reciting his Miranda rights. He, of course, started yelling at me. I kneed him in the groin, and while he was bent over, shoved him frontwards onto the couch, my knee in his back as I continued reading him his rights and cuffing him. Emily, meanwhile, was pounding on my back and yelling at me. Before I had a chance to cuff her, Dalton Pettigrew and Nita Skitteridge showed up, as well as an ambulance. I yelled for Jasmine, who was still back with Rachael and the little girl, and she came out to get the paramedics while Nita grabbed Emily McKinsey and cuffed her.

I sent Michael and Emily out with my deputies, grabbed a butcher knife from the kitchen and went back to the little room by the kitchen.

The paramedics, Jason Pool and Liz Johnson, took Rachael's vitals and were dead set on getting her to the hospital. I told 'em to go on but to come back in case there were more problems. They left, and while I worked on the lock to get the little girl out of the crib, I sent Jasmine to check the other rooms.

I used the butcher knife as a lever and was able to break the wood around the padlock and thereby open the lid. When I reached in for the little girl, she cringed at my touch. 'Hurts,' she said in a subdued voice.

I was having daydreams about my interrogation of Michael McKinsey. I told the little girl, 'Lie flat, honey. I'm gonna pick up the mattress so I don't hurt you, OK?'

She nodded her head. It was a piss-poor mattress, not more than a couple of inches thick, so I was able to cradle it around her as I lifted her out. She winced but didn't cry out. I was thinking this was one hell of a brave little girl.

Jason and Liz got back as I was bringing the child out of the house. Following close behind me was Jasmine with four other children. Jason had the child I'd brought out on the mattress in the back of the ambulance while me and Jasmine and Liz checked out the other four kids. The oldest was a youngish teenaged boy. His clothes were tattered. On further inspection, we noted his ribs were showing and his abdomen distended. The other kids were also malnourished and looked more like third-world children than residents of the US of A. I was real close to puking at this, and I don't puke as a general rule.

I left Jasmine to help with the kids, telling her I'd send back the SUV to pick 'em all up, and I headed to the station. I was ready to charge Michael McKinsey and his little wifey with battery and the attempted murder of Rachael McKinsey, child abuse, and the murder of Mary Hudson. I was also going to charge him with the vandalism at the Smithfield Grocery Store that happened a couple of weeks ago, and the rustling of three head of cattle I still had on the books from 1984.

Before I went into the cell with Brother Michael, I called Bill Williams in Tejas County and asked him if he'd be so kind as to bring Brother Earl Mayhew to me. I figured as the leader of this flock of assholes, he had to have *something* to answer for.

We have one interrogation room with a two-way mirror between it and the break room. It was two-paned and had some kind of tinted air in the middle that could be turned on and off so you couldn't see through without flipping a switch, and waiting longer and longer the older the damned thing got. Dalton had put Michael McKinsey in the interrogation room, and Nita Skitteridge was watching over wife number two in the break room. I went into the interrogation room and slammed the door hard behind me.

Michael McKinsey's hands were cuffed in front of him, a courtesy I wouldn't have given him had I been the one who'd placed him here. I woulda let him just sweat it with his hands cuffed behind his back. He was leaning forward, his hands on the table in front of him, and smiled when I entered the room.

I just stood there for a minute, looking at him.

Coaxing myself not to start beating on an unarmed and cuffed prisoner. Just wasn't right, I kept telling myself, but in my head I kept seeing the shaved head and naked and bruised body of Rachael McKinsey and the emaciated bodies of the five children. Somehow beating the shit out of this guy seemed a lot more humane than what he'd done to his family.

'You know,' I told him, 'I'm going to do everything in my power to make sure you never see the outside for the rest of your life.'

'For what?' he demanded, a scowl replacing the smile.

'What you've done to your family,' I said, not raising my voice. If I raised it, I might not be able to stop the violence that was bubbling up inside me.

'My family is *my* business, Sheriff! You got no call messing in where you don't belong! My wives and my kids are *my* business, not any of yours! I want my lawyer and I want him now!'

'If your wife dies—' I started.

And he laughed. He shouldn't have done that. I lunged across the table and grabbed him by the shirt front, pulling him onto the table, where my hands went around his neck . . .

It took but a minute for Dalton Pettigrew and Holly Humphries to be in the room. Dalton pulled me offa him and Holly set the prisoner back in his chair. He had a bloody lip and his hair was mussed. I guess I'm getting old. The man wasn't near dead, and I was sorry for that.

'I'm gonna sue you personally, Sheriff! And the county! And maybe the State of Oklahoma!'

'Now how are you going to spend all that money in jail?' Holly asked him sweetly.

'I said I want my lawyer and I want him now!' McKinsey screamed.

Holly put her arm in mine and let me escort her out of the room. Dalton followed, slamming the door harder than I did.

When we got into the big room – where the front door opens in and there's a waiting room, and a counter that closes off a bullpen of sorts – Holly patted my hand and said, 'Sheriff Williams from Tejas and Pastor Mayhew are in your office, Sheriff. I'll find out Mr McKinsey's lawyer and give him a call. When I finish my nails,' she said.

I headed down the hall to my office, stopping halfway there to do a little deep breathing. I had questions for Brother Earl, but I didn't want to take my wrath out on him. Not until I knew what he knew about the McKinsey household.

The two were sitting in my visitors' chairs when I walked in. I said, 'Hey' then rounded the desk to my chair and sat down.

'Why have I been drug here, Sheriff Kovak?' Brother Earl Mayhew said immediately, leaning forward over my desk.

'I'm arresting a member of your flock and I thought you would want to be here,' I said. By the look on Bill Williams' face, I knew my speech pattern wasn't normal yet. Maybe my voice was a little heavier than usual, or something.

Earl Mayhew leaned back in his chair. 'For goodness' sake,' he said. 'You found out who murdered Sister Mary?' he asked.

'Possibly,' I answered. 'But the immediate arrest is for spousal abuse and child abuse.'

And I got my answer. Brother Earl turned red in the face and looked at the floor. And didn't say a word.

'I suppose you know who I'm talking about,' I said.

He got his face under control and looked up. 'No, Sheriff, I do not. I can't imagine a member of our church behaving in such a way. Now you might just be confusing parental discipline with abuse. It's happened before. Some people don't believe in "spare the rod, spoil the child," but we live by that credo in our church, Sheriff.'

'How about starve the child, anything about that? Or beat the wife and shave her head? Got any homilies about that, Brother Earl?' My voice was getting louder so I stopped talking and looked at my desk. I had to calm myself down. So I started counting, something Jean had taught me. When I looked up, Brother Earl was shaking his head and looking at his feet.

'So what family you think I'm talking about, Brother Earl?' I asked, and I couldn't help myself, the 'Brother Earl' was still coming out sounding sarcastic.

He looked up at me. 'I'll venture a guess,

Sheriff. The McKinsey family?'

'Now why would you think that?'

He sighed. 'I'm sorry; I've done all I can for that family! Brother Michael's first wife, Nalene, ran off four years ago, right after he took Emily on as his second wife. Nalene never did have children, which was her reason for leaving – she felt so guilty, and then Emily was there for two years and never conceived either. And I got a call from a group in east Texas that had a widow with five children who needed a husband. So I talked to Michael about it and the two of us, we figured the woman already had five children, so obviously she could conceive, so Michael went down to east Texas and they got married there and he brought the whole family back. That had to be two years ago. And the whole family came to church regular for over a year, and then just Rachael and some of the children, and then less and less. Till around last Christmas, Rachael started coming by herself every once in a while with just Michael and Emily. And every time I asked about the children, Michael would just say that with that many kids, there was always something going around. Flu, a cold, something like that.'

'And did Rachael conceive in the two years she was with Michael?' I asked.

Brother Earl shook his head. 'Not that I know of.'

'Did anybody ever think,' Bill Williams said, standing up from his chair, his voice hoarse with probably the same emotion I'd been fighting for hours, 'that this Michael, the husband, that *he* was the one who was shooting blanks? Huh? Jesus H. Christ on a bicycle!'

'Well, now, no, I never thought about that,' Brother Earl said.

'Then you're as dumb a fuck as he is!' Bill said, and sank back down in his chair.

Jean McDonnell – Thursday
Holly Humphries called me to let me know that Rachael and the children were coming into the hospital. The daycare was getting ready to close, so I asked my secretary to pick up John and bring him to my office, then I notified the ER and headed down there myself. Rachael was immediately rushed to intensive care and the children treated with emergency care then sent to the pediatric wing. I went with them upstairs. There were two boys and three girls. The boys shared a room and a third bed was brought into another room so all three girls could be together. The girl with the shorn hair and black dress was named Melissa. It took about an hour of hydration before she began to talk, and this young lady seemed to have no desire to ever stop talking.

'They're horrible people!' she told me in a hoarse voice. 'He beats on my mommy and she doesn't feed us all day sometimes! She calls my mommy names and sometimes she hits her too! And she locked me in the cellar for two days

150

one time and then she started shaving my head, but my mommy made her stop, and then she started hitting my mommy! And then Papa comes in – he made us call him papa, but he isn't our papa! Our real daddy died when he fell off the tractor and it ran over him! There was blood everywhere; I heard my mommy tell our preacher! And not that Brother Earl either, our real preacher back in Tyler! Brother Timothy! Brother Earl's always saying that girls are unclean and should be kept away some of the time. I don't know when, but I don't wanna ever be kept away, but I'm not even sure what I'm supposed to be kept away from! He just don't make any sense, that Brother Earl! Brother Timothy was always nice and talked about heaven and Jesus and stuff, not about the Devil and damnation and how bad women are! My mommy's a woman and she's not bad at all!'

She stopped and I took a long breath. 'Wow,' I said.

'And that's not all...' she said, starting up again.

I touched her arm. 'Melissa, you need to rest, you've been through a horrible ordeal—'

'I don't know what an ordeal is, but I can tell you this, Papa's a bad man! He hits all the time, and not just me and Mommy, he hits the boys a bunch! Mommy would get mad and try to stop him, and then he'd just start hitting her! I don't like Papa one little bit, and you can tell him I said so!'

I could see why Michael and Emily had abused this child more than the others: Melissa had spunk. She stood up to them and probably talked back to them – certainly talked back to them. I patted her hand and told her I'd be back in a minute, and went into the next room to talk to the boys.

The oldest at fourteen, Matthew, was subdued, but the anger he was feeling radiated off his body like a high fever. 'May I talk to you?' I asked him.

He nodded his head but didn't say anything.

'I'm trying to find out what went on in that house. The more information we have, the longer we can put Michael and Emily away for. What can you tell me?'

Matthew shrugged his shoulders but didn't open his mouth. I turned to his brother, Luke, who was twelve. 'How about you?'

He looked to his older brother for guidance and then just shrugged his shoulders.

'I don't know why you two won't talk to me,' I said, 'but I want you to know that Melissa already has.'

Luke snorted, and I looked at him. 'What?' I asked.

He again looked at his brother, then back at me. 'Melissa don't suffer fools gladly,' he said.

'And that means...?' I started.

'It means,' Matthew said, rising up on his elbows, 'that she's braver than me and she took them assholes on when I was too chicken shit to

152

do it, and she got beat for her efforts. And her hair was all cut off!' There were tears in his eyes when he threw his body back on the bed.

'That's not your fault, Matthew,' I said. 'If you had interfered they would have just beaten you and still hurt Melissa.'

'I'm the man of my family,' he said. 'At least I'm supposed to be. Instead, looks like Melissa turned out to be.'

The gender roles in this family were so tightly specific that it was hard to find a toehold to give the boy some comfort. Luke just looked at the floor, refusing to look at either his brother or me. I'm sure he felt the same as Matthew, that Matthew had messed up and that he, Luke, should have taken his place but didn't. And they both felt shame that a *girl* had to take up for the family.

I forget sometimes how far we've come, even in a small town like Longbranch. Gender roles are probably a bit more specific here than in a large city, but still there are women deputies at the sheriff's department and male nurses at the hospital, and I saw a young woman up on a telephone pole just last week. We accept these things. Sure, there are a lot of stay-at-home moms, but these days it's mostly their choice, and there are some men who chose to stay at home with their children as well. These things are commonplace now, so much so that it's a shock when you find families, such as some of these plural ones, locked in nineteenth-century gender roles.

But the McKinsey family was dabbling in more than gender preference: what they'd been doing to the family from Tyler, Texas, amounted to slavery. It was going to take these children, and their mother, a long time to recover from what Michael and Emily McKinsey had put them through.

Milt Kovak – Thursday
Around eight o'clock that night, about an hour after Bill Williams had taken Brother Earl Mayhew back to Tejas County, I got a text from Holly Humphries, who was working some overtime.

'Mr McKinsey's lawyer's here, Sheriff,' she said.

Oh, goodie, I thought, wondering who would be stupid enough to admit they were that asshole's lawyer. 'Send him in,' I told Holly.

I was looking down at some paperwork when a shadow was cast across my office floor. I looked up to see David Bollinger, the only father of a normal-looking plural family, standing there.

'Hey, Sheriff,' he said, smiling big at me. 'I'm Mike McKinsey's attorney. Can we talk?'

I halfway stood up and waved my hand at one of my visitor's chairs. 'Have a seat,' I said.

He did and then breathed a big sigh. 'Now this is a real kettle of fish, don't you think?'

'If you're referring to the charges against Mr

McKinsey,' I said, 'I think it's a bit more than a kettle of fish. Or even a barrel of monkeys. It's more like a cage full of abused and neglected children.'

Bollinger shook his head. 'Brother Earl Mayhew, our pastor?'

I nodded my head.

'He called me. Told me what had happened. I had a message on my phone from Mike saying he was in trouble and at the sheriff's office, but he didn't say what for.'

'Have you been in to see him yet?' I asked.

'No, sir,' he said, shaking his head for emphasis. 'I wanted to hear it from you first.'

Since he was the defense attorney, I just gave him the basics. I'd already talked to our DA and he was working up as many charges as he could come up with, so I didn't want Bollinger to know all the aces up our sleeves.

Bollinger shook his head all through what I had to say. When I stopped, still shaking his head, he said, 'There's got to be some mistake. I've known Mike since we moved here. Good man. Real good man. Not a bit of violence in him. I'd stake my reputation on that.'

'You do that a lot?' I asked. 'Stake your reputation on the vagrancies of assholes?'

Bollinger stood up. 'I'd like to see my client now,' he said.

I pushed the button on our new telephone system that got me to Holly. 'Yes, sir?' she said.

'Mr Bollinger, the attorney, is coming out

now. Please let him see the prisoner,' I said. I thought the words 'the prisoner' rather than 'his client' sounded lots better.

'Yes, sir,' Holly said.

I pointed at the door and Bollinger nodded his head. 'Thank you, Sheriff.'

I just nodded back.

Twenty minutes later, Bollinger came out of our little cellblock and strolled down to my office. He was grinning as he leaned against my doorjamb. 'You're not getting sued,' he said.

'That's good,' I said, leaning back in my chair.

'County's not getting sued.'

'That's good too.'

'Oklahoma's not getting sued.'

'That works.'

'Other than that, what can I say?' he said.

'Well, you could say the asshole pleads guilty to all charges, including the murder of Mary Hudson,' I said.

Bollinger was shaking his head before I got all my words out.

'Not going to happen,' he said. 'I'm a tax attorney, not a criminal attorney, so I'll have to find him one.'

'Who's gonna pay for all this?' I asked.

'All what, Sheriff?'

'Your services, the criminal attorney's services, all that?' I asked.

He smiled but shook his head. 'That's not for me to say.' He straightened up from my doorjamb. 'I'll call you in a couple of days, let you know the new attorney's name, or he or she will call you. Got any referrals?'

I just smiled and watched as he left the office. Then the question became, did Michael McKinsey kill Mary Hudson, or was it someone else? Did I formally charge McKinsey with it or not? I needed to have a talk with our little assistant district attorney.

I usually only have a deputy on duty till midnight, then we got somebody on call, which means the phone calls, if we get any, are directed to that person's cell phone. Back in the old days, we had to either have somebody on duty all night or, for a while, we just went with a sign on the door saying call this number in an emergency. Now we've got all these new gadgets that do everything but blow your nose, and then half the time they don't work. OK, half the time they don't work *for me*. I'm snake-bit when it comes to electronic bullshit. I put a finger on a computer or one of them fancy cell phones or a BlackBerry or any of that other crap, and it's just gonna up and die. Hand to God.

Anyway, with two people in lock-up we had to have round-the-clock babysitting so, since Dalton had come on at three in the afternoon, he'd stay till midnight. Jasmine had come in early that morning so I let her go early and told her to go home and get some rest, 'cause she'd be taking the midnight to six a.m. Nita was new; I figured she owed it to me to come in at six in the morning. Prove she could power through – or whatever.

I wasn't sure how long we'd have to do this, and I was thinking if it took a while we could transfer the prisoners to the Longbranch city jail, because they've got a permanent round-the-clock staff. But the chances of Michael and Emily McKinsey getting bail were pretty big; I didn't have any real evidence to charge 'em with murder – only attempted murder and child endangerment, which I thought was enough to have them put *under* the jail, but some judges tend to disagree. Meanwhile, since we don't have separate areas for male and female prisoners, this being the first time we ever had one of each at the same time, Mr and Mrs McKinsey were in neighboring cells, which I think was breaking some State law, but I wasn't sure. Have to check that.

I headed home around nine. Jean had taken her own car in to work that day, so she and Johnny Mac were already home. She'd told me earlier she'd be leaving once she'd got the McKinsey kids settled at the hospital for the night.

Being as late as it was, Johnny Mac was already in bed, bath time and teeth brushing time already taken care of. Jean has a hard time on the stairs up to his room, so she'd read him stories in the living room and send him up to bed on his own. He called out my name when I walked in the door, so God only knows what he'd been doing up there, 'cause sleeping was obviously out of the question.

Since eight o'clock was his bedtime, I made it upstairs and into his room, saying, 'What are you doing up, Bucko? You should have been asleep an hour ago!'

'Daddy?' Johnny Mac said.

I sat down next to him on the bed. 'Yeah, son?'

'Can I call you Dad instead of Daddy?'

I felt my stomach heave and I didn't know why. Maybe because I still called my father Daddy even though he'd been dead for over twenty years. So I said, 'Well, honey, you know, Dad is what really big kids, like teenagers, call their daddies. And I really like it when you call me Daddy. Can we keep that for a while longer?'

Johnny Mac stared at me hard, then sighed. 'I guess so,' he said. 'Mommy said the same thing. Weird, huh?'

I kissed him on the forehead. 'Double weird,' I told him.

'Daddy?'

'Yeah, son?'

'My friend told me that a lady, a mommy, got killed – murdered, like on TV. Did you hear about that?'

'It happens sometimes honey, but it's nothing for you to worry about,' I said, wondering if there was already talk about Mary Hudson's murder at the grammar school.

He sat up, getting excited. 'And my friend told me she had a hundred million kids and one of them killed her. With a laser gun!'

'Whoa!' I said. 'Now I didn't hear anything about something like that!' I told him.

'Yeah, and there was blood everywhere! And then the kid, the one who killed her, turned the laser gun on all the other hundred bunch of kids, but then they got together and jumped him and—'

'Now this is getting into the realm of story-telling, Johnny Mac.'

'It's not a story, Daddy, it's true!' he insisted.

'So how much of this true story did your friend tell you, and how much of it did you tell him?'

Johnny Mac thought about it for a moment. 'Well, he told me about the lady and that she got killed and all, but we sorta made up the rest of it. It's just a joke,' he said, lying back down.

'Not a funny joke, is it?' I said.

'No, I guess not.'

I gave him another kiss on the forehead. 'You get some sleep, son.' And I headed downstairs to the living room. Jean was on the couch, her laptop on her lap.

'What'ya doing?' I asked when I came in.

'Checking out the foster care system.'

'You gonna stick those kids in foster care?' I demanded. I'll admit to being a little het-up at this.

'No, I'm trying to keep them out,' she said,

giving me a look. I sat down next to her. 'But the problem is what if Rachael doesn't *get* better? Can we send them back to Texas, to their church family there or, since Rachael was married to McKinsey—'

'Ah ha!' I said. 'Not legally married. He had a first wife who ran off, and unless she divorced him, she's his only *legal* wife. If she did divorce him, then I think Emily would be next in line to be the legal wife.'

'Well, now wait,' Jean said. 'If he married Emily while legally married to the first wife, that negates his marriage to Emily, right? Which means if the first wife divorced him while he was married to Emily, and he didn't remarry Emily, then when he married Rachael she'd be his legal wife. Right?'

I stood up. 'I'm tired. I'm going to bed. And don't wake me in the morning. I'm taking a couple of hours.'

She grinned. 'Got you all confused, didn't I?'

'You're a mean woman,' I said as I headed out of the room.

'Oh, but you like a mean woman,' she said and laughed.

What could I say? She was right.

Jean McDonnell – Friday
First thing Friday morning, after dropping off my briefcase in my office, I went upstairs to check on the McKinsey family. When I got to the girls' room, all was not well. Melissa, the

161

nine-year-old who had been locked in the cage/crib, was quiet. Doctors and nurses surrounded her bed and a crash cart was there. The two other girls were together on one bed, holding each other and crying. I went to that bed and sat with them, holding them.

One, June, at eleven was older than Melissa, and the other, Samantha, at seven was younger. Both had long blonde hair and big blue eyes, and were dressed in hospital gowns that weren't that different from the clothes they normally wore, except their normal clothes did have backs. With my arms around both backs I could feel their ribs jutting out.

I tried to ignore the orders the doctors were yelling out, the answers of the nurses, and all the life-saving things that were going on in the next bed. I got the girls to sing songs from their church in Tyler, Texas, uplifting songs of praise and peace. They held on to me for dear life and I kept my arms around both of them, finding some of the words and singing the chorus with them.

Finally all the excitement from the next bed stopped. The girls were still singing, and I couldn't hear if the machine monitoring Melissa's heart was still making the straight-line sound or the beat-to-beat. The two sisters noticed the quiet in the next bed and stopped singing.

Then I heard it. A strong beat-to-beat sound coming from the monitor. There had been only seconds of quiet, but it had seemed like years.

Then there was the stampede to get her up to the ICU, bed rails coming up, connections being severed, IV being taken from its stand to the side of the bed – all the things necessary to move Melissa to intensive care.

The two sisters were on their knees on the bed. 'Where are they taking Melissa?' Samantha, the seven-year-old, asked.

'Is she OK?' demanded June.

'She's better,' I told them. 'They're taking her to a part of the hospital where she'll get special care. The same place your mother is. They might put her in the same room. That would be good,' I said.

'Why does she get to stay with Mommy?' the seven-year-old asked.

'Because she's sicker than us!' June answered. 'Don't be selfish, Samantha.'

The two boys hurried across the hall into the girls' room. 'Was that Melissa?' Matthew asked. 'What happened?'

'We have to wait for the doctors to tell us,' I said. Would they, I wondered? Would the doctors think to come tell these children what was happening with their sister? Who had authority over these children now? Their mother was in ICU, their father was dead, their stepfather and Emily – whatever she might be to them – were both in jail.

I excused myself from the children and went into the hall to use my cell phone. When the person on the other end of the line said,

'Hello?' I said, 'Carol Anne, it's Dr McDonnell.'

Dalton Pettigrew – Friday
The ME's report was on Dalton's desk when he got in that Friday morning. He opened it and began to read. There was a lot of gobbledygook he didn't understand, but in the remarks section it said: 'The victim appears to have been hit on the head by a hard object that was not the cause of death, but may have stunned him. Cause of death was suffocation.'

It also said the man was anywhere from fifty to sixty years of age, had type two diabetes, and probably suffered from high blood pressure. He only had seventeen original teeth, five replaced with a broken partial denture. And he was missing his baby toe on his right foot. Dalton figured with all this information, or these parameters, he should have no problem finding a missing person report on this guy. He smiled and walked over to Holly's desk.

'Hey, Holly,' he said boldly.

'Hi, Dalton,' she said, returning his smile.

'Could you help me check missing persons' reports for these parameters,' he said, grinning with his choice of words. He gave her the description he'd received.

'Sure,' she said, taking the sheet of paper where he'd written down the man's description. 'It might take some time.'

'Hours?' he asked.

Holly sighed. 'More like days,' she said. 'The service is way backed up, and just trying to log in can cause major frustration. But I'll keep at it.'

'Don't get stressed out,' he said.

She looked up at him and smiled. 'Thanks,' she said. 'I'll try not to.'

'Good,' he said.

He stood there for a long moment, each of them looking at the other. A million comments flew through his mind but none landed. Finally, Dalton turned and walked away.

Milt Kovak – Friday

I stayed so late at the shop the night before that I decided to sleep late Friday morning. I left a message with Dalton, who was on call, told my wife, and shut off my alarm. I was wide awake at seven thirty. OK, I usually get up at six thirty, so I slept in an hour. Not what I'd planned on. But the whole mess of what was going on with these church people was getting to me. Somebody killed a woman everybody seemed to love. So what did that mean? Was it an accident? Was somebody after someone else and accidentally killed Mary Hudson? Or *was* it some vagrant after money or jewelry? The Branches is an exclusive neighborhood with lots of rich people. Was it an accident that this asshole broke into one of only three houses in all of The Branches that didn't have cash-and-carry loot? I tried to remind myself that shit happens. It could have been a vagrant. Or maybe teenagers? The Branches teenagers would be more likely to get stoned and run somebody over in their brand-new Beamer than break into a home and kill a woman for no reason.

Of course, there's always the scenario of the thrill-kill teens. Knew the Hudson children from school, thought they were weird because of the way they dressed, decided to get 'em, got to the house and only found Mary. And killed her.

I sighed and got out of bed and took a shower. That didn't help much. I smelled better, but that was about it.

When I got to the shop, about an hour and a half later than usual, all hell had broken loose.

I came in the back door and could hear a commotion going on in the front. I dropped my crap on a chair in my office and walked to the bullpen. Holly was behind the counter, literally wringing her hands. In front of her stood Emmett Hopkins, trying to calm a very upset lady.

'What's going on?' I asked Holly.

'This lady's father disappeared...' she started but I tuned her out when I recognized the lady.

Brenda Burdy, as I live and breathe. I'd had a mad crush on her in my freshman year in high school, before I started dating my first wife, La-Donna. Brenda was the prettiest girl in school, already with a Marilyn Monroe figure at fourteen. She had naturally blonde hair, big blue eyes, gorgeous lips, righteous ta-tas, as we used to say, and an ass that looked damn good in a straight skirt. There wasn't a boy in school who didn't salivate when she walked by.

I recognized the blue eyes and the lips. The righteous ta-tas and the gorgeous ass had blurred a bit, rounding out to one very large body. 'Brenda?' I said.

She turned to me, eyes rimmed with red, face haggard. 'Sheriff?' she said.

'Yes, ma'am. Can I help you?'

'My daddy's disappeared! I don't know what happened to him! His bed hasn't been slept in!' She was clutching my arms, her face wet with tears and, forgive me, snot.

'Was he living at home or in a nursing home?' I asked her. This is when I happened to notice Emmett Hopkins making hand signals over Brenda's head. I don't read hand signals so I'm not sure what he meant, but I did interpret that something was up.

'The nursing home out on the highway!' she said.

'Which highway?' I asked.

That's when she started shaking me. 'You know! The one on the highway! Help me!' And she started sobbing.

'Brenda, come on, let's go sit down over here,' I said, trying to lead her to the bench in the reception area.

'No! No!' she said, pushing me away. 'I've got to find my daddy!'

She headed for the front door, but Emmett

blocked her way. 'Ma'am,' he said, 'we're gonna do everything we can to help you find your daddy, but right now, we need you to sit down so we can figure out where he is, OK?'

She turned and looked at me, squinching her eyes half-closed. 'Do I know you?' she asked.

'Yes, ma'am,' I said, 'I'm the sheriff. We also went to high school together, but that was a long time ago.'

Her eyes slowly opened and she smiled and, Lordy, she was Brenda Burdy all over again. 'You're on the football team, aren't you? You're LaDonna's boyfriend!'

I looked over her head to Emmett, and he just shrugged. Finally, looking back down at the former beauty queen of Longbranch High School, class of none-of-your-business, I smiled and said, 'Yeah, that's me. How you doing, Brenda?'

'It's my daddy,' she said as I led her to the bench and we sat down together. 'I can't find him.'

'I'm sorry to hear about that. When did you see him last?' I asked.

Her eyes narrowed and she appeared to stare off into space. 'I'm not sure,' she said. 'This morning? Or maybe yesterday morning?' She shook her head hard, like she was trying to shake something loose. 'It's so hard to remember sometimes.' She looked at me and smiled again. 'But I remember you!' Then she put her hands on either side of my face and kissed me

168

smack on the lips. When she finished, she whispered, 'Don't tell LaDonna!' and giggled.

I whispered back, 'I won't.'

Then the door opened and Steve Burdy, Brenda's little brother, quarterback three or four years behind our class, came in.

'Brenda!' he said, running to where we sat on the bench. He knelt in front of his sister. 'You OK, honey?'

'Hey, darlin',' she said, patting the top of Steve's head. 'I've been looking for Daddy.'

'That's OK, honey, I found him,' Steve said.

'You did?' Brenda said, clapping her hands and squealing with delight.

And then I remembered.

Steve pulled his sister up from the bench and I stood up. He said, 'I'll take her home, Sheriff. I'm sorry, this won't happen again.'

I nodded my head. 'You call us any time you need to, Steve.'

'Yes, sir.' He frowned. 'Do I know you?'

'Brenda and I went to school together. I was on the team a few years ahead of you.'

'Kovak – Milton Kovak?'

'Yeah, that's me.'

He grinned and held out his hand and we shook. 'You had a great rep, Sheriff.'

'Thank you,' I said, trying hard not to blush.

'He's LaDonna's boyfriend,' Brenda said. Then she whispered, 'And I kissed him! Shhhh, don't tell LaDonna!' Then she laughed.

'Come on, Bren, let's head home,' he said.

'I can't wait to see Daddy!' Brenda Burdy said as she and her brother left the office.

Emmett, Holly and I stood there watching. When they were out of the building and out of sight, Emmett said, 'The brother called just as she walked in, said she was confused. I've seen confused. What the shit was that?'

'The prettiest girl at Longbranch High School. Miss Everything. Senior year she was driving her father someplace – work, I think – when they got hit by a semi. She was stuck in the car for over two hours, totally conscious and miraculously uninjured, with her father's decapitated body. She never came back to school, and I'm ashamed to say I haven't thought about her in all these years. Looks like she never left that day.'

'God almighty,' Emmett said under his breath. And Holly burst into tears.

Just another day at the shop.

Jean McDonnell – Friday
I explained to Carol Anne Hudson what had been going on at the McKinsey house.

'Oh, dear God! That's horrible! And Emily was part of this?'

'It appears so,' I answered. 'The problem now,' I told her, 'is the children. I would hate for them to go into the system and be sent to separate foster care situations while their mom's in ICU, but I can't see what else to do. That's why I called you.'

There was dead silence on the other end of the line.

'Carol Anne?' I finally said.

'What?'

'I'm sorry, this is too much...' I started.

'I was just thinking,' she said. 'We could make my old house a temporary boys' dorm and my mom and Dennis could watch the boys, and we could make our house the girls' dorm. Hallelujah!' she cried out. 'I think that will work! I'll keep Mark here, of course, he's just a baby. How old is Rachael's youngest?'

'Seven. A girl,' I said.

'That's right. Samantha. How long do you think Melissa will be in ICU?'

'I really don't know about either of them – Melissa or her mother. I can find out tomorrow, though.'

'And the other children?' she asked.

'They're being hydrated right now, and fed and given vitamins. They'll probably be released later today.'

'Whoa, then I better get the kids and get to it! We need to figure out beds and bedding, and towels. Oh, Lord! I need to go grocery shopping!'

'Carol Anne?'

'Yes, Dr McDonnell?'

'Thank you,' I said.

She laughed. 'The Lord never gives a person more than they can handle, Dr McDonnell. You should know that.'

SEVEN

Nita Skitteridge – Friday

I rode with the sheriff to the hospital in the van we use to transport prisoners. We picked up the McKinsey kids, but there were only the four since little Melissa was in ICU with her mother. The sheriff sent me inside to deal with getting the kids released, which meant me signing a bunch of papers as temporary guardian, representing the sheriff's department, and then signing more papers to prove I was with the sheriff's department and had the right to represent the sheriff's department as temporary guardian of these children. Then, finally, we got to the medical releases. It would have been a lot easier if the sheriff had come in, but he was out in the van, listening to the radio – and I don't mean police calls either – I'm talking that awful country music he listens to. Sounds like somebody choking on their biscuits and gravy, if you ask me.

When we finally got to the McKinseys' house, the oldest boy, Matthew, said, 'I'm not sure where anything is, Sheriff. When we got here we had our clothes and stuff, but Mr

172

McKinsey didn't approve of our clothes and he took them away, and all the little kids' toys and stuff. And my books.' He shook his head. 'I don't know where he put everything.'

'I bet Melissa does!' Samantha said.

Matthew stiffened, but June, the eleven-year-old, ruffled her younger sister's hair and said, 'I know she does!'

'So tell me about the house,' I said to Matthew.

He shook his head. 'We were only allowed in the dining room and our bedrooms,' he said. 'And one bathroom.'

I noticed June had her hand up. 'June?' I said.

Her face turned red as she spoke. 'Melissa was always exploring, going places she shouldn't.' Her head was down when she said this, but then she looked up, grinned slightly and said, 'And I went with her once!'

'You did?' I said, surprised-like. 'That was very brave!'

'I know!' she said, her eyes wide. 'And we didn't even get caught!'

'So,' I said, 'where do you think he might hide y'all's stuff?'

'I don't *think*, I know!' she said. 'There's a bunch of rooms in the garage, and one of 'em has our stuff. We found Sammie's Pinky-Bear and brought it to her.'

Everyone looked at Samantha. The child blushed, then said, 'I hide him under my mattress, back by the wall so Emily won't find him.'

'Not like she would!' June said defiantly. 'We had to make our own beds and clean our own rooms, and wash and scrub our floor. She hardly ever came in our room!'

'So,' the sheriff said, opening the doors of the van, 'Samantha, you go to your room and get Pinky-Bear—'

She began to cry. 'Not by myself! He'll get me!' She grabbed Matthew around the waist and held on, crying into his shirt.

'That's OK, Sammie. I'll go with you. Remember, he's in jail!' Matthew said.

'That's right, Sammie!' Luke said. 'He can't hurt any of us now!'

'But what if he gets out?' Samantha said. 'He'll come get me!'

I squatted down next to her. 'He's not going to touch you again, honey. Even if he gets out on bail, you'll be where he can't hurt you.'

'He's getting out on bail?' Matthew demanded.

'It can happen,' the sheriff said. 'But there's no way he's going near any of you. You'll be in Bishop, not even in Longbranch, OK? And you'll be protected by Mr Hudson. Do you know him?' They all nodded. 'He won't let McKinsey get anywhere near you.'

I prayed the sheriff's words were near as true as I wanted them to be.

The sheriff used the key confiscated from Mike McKinsey to get in the house, and Matthew took Samantha down the hall to the girls' room to get her bear, while I took the others into the garage to find the room June spoke of.

The garage was full of man-crap. Engine parts, tools, one of those six-foot-high Craftsman tool cases my husband lusts after, ban saws, standing drills, a whole rack of power tools, broken lawn furniture, and boxes of unknown crap. There were three doors at the back of the garage, and June couldn't remember which one had their stuff. Opening the first door revealed the laundry room, full of baskets of clothes, but they appeared to be those of the McKinseys – Michael and Emily. The second held the hot-water heater, and the third was full of boxes of the kids' and their mother's stuff. As I began to pull clothes out of one box, I noticed a terrible odor.

'Oh, Lord,' I said. 'Kids, start a stack over here. We gotta wash this stuff.' Then I saw the bugs: roaches. Not the huge outdoor kind that can get in occasionally, but the nasty little brown ones that get in your house and breed. My first instinct was to pull the gun riding on my hip, but even I knew that could be overkill.

'Matthew, Luke, you boys look for some bug spray, quick!'

They ran looking while the girls squealed and I tried not to – squeal, that is. They found some Raid and came back spraying the dickens out of all the clothes. We stood around and watched the little buggers fall over and die. It was truly family entertainment.

I went in the laundry room – the first door – and took the baskets of the McKinseys' clothes and dumped them in the center of the garage, and used the baskets for the kids' clothes. We loaded up the washer and all stood around feeling righteous.

'Hey, Junie,' I said.

'Yes, ma'am?' she said.

'Why don't you get a broom and sweep those nasty things on over there?'

'Where, Ms Deputy?' she asked.

'Well, on those old clothes there would be fine,' I said, indicating the McKinseys' dirty clothes. I mean, after all, they were already dirty.

Milt Kovak – Saturday

After Nita took the kids into the garage, I decided to entertain myself. I started with Michael McKinsey's desk that sat in a corner of the living room.

Everything on the desk and in the desk was neatly labeled and organized. I doubted McKinsey had done this himself; he wasn't the organized type. One of the women had done it, and I doubted if he would have allowed Rachael near his personal papers. Emily may have been messy when it came to the belongings of the family from Tyler, Texas, but she was pretty damn anal when it came to hubby's desk. And I shortly became thankful for that.

There was a file on Rachael Owen, which I knew to be the married name of the kids' mom before she married McKinsey. I pulled it up on the desktop and sat down in McKinsey's chair, turning on the desk lamp to see it all better. In the file were bank records and check stubs from social security and the late Mr Owen's pension statements. Rachael wouldn't have received social security after she married McKinsey, but the kids would have. In the two years Rachael had been married to McKinsey, he had pocketed more than a hundred thousand dollars. Somehow, I promised myself, that was coming back to Rachael and the kids – if it had to come out of the sale of this house or whatever, she was getting her money back come hell or high water.

Then I found something curious. A file on Nalene McKinsey. That was the name of McKinsey's first wife, the one who ran off after he took Emily for his second wife. I pulled it out and put it on the desktop. Strangely enough, there were bills for cremation from an outfit out of Oklahoma City, and record of an insurance payment of $150,000, payable to Michael McKinsey.

So he lied, I figured. To his preacher and to me. Nalene didn't run off, she died – either on her own or with a little encouragement. I was leaning towards the encouragement scenario since they went all the way to Oklahoma City to cremate the body, rather than have a nice little ceremony with their own church. It might be hard now to prove it, but it looked like Michael McKinsey might have two murders on his conscience – or whatever he had that passed for one.

Jean McDonnell – Friday

Milt was supposed to pick me up at the hospital on his way to take the McKinsey kids to Bishop. While I was waiting, I checked on Rachael and Melissa and found Melissa doing well, but since Rachael, who was finally conscious and responsive, was still not out of the woods, the doctors had decided to leave the child with her mother, rather than cause more trauma by putting her in a room by herself. I had encouraged them towards this decision, so was quite pleased that they had acquiesced.

I sat down next to Rachael's bed and said, 'Sister Carol Anne Hudson has come forward to take care of your children until you're out of the hospital.'

'Thank her for me,' Rachael said in a weak voice.

'I'll do that. Melissa is going to stay here in the ICU with you, although she's healthy enough to go to a regular room. The doctors and I all agreed that it would be better for her emotionally to be here with you.'

'Yes,' she said, taking my hand. 'I want her with me, and she'll do better here.'

I smiled. 'The sheriff is coming by here to

pick me up. Would you like the other children to come up?'

She smiled back at me. 'Very much,' she said. Then, touching her head, which was now covered with a gaily colored turban, she said, 'And thank you for my hat.'

I laughed. 'You're very welcome. We found it in lost and found and one of the nurses washed it. It's quite colorful!'

'Isn't it?' she said, laughing back. 'I love it!' She sobered. 'I haven't seen color in a long time. And I've had very little to laugh about.'

Sometimes I believe a professional needs to feel free to be unprofessional. Or possibly that's just an excuse. I leaned over and hugged her. 'That's all behind you now,' I said.

Out in the hallway I called Milt, asking him to bring the children up to the ICU floor when he got there.

Ten minutes later Nita Skitteridge stuck her head around the corner of the door to Rachael's room. 'Got room for a whole bunch more?' she said with a smile.

I stood up and Rachael and Melissa both sat up in their beds. 'Definitely!' Rachael said.

The four other children came in the room, all dressed in 2011 street clothes – Matthew in baggy jeans and a big T-shirt, Luke in much the same, June in a short, ruffled denim skirt and a pink flowered T-shirt, and Samantha in blue jeans with a pink belt and pink hearts stitched on the butt and a puffy-sleeved pink T-shirt.

They wasted no time in rushing to their mother and sister. I left the room, going into the hall with Nita.

'Where's Milt?' I asked her.

'In the car,' she said. 'I think he has a problem with the mushy stuff.'

I laughed. 'Oh, yes, that he does. And the mushy stuff is open to interpretation. You wouldn't believe what all that encompasses.'

'Oh, I'd believe it!' she said, laughing back.

It was as if we'd all had a load taken off our shoulders. Rachael was getting better, Melissa was definitely on the mend, and the other children would be in good hands. And Michael and Emily McKinsey were behind bars where, hopefully, they would stay for a long, long while. And even if they did get out, on bail or, God forbid, acquitted, the children would be safe from them.

Personally, I was of two minds when it came to who was responsible for the injuries incurred by Rachael and her children. I was fairly sure that Michael had done much of the damage inflicted upon Rachael, but I wondered if Emily hadn't been the one to discipline the children and shave Rachael's head. The cutting of the hair and shaving of heads seemed more like something a woman in that sect would know to do to inflict the maximum emotional damage. Even in the 'normal' world, cutting a woman's hair against her will or, God forbid, shaving her head, would be a demoralizing punishment.

I've counseled women who have had to have their heads shaved due to chemotherapy, and in some instances that action has been as demoralizing as the cancer itself.

Women think of their hair as their crowning glory. We spend entirely too much time agonizing over how it looks, buying just the right product to make it shine, give it body, make it thicker, color it the color it *should* have been by nature, fixing it this way and that, teasing it, blow drying it, curling it, or straightening it.

I keep my hair short and spend very little time on it. Shower and shampoo in the morning, toss it a little and let it dry naturally. That's my hair day. But, and this is a big but, it looks cute. It's a cute cut. Tossing it makes it cuter. The cut was my decision. If someone were to strap me down and shave my head, I would be outraged – as well as humiliated and ashamed. Why? It's a temporary thing – hair grows back. It is in no way equivalent to a man losing a testicle or having his penis removed. But yet it would feel as if I'd lost my womanliness. I've had a hysterectomy, I've lost that part of my womanhood, but having someone forcibly shave my head would be like losing it all over again.

A man would not know this. He would not be able to relate to this. Only another woman could know this feeling. That's why I was as positive as I could be that Emily had been the one to shave Rachael's head and snip away nastily at Melissa's hair.

181

The doctor broke up the family reunion rather quickly as the kids were disturbing the other patients in ICU, so we headed out to the county van to take us all to Bishop and the Hudsons' house.

I let Nita Skitteridge ride up front with Milt, while I rode in the back with the kids. The meeting with their mother had perked them all up. While we were driving along, I heard Luke say, 'June's not gonna mind this at all, huh, Matt? She's gonna have Nathaniel all to herself!' And he laughed, as only a brother can at a sister's expense.

June started to protest, but Matthew spoke up. 'Hey, Luke, don't be mean. 'Sides, it's Daniel she's after!'

June swatted at both boys, then let loose with the female comeback: 'Too bad Lynnie's too old for you, Matt. I know you *drool* over her!'

Matthew blushed and Luke laughed with his sister until she said, 'Lynnie's too old for him and Candice is too young for you. Poor baby!'

And so the punching and slapping began. I'd barely gotten that stopped before Samantha started crying for her mother.

The Hudsons were out to greet us as we pulled into the cul-de-sac. Mary Hudson's driveway was crowded with kids. Both Carol Anne and Rene were there; Rene's little girl, Cheyenne, was clinging to one leg, while the baby, Michael, sat on Rene's hip checking out the antics of his family. Carol Anne had baby

Mark in her arms.

The kids piled out of the van and there was a lot of arm punching going on with the boys, hugs going on with the girls, and Carol Anne Hudson had Samantha in her arms, drying tears. Rene looked like she wanted to rush into the fray. I held out my arms for the baby boy, who came willingly. Rene and her two-year-old, Cheyenne, moved into the crowd while I held six-month-old Michael. It had been five years since I'd held a baby this age and it felt good. He was tiny and cute as a button, with light brown hair that curled around his ears, green eyes that shone like a grassy field, a tiny cleft in his little chin, and three teeth that were always present since he seemed to smile constantly. What we in the business call 'a good baby.' And the business I'm speaking of at the moment is not psychiatry but motherhood – the best of the two.

And, of course, now I regretted the hysterectomy and wished I could give my son John a sibling – a brother particularly. Watching these boys interact, I wanted that for my son. His cousins here were so much older than him that he would never have that feeling of comradeship that these boys had, and the cousins nearer his age were all up north in Illinois, where my brothers and sisters lived. He would be lucky to see them once a year.

I saw Milt looking at me as I held Michael, and knew he was thinking the same thing.

Milt Kovak – Friday

I looked over at my wife and saw that she was holding Rene's baby, and turned to look for Rene. Couldn't help it, a man has a right to gaze at a cute butt – I think that's in the constitution somewhere. I found her in the middle of the bunch of kids, her little girl in her arms, talking to Rachael McKinsey's kids and giving pats here and there. Couldn't see her butt though; too many kids in the way.

Then out of nowhere, the big yellow dog came galloping at me and threw himself in my arms, I swear to God. I almost lost my balance. He was licking my face and I was holding him fore and aft, and let me tell you he was heavy.

'Butch!' Carol Anne yelled. She ran over to me. 'Just put her down. Butch, what were you thinking?'

Butch turned back to me and stood up, his – I mean her – paws on my shoulders and licked my face some more.

'Hey, Sheriff!' one of the boys called. 'She likes you!' And all the kids laughed like – well, kids.

'Butch!' Carol Anne said, pulling at her collar, 'Get down! The sheriff doesn't want you drooling all over him!'

I looked over at my wife who was laughing along with the kids. She caught my eye and I gave her a mean look. That just made her laugh harder.

Enough falderal, I thought. I needed to be

getting on back to the shop. I had a few more questions for ol' Michael McKinsey – like, what the hell happened to Nalene, his first wife? How'd she happen to die? That sort of thing. The circumstances seemed a little more than suspicious, if you ask me. Of course no one has – asked me, that is.

I radioed in and asked if anyone was near Bishop and found out Dalton was. I told him to come pick me up at The Branches asap. I thought I'd leave the van for Nita and Jean.

I told the women what I was up to, just in time for Dalton's squad car to come screeching into the cul-de-sac. I waved goodbye and sat riding shotgun. Once we were on the road and I'd filled Dalton in on everything that had happened that morning, and he'd told me why he'd been out this way (a carjacking outside Bishop in the country – a Bishop cardiologist and his wife, both shaky but at home, who promised to come to the station in the morning to look at mugshots), I said, 'Dalton, I got something I need you to do.'

'Sure, Milt. Anything you say,' Dalton said.

'You know that dance coming up next month at the Veterans of Foreign Wars Hall?' I said.

'Sure, Milt. I heard about it.'

'You going?'

'Ah, hadn't thought about it much,' he said. 'I took Mama a couple of years, since she knew people there, but most of them are gone now and it just depresses her, so I doubt if she'll

185

want to go.'

All I could do was shake my head. 'Well, Dalton, I think you should go this year, but I don't think you should take your mama. I think you should take Holly.'

All was silence behind the wheel. I let it go for close to five minutes, like you do in an interrogation when you want the perp to talk; you be silent and then the perp has to fill the silence with something. Well, it didn't work. Dalton could out-silence me. So I finally said, 'Dalton, did you hear me?'

'What's that, Milt?'

'Did you hear what I said about taking Holly Humphries to the VFW dance next month?'

Silence.

'Dalton, you have to acknowledge that I said something.'

'Well, yeah, Milt, you said something,' he finally said.

'Good. What did I say?' I asked him.

Silence.

'Dalton!' I yelled at the top of my lungs. He swerved all over the road, but it was empty so we didn't hit anything.

'Milt, don't yell at me!' he said, once he had the car straightened out.

'So, you can't stand Holly, is that what you're saying?' I asked.

'No,' he said, 'that ain't it.'

'You just don't like her much?'

'Noooo,' he said, 'that ain't it.'

186

'Then what *is* it?' I demanded.

'Milt,' he said, looking over at me, his face tormented, 'it's a Sadie Hawkins dance. You know, where the girls ask the guys...'

'I know, I know!' I said, and threw my head back against the headrest. 'Shit,' I said. To get off that subject, I asked him, 'So how's your ID of that DB going?'

'Not so good,' Dalton said. 'But Anthony gave me an idea, and I think I can get Holly to help me with the computers...'

'Good, good,' I said, cutting him off. If you let Dalton go, he could talk your ear off and I wasn't in the mood.

We rode the rest of the way in silence and once at the shop, I told Dalton to bring McKinsey to the interrogation room and went in there to wait for him.

He came in five minutes later, dressed in county-blue coveralls, hands cuffed in front, leg irons intact, and Dalton placed him in the chair opposite me. 'Milt?' Dalton said. 'You want me to stay?'

'No, Dalton, that's OK,' I told him. He left and I turned to McKinsey. 'Bollinger find you a criminal attorney yet?'

'Yeah. I talked to him on the phone. Said I shouldn't answer any of your questions and to keep my mouth shut until he gets here. Which I'm doing.'

'When's he supposed to get here?' I asked.

'This afternoon,' McKinsey answered.

I nodded my head. 'OK,' I said. I stood up. 'I can tell him then about the murder charges.'

I started toward the door and McKinsey said, 'Now, hold on, Sheriff! What murder charges? Rachael ain't dead, is she?'

'No, your – excuse the expression – wife is doing real fine, under the circumstances, those being that you beat the shit out of her and the kid, Melissa.'

'The kid? I never touched that kid!'

'Yeah, I figured Emily for that,' I said.

'I never said that!' McKinsey shouted. 'Who the hell you think I murdered, for God's sake?'

'Mary Hudson, of course,' I said. 'I figured she found out what you were doing with the Owen family – stealing their money and beating 'em up and all – and said she was gonna turn you in, so you killed her.'

McKinsey tried to stand up. 'Listen! Listen, Sheriff! I never in my life even spoke to that Hudson woman, I swear to God! OK, I mighta done some of what you're saying, I mighta been a little hard on Rachael for talking back and such, but I never, ever killed anybody! And I never stole anything from her! The woman didn't have a pot to piss in, for God's sake. Now that Hudson woman, I saw her in church with her family, that's all. I barely spoke to her husband, and I'm a married man – I don't talk to another man's women.'

I sat down across from him and he too sat back down. 'So, I can talk to you right now without your lawyer?' I asked.

'Yeah, sure! I don't want you thinking I killed somebody, for God's sake!'

'So you never killed anybody?'

'That's what I'm trying to tell you!' McKinsey shouted.

'So what happened to Nalene?' I asked.

'Huh?'

'Nalene. Your first wife? The one before Emily? The one y'all had cremated in Oklahoma City, the one you told the church ran off, the one you collected $150,000 insurance payment for. You know, Nalene.'

McKinsey's face turned red, a different shade than the one he turned when he got mad – I think this was the embarrassment shade of red. 'I didn't have anything to do with that,' he said. 'Nalene just up and died in her sleep one night. I was with Emily so I didn't find her. Emily found her when she didn't come to breakfast and she went to check on her.'

'How old was Nalene?'

'Close to forty,' McKinsey said, like forty was a good age for a first wife to die.

'What did she die of?'

McKinsey shrugged his shoulders.

I rubbed my face with my hands, trying to keep patience with this dumbass. 'Y'all had her cremated. Nobody's gonna do that without a death certificate. So y'all had to call the ME or something. There had to be some record.'

'Emily said we couldn't call the ME here

'cause everybody would be snooping into our business. She said we should drive Nalene to Oklahoma City, check into a motel, move the body in at night, then call an ambulance in the morning. Which is what I did. Emily stayed in the bathroom so there wouldn't be any questions. The ambulance guys said Nalene had a heart attack, a JP signed off on it, and I had a funeral home come pick her up. Told them we were from out of town and I wanted her cremated and I'd take the ashes home to bury.'

'What *did* you do with the cremains?'

'Ah, I haven't picked 'em up yet,' he said.

'What do you think Nalene died of, Michael?' I asked.

'I guess a heart attack, like the ambulance people said.'

'You don't think Emily had a hand in it?'

'No!' he all but shouted. 'Emily's the love of my life! She'd never do anything like that.'

'So why did you have Nalene insured for so much?' I asked.

'Insured?' he asked.

'Yeah. There was a $150,000 insurance policy on her,' I said.

'No there wasn't,' he said, a confused look on his face.

I sighed. If he didn't know about the insurance money, was it possible he didn't know about the social security or pension money Rachael should have been receiving? Was little Emily that good? Maybe she was.

EIGHT

Jean McDonnell – Friday

We got the kids all straightened out – boys off to Carol Anne's former home, where her mother and brother now lived, and the girls in Carol Anne's new home, Sister Mary's former home. Carol Anne explained to me that with her four boys and Mary's three boys (not counting Little Mark), she and Jerry had thought seriously about making Carol Anne's former home into a permanent home for the boys, with Denise and Dennis as chaperones, leaving the four girls and Mark at Carol Anne's new house.

'I still think of this place as Mary's house,' she said, looking around the kitchen where the two of us sat at the breakfast table.

I looked where she looked, and couldn't help agreeing with her. 'This *is* Mary's house,' I said. 'You need to make it your own. If you'll excuse my saying so, your house was very different from this one – more lively, more exciting. You need to make your mark on this one, even if it means moving some of your stuff over here. Or,' I said, grinning at her, 'maybe just mess up some stuff in these cabinets. That would be a start.'

Carol Anne laughed. 'Sister Mary *was* very neat,' she replied. 'It's like pulling teeth to keep all this the way she had it.'

'You're too young to have your teeth pulled,' I said. 'So don't. This is no longer Sister Mary's house. It's yours and Jerry's. Talk to him – ask him what he likes best about this house, and what he likes best about your old house. Compromise.'

Carol Anne was slowly nodding her head as I talked. 'That's a good idea. Now that we're moving children around, maybe it *is* time to move some furniture and stuff around too.'

I squeezed her hand as the kitchen door swung open and Lynnie, Mary's oldest daughter, came in. Her face was very serious. 'Mama Carol Anne, we need to talk.'

'We have company right now, Lynnie,' she said.

I started to stand up but Lynnie shooed me down. 'No, Dr McDonnell. Please stay. I think you might be a good referee for this,' Lynnie said.

I sat back down. 'If it's OK with Carol Anne,' I said.

Carol Anne nodded. 'Of course, although I can't imagine—'

'I want to wear real clothes!' Lynnie all but shouted. 'June and Sammie and the boys wear real clothes, why can't we? We stand out like sore thumbs at school. I don't have any friends because they think I'm some sort of weirdo! We used to wear regular clothes before we moved here!' Lynnie stopped and took a deep breath. 'That's it,' she said. 'That's what I have to say.'

Carol Anne nodded her head and looked down at her baggy black dress, the one she'd been wearing (or one of many she'd been wearing) since Mary's death. 'I'll talk to your father.'

'Mama Carol Anne, that's not enough! You have to be on our side when you talk to him! Can't you see how none of us have any friends because of these stupid clothes?'

'Clothes do not make the person, it's what's in—'

'Oh, bull!' Lynnie said. 'Even you don't believe that! Think back to when you were a teenager! Would you have been accepted by your peers wearing this crap?'

'Lynnie, your language. Please don't use those words, they're offensive.' Carol Anne sighed. 'Yes, I understand what you're saying. And I sympathize. Like I said, I'll talk to your father.'

'OK,' Lynnie said. Then she looked at me. 'Dr McDonnell, do you have anything to add?' she asked.

I shook my head. 'No, I think you covered the issue nicely,' I told her.

She nodded and walked out.

Milt Kovak – Friday
I got a call from Charlie Smith, police chief of

Longbranch. 'Milt, Charlie.'

'Hey, Charlie,' I said. 'What's up?'

'Tatum Barclay's dander,' he said.

'What's his problem?' I said, not the least bit interested. Tatum Barclay was a lawyer, and a pretty bad one. I think he mighta won a case once, but it woulda been a long time ago.

'Seems you got his clients in your jailhouse that should be in my jailhouse,' Charlie said.

'Oh, 'cause they live inside the city limits, you mean?' I asked.

'That's Barclay's point. Personally, I don't need 'em and I don't want 'em.'

'Oh, I'd happily give 'em up, Charlie. Bring 'em over to you all tied up in a pretty bow. 'Cept the murder I think one of 'em committed was in the county, which is why I'm holding 'em.'

'Good enough for me. I'll call Barclay back and tell him to bug you and not me.'

'You're a peach, Charlie.'

'I try to please,' he said as he hung up.

I sighed. I truly did not want to have a pow-wow with Tatum Barclay. But I had to wonder, why in the world would David Bollinger hire that nincompoop? Barclay *had* to be the worst lawyer in Oklahoma, maybe the entire Southwest, if not the United States of America. Hell, maybe the universe, I don't know. But he was bad. He was the kind of lawyer who sounded good – a real fast talker, but when it came right down to it, he didn't know a brief from his shorts.

Why would Bollinger hire him? I looked in the Longbranch phone book. Barclay was the first lawyer listed. Maybe that was why. Bollinger had been in Oklahoma, how long? I couldn't remember exactly, but not long. So he picked the first lawyer he came to. Not very professional, I thought, but under the circumstances, a worthy attorney for the likes of Michael McKinsey and his little bride.

My private line rang and I sighed. Tatum Barclay had been a half-assed friend of my predecessor, Elberry Blankenship, and would have the private number to this office. I picked up the phone and said, 'Sheriff Kovak speaking.'

'Kovak, this is Tatum Barclay,' he said. 'I understand you're in charge now.'

'Yes, sir, have been for about six years now.'

'Whatever. You got two of my clients in your jailhouse, Michael and Emily McKinsey,' he said.

'Yes, sir, I do,' I said, although it hadn't been a question but a mere statement of fact.

'I want them released immediately. Anything you could charge them with would have occurred within the city limits of Longbranch, and therefore should be the purview of the Longbranch police department and not the county sheriff's department. I'll have the paperwork on your desk—'

'Mr Barclay, excuse me for interrupting, but

195

the most pressing charge against them is the murder of Mary Hudson of Bishop, which is under the sheriff's department jurisdiction.'

'You got any evidence against either Michael or Emily McKinsey regarding the murder of Mary Hudson?' Before I could answer, he continued, 'No, sir, you do not. Because there isn't any. They barely knew the Hudsons. You need me to go before the judge today and have that charge thrown out?' Again, before I could answer, 'Because that would be no problem for me. Of course, you'd have to come up to the courthouse with what evidence you have – which you don't – and that would look bad next time you need to go before that same judge with any *real* evidence on some other case. Make you look like an ass. So, Sheriff, and I use that term loosely, why don't we get my people moved over to city jurisdiction?'

I sighed inwardly. 'Tell you what I'll do, Barclay,' I said, like I was doing him a favor, 'I'll have the McKinseys transferred to the city facilities until such time as I have sufficient evidence against them for the murder of Mary Hudson. Then we'll move 'em back.'

'Whatever,' Barclay said. 'I'll be over there in fifteen minutes.'

'Fine. I'll call Police Chief Smith when I get a minute. Which will probably be in about an hour,' I said and hung up. Then the thought of Tatum Barclay hanging out in the station for an hour began to give me the shivers, so I called

Charlie Smith to get the ball rolling.

'Ah, fuck, Milt! I don't want that asshole and his wife! And I sure as hell don't want to have to deal with Barclay!' Charlie said when I informed him of the situation.

'They shouldn't be there long,' I told him sadly. 'Judge'll give 'em bail on the charges of assault and child endangerment. Mark my word, they won't be there more'n a day tops.'

'From your mouth to God's ear,' Charlie said and hung up.

He thought bail was going to be a good thing. All I could think of was Rachael and Melissa all alone in the ICU.

The county had started up a program last year of auxiliary deputies, people we could call on to direct traffic at a wreck, in case of a national emergency or natural disaster, or the like. One of the auxiliary deputies was a guy named Roy Donley, a long-haul trucker who had a lot of down-time he wanted to fill with the excitement of directing traffic. Roy was six foot eleven inches (which had a lot to do with his down-time – he had serious back problems from the long-haul trucking), close to 300 pounds, had a full beard, a deep, gravelly voice, and looked and sounded like he had an attitude, which he didn't. Roy was a hell of a nice guy; you just couldn't tell that by the way he looked.

I called him up to see if he was on down-time, and he was. 'Roy, I got an assignment for you,' I told him.

'Sure, man, whatever. Always glad to help out.'

'I got an abused woman and her abused daughter in the ICU at the hospital, and their abusers are getting out of jail, probably today. I just need you to find a comfy chair and sit outside their room.'

'Son-of-a-bitch!' he said. 'Hell, man, you got it. Son-of-a-bitch tries to get anywhere near them two he'll be looking backwards for a time to come!'

I smiled. 'That's good, Roy. I'll call you when they get out.'

'Use my cell phone, Milt. I'm gonna head on over to the hospital and introduce myself. Get ready, ya know?'

'That sounds good, Roy. I'll call you.' I gave him the pertinent information, then sat back in my chair with what I can only assume was a satisfied look on my face. And, Lord yes, I did want Michael McKinsey to try to get in that room.

Jean McDonnell – Friday

I went up to the ICU to check on Rachael and Melissa. Melissa was sitting up in bed, her head newly shaved, talking a mile a minute. When she saw me, her smile broadened and she pointed to her head.

'Look!' she said. 'I asked the nurse to fix my hair and she made it look just like Mama's!'

'Wow!' I said. 'You both look great! We can

198

put some lotion on your heads and make them both shine!'

'Ooo, Mama, let's do that!' Melissa said, bouncing in her bed. 'You'd look real pretty with a shiny head!'

Rachael laughed. 'What a grand idea,' she said.

I pulled up a chair between the two beds so we could talk for a while. I'd only been there for fifteen minutes or less when I saw the strangest thing: a giant man walking toward Rachael's room. Melissa saw him about the same time as I did, and for the first time since my arrival, stopped talking. Rachael turned to where both Melissa and I were looking, and her smile faded.

'Excuse me, ma'am,' the giant said in a deep, gravelly voice, as befitting a giant, 'my name's Roy Donley. Sheriff Milt said I should come over here and sit. Something about your husband getting out on bail.'

Rachael and I looked at each other and both sighed our relief. He wasn't a giant hit man; Milt had sent him.

'Mr McKinsey's out of jail?' Melissa said in a whisper.

'Now, don't you worry, little darlin',' the giant – excuse me, Roy Donley – said, moving closer to Melissa's bed. 'I'm not a mean man, I'm just big. But guys like Mr McKinsey don't know that. They take one look at me and run like the cowards they are.'

Melissa held out her hand. Roy took it and placed it on his palm. 'Boy, you're big,' she said, her little hand in the center of his palm, with lots of room left over.

'Yeah, little darlin', I am big, that's just a fact of nature. Like a skunk's got a white stripe, and a porcupine's got quills. And you've gotta a pretty bald head.'

Melissa giggled. 'That's not nature! The nurse shaved it so I'd look like Mama.'

Roy Donley looked over at Rachael and smiled. 'Two of the prettiest bald-headed women I've ever seen,' he said.

Rachael smiled back.

Milt Kovak – Friday
I got Holly to do the paperwork we needed and by the time Tatum Barclay slithered through the door we had the prisoners out of their county-blue jumpsuits and into street clothes, and the paperwork sealed in a manila envelope. It took less than five minutes to get them out of there and I was grateful for that. I hadn't seen Tatum Barclay in a while. Ten years ago I woulda sworn it was impossible, but the man was even uglier than he used to be. Short to begin with, he was even shorter now, his back hunched up with osteoporosis, his head poking up like a turtle's, his long, thin nose sticking out of his face like an antenna. He looked like a caricature of himself. Even Emily McKinsey shied away from him, and that woman liked to inflict ugly.

But they were gone, and that was some sort of good news. I called Charlie to tell him they were on their way, and he said, 'We're gonna have to keep 'em the night. Judge is out of town till morning. Got any recommendations on how to treat 'em?'

'Don't let 'em get wet and don't feed 'em after midnight,' I said as I hung up, not caring really if Charlie got my movie reference or not. It was an old movie, after all.

I called Roy Donley next. When he answered the phone, I said, 'Roy, Milt Kovak.'

'Hey, Sheriff,' he said.

'You at the hospital?'

'Yes, sir. Everything's copasetic here.'

'Well, the prisoners have been transferred to the city jail, but they won't even go before a judge to set bail until morning. So you can go on home,' I said.

'Oh,' he said, sounding dejected. 'OK, then.'

'You gonna be OK to come back tomorrow?' I asked.

'You got me twenty-four/seven, Sheriff Milt,' he said.

I thanked him and hung up, thinking, bald or not, Rachael McKinsey was still a pretty woman and that maybe Roy Donley had picked up on that.

Which still left me with trying to prove that Michael McKinsey, or possibly Emily McKinsey, had killed Mary Hudson. Somebody sure had, and if it wasn't the McKinseys, which I was kind of afraid it wasn't, then I was right back where I started. Which was nowhere.

I sat back and contemplated the situation as I knew it. The city police forensics guy found no fingerprints in Mary's kitchen other than hers, her children's, her husband's, and the two sister-wives' and their children's. In other words, so many damn prints he probably lost track. The only footprints in the blood were those of Lynnie Hudson, Mary's daughter who discovered her. Basically, no forensics evidence to point at anyone, much less specifically at the McKinseys. Michael McKinsey's alibi (being at work) could be fudged; he didn't clock in, being a supervisor, but this or that employee saw him most of the day. Emily, on the other hand, didn't have much of an alibi. She was at home abusing Rachael and her kids, and since none of them were allowed to see a clock, they certainly couldn't vouch for her whereabouts at any given time. Since she took breaks from her torture of the family, she would have had the opportunity.

The only motive I could come up with for either McKinsey having done the deed was the obvious one: Mary had found out about the abuse or the theft of funds or the death of Nalene McKinsey, or any of the other nefarious stunts pulled by the couple, and was going to turn them in. As more and more information about the torture of Rachael and her children came out, suspicion fell more heavily on Emily than on Michael. Michael was a beast who beat his wife; Emily tortured the wife and the children and stole money from them, as well as from Michael, and may be responsible for Nalene's death. Emily was not a very nice young lady.

Any other suspects, I asked myself? Just church people. Like their preacher, or whatever he called himself, Earl Mayhew, or his boy Earl Jr, or Thomas Whitman, who Jean said probably had nothing to do with it. He didn't talk to women unless he was married to them, she'd said, which was the same thing Michael McKinsey had said. 'I don't talk to the wives of other men.' Then there were the Bollingers. They were more modern – wore street clothes, had normal haircuts, etc. So maybe David Bollinger didn't have a problem with talking to other men's wives. Have to look into that. And Bollinger brought it back full circle to Earl Mayhew, as one of Bollinger's three wives was Earl Mayhew's daughter, Naomi Ruth. Who was also Earl Jr's sister.

Interesting, I thought. Interesting enough to take another look at the Earls. Earl Sr knew something was wrong at the McKinsey house and never said anything. If he wasn't directly involved in Mary Hudson's death, he was surely guilty of not reporting child abuse. Earl Jr had been spying on or stalking Mary Hudson. And then he up and lied to me about it. I'd like to talk to him alone.

And then, of course, there was Brother Bob Nathanson, pastor of the United Brethren of the Holy Church of Jesus Christ in His Almighty Goodness, or just the Brethren as they were known locally. Brother Bob was the one who burst in my office demanding I arrest somebody for the killing of that 'wanton woman.' That being Mary Hudson. I never did find out what he and his congregation were up to that Monday.

I thought about the whole thing for way too long. After about an hour, Holly called me to tell me there'd been a wreck right in front of the station and I was the only one here. I sighed and headed outside to deal with it.

It was a two-car wreck, and I knew both participants. Kyle Davies was seventeen and he and his family went to the Catholic church where me and Jean go every other Sunday; the kid was a straight arrow. The other vehicle belonged to Jessica Anderson, who was twenty-two, a party girl, spent most of her nights at the Dew-Drop Inn and her days nursing a hangover while checking out groceries at the Stop-N-Shop. I only knew her because she'd been the cause of several bouts of fisticuffs at the Dew-Drop over the past couple of years. Longer than she's been of drinking age, that's for sure. As it was her quitting time at the grocery store, I figured she might be in a hurry to get to the Dew-Drop.

'Hey, y'all,' I said, as I looked both ways

while crossing the highway to get to where they'd pulled their vehicles off to the side. Kyle drove an antique 1980s Ford F150 pick-up truck; Jessica drove an antique 1980s Datsun (before they were called Nissans). Kyle's truck didn't have a dent; Jessica's Datsun looked totaled. 'What happened?'

I shoulda known better. They both started talking at once, pointing at each other, their voices getting louder and louder. I did a two-fingered whistle and they stopped. 'Ladies first,' I said.

'He pulled out in front of me and slammed on his brakes!' Jessica said.

'I did not!' Kyle all but shouted. 'I pulled in front of her back by the courthouse, and then we get here, and a car's turning in front of me, so I put on my brakes and she slams into my rear!'

I thought, *He should be so lucky*, but didn't let my garbage mind spill out of my mouth. 'That's the way it happened, Jessica?' I asked.

'No! Well, not exactly!' Hands on hips, she blustered a bit.

'You speeding, Jessica?' I asked, since she'd been stopped for that a couple of times.

'No! Not really,' she said.

'What does not really mean?' I asked.

'I was just going maybe a mile or two over the limit,' she said, looking behind her at nothing. 'The limit changes right up there.'

'Yeah, right up there,' I said, pointing at the

fifty-five-mile-an-hour sign a hundred or so yards up the highway. Here in front of the sheriff's office, although out of the city limits, the speed was still forty.

'Sheriff, pleeeeez don't give me a ticket! Pleeeeeez! I'm gonna lose my insurance.'

'Seems like you don't have much of a car to insure, honey,' I said, looking at the Datsun.

Jessica turned around and looked at it and burst into tears.

Kyle was rubbing the toe of his Tony Lama in the dust of the highway shoulder. 'Don't cry, Jessica,' he said, which just made her cry harder as she turned around and threw herself against Kyle's scrawny chest. He patted her back and looked at me. 'Maybe we can say it was my fault?' he asked. 'So my insurance can pay to fix her car?'

'Kyle, that's called insurance fraud,' I said.

'Oh,' he said.

'What am I gonna do?' she wailed.

'Both of y'all call your insurance companies,' I said. 'I'll call a wrecker for your car, Jessica.'

'How am I gonna get home?' she wailed, while I was thinking 'home' might be a euphemism for the Dew-Drop Inn.

'I'll take you,' Kyle offered.

'That's OK, Kyle,' I said. 'We'll make sure she gets home OK. Since your truck's fine to drive, why don't you get on your way after you give me your insurance information.'

He did while Jessica lit up a menthol cigarette, getting pissed now, arms crossed under her already ample bosom, making them look even larger. 'Kyle, call your agent,' I said, 'then go on about your business.'

'Yes, sir,' he said, looking longingly back at Jessica.

I walked Jessica back across the highway to the station, had her put out her cigarette in the ashtray in front of the building, then took her inside and sat her down on the bench. Holly was the only one in the big room and she was filing and pretending not to pay attention.

'Jessica, you've been stopped three times for speeding. Nobody ever gave you a ticket but you've been warned. This time, I'm afraid, you're getting two tickets, one for speeding and one for rear-ending Kyle.'

She welled up again. 'Honey, I'm married to a psychiatrist,' I said. 'I've learned not to let female tears affect me. So here's the deal. Since I personally did not see you speeding, I'm just gonna give you a ticket for causing a wreck. You got anything other than liability insurance?'

The tears began again as she shook her head. 'Now I'm without a car, huh?' she said, looking into my eyes. 'What am I gonna do?' and she began to wail righteously and loud.

'What you're gonna do is this,' I said. 'While you're sitting here waiting for Holly to take you home, you're gonna call your insurance agent. Got that?'

She sniffled but nodded.

'Meanwhile, I'm calling a wrecker to come get your car.'

Again, she sniffled but nodded.

I walked back to the bullpen and spoke softly to Holly. 'Get her address off her ID and take her to that address, not to the Dew-Drop Inn, which is where she'll wanna direct you, got it?'

'Yes, sir, Sheriff,' Holly said.

I used Holly's phone to call for a wrecker, watching while Jessica made a call, hopefully to her agent and not to her hunk-of-the-month to drive her to the Dew-Drop. But it was really none of my business. The girl was over twenty-one.

I told Holly, 'You go on home. Go get your purse and take off.'

'But, Sheriff, I'm not through—'

'It'll be here in the morning. I'll switch the radio and the phone over to the duty officer.' She looked at her computer longingly and I said, 'Now, get, girl.'

'See you in the morning,' she said, as she picked up her purse that rested on a shelf under the counter, and headed out to the waiting room to get Jessica. I figured by morning I'd hear from Jessica's mother, a city councilwoman who expected favors.

I called Emmett, tonight's duty officer, to let him know I was switching over early, did the deed, then went back to my office to listen to the silence. That didn't last long. My stomach rumbled and I remembered a new Mexican restaurant just opened the other side of down-town. I called my wife and suggested she and Johnny Mac stop by here and we'd drive there together. My wife thought that was a wonderful idea.

NINE

Milt Kovak – Saturday

The next morning I got Nita Skitteridge to ride with me back to Tejas County and the New Saints Tabernacle. I called Bill Williams to let him know I'd be going into his jurisdiction.

'Well, hell, Milt. I got my own stuff to worry about right now,' he said when I told him I was on my way.

'Truthfully, Bill, it's closer if I just go to the church than come all the way to your shop. And I don't see that we need more than you saying it's OK.'

'You gonna arrest the preacher for anything?' Bill asked.

'I don't think so,' I said. 'Just need to ask some more questions.'

'You gonna arrest his wives or his children?'

'I have no plans to arrest anybody,' I said. 'Except maybe you for running up my cell phone minutes.'

'OK then, go ahead. But call me when you're through.'

'You got AT&T stock, dontcha, Bill?'

'I wish,' he said and hung up.

There were several cars in the parking lot of the church when we got there. Earl Mayhew himself opened the door to the double-wide.

'Well, hey, Sheriff Kovak,' he said, still chewing from, I suppose, the sandwich he held in his hand. 'What can I do you for?'

'Wondered if we could have a word, Brother Earl,' I said.

'Well, now, I'd invite you in, but...' He shrugged his shoulders.

'But what, Brother Earl?'

'Well, now, I know it ain't politically correct,' he said, 'but it's in the scriptures that we, and by we I mean God's chosen, don't consort with mud people.'

'Here we go again with this mud people shit!' Nita said, hands on hips, a couple of fingers I noticed caressing the butt of her .45.

'Now, I don't mean to offend, Deputy, you got ever' right in the world to do just about anything you want ... Except come inside my home.' He looked at me. 'You understand that, Sheriff?'

'Not a bit,' I said. 'But I don't figure I have time to get a warrant, so get your ass out of the trailer on your own, or I'll slap cuffs on you and take you in. 'Course, Deputy Skitteridge'll have to sit in the back with you.'

Nita smiled. 'And I like to rub legs with my felons,' she said.

He handed his sandwich to someone behind him and walked down the steps. He was wearing pleated front trousers with cuffs and one of those sleeveless T-shirts I've heard called wife-beater, his graying hair too long and not yet blown-dry and sprayed stiff. It bounced around his face as he came down the steps.

'I think I done answered all the questions you had, Sheriff. And I tried to help you with the whole problem with the McKinseys.'

'If I were you I wouldn't speak of the McKinseys,' Nita said. 'The sheriff is not happy about that whole thing and how you could have prevented most of it by saying something months ago. So, shush,' she said, holding her finger up to her lips. 'Be very careful what you say,' she whispered.

'This woman is harassing me, Sheriff,' Brother Earl said. 'I am formally asking you to make her stop.'

I slapped my arm over Brother Earl's shoulders, and told him in a right friendly manner, 'Naw, Brother Earl, she's just giving you facts. What you do with 'em is your business.'

'I wanna call Sheriff Williams...'

'He told me to tell you how sorry he was that he couldn't make it today,' I said, arm still around his thin shoulders, 'but to tell you hidy.'

We'd made our way inside the metal building that served as the sanctuary. I pointed to a metal chair sitting by the front door, and Deputy Nita influenced Brother Earl to sit in it.

'I got questions, Earl, and you *will* have answers, understand?' I said.

212

'How can I have answers if I don't know any, Sheriff? That's just plain dumb—'

Nita kicked the bar on the chair between his legs, shoving the chair back a foot or two and getting a nice shade of pale on Brother Earl's face. 'Are you calling the duly elected sheriff of Prophesy County dumb?' she shouted at him.

'No, of cour—'

'Then answer his fucking questions!' she shouted.

'Of course, yes, no problem...' Earl stammered.

'Who killed Mary Hudson?' I asked him.

'I don't know!' he said.

'Who killed Mary Hudson?' I asked again.

'I don't know! Really...'

'Why would they do it?' I asked, getting up close in his face.

'Who? What?' he said, cringing back in the chair.

'Why would someone kill Mary? What did she know?'

Brother Earl pulled up his shoulders, like a turtle trying to hide in his shell. 'I don't know, Sheriff, honest I don't. I never talked to the woman. But maybe one of my wives...' he said, his face showing how eager he was to throw his wives to the wolves – namely me and Nita.

'Keep him here,' I said to Nita, and headed for the trailer.

'Now wait, Sheriff! This is a house of God and this heathen mud woman is cussing and just

213

being here—'

'It's OK, Sheriff,' Nita said as I headed for the door. 'Me and Earl here are gonna be just fine.'

And I didn't doubt it one bit.

Nita Skitteridge – Saturday

Now I needed to rein myself in. I'd been letting loose a bit with the sheriff being there, playing up to this old geezer like I was some kind of mad woman – as opposed to mud woman. But underneath, deep down, yeah, I wanted to hurt this guy, and I knew it. And I knew I had it in me. That's why I went to the academy instead of dental hygienist school. It'd be mean to take out my frustrations on somebody strapped down with my hands in their mouth. No, being a deputy, I got to vent my frustrations a little bit. But I had to watch it. Couldn't let it get out of hand. Not like I knew it could. Not like it did back home that time.

'Be still!' I told the preacher, who was squirming around like he was gonna make a break for it. 'You want me to tie you up?'

'I'm gonna have your badge!' he shouted.

I took it off my breast pocket and handed it to him. 'Whatcha gonna do with it?' I asked him.

He threw my badge on the floor. That kind of disrespect – not for me in particular, but for what the badge represents – well, that just got all over me.

'What do you call yourself, preacher?' I asked him. 'Are you the Right Reverend Earl May-

214

hew, or are you Father Earl Mayhew, or are you Pastor Earl Mayhew, or are you just that Jackass Earl Mayhew? Now which do you want me to call you?' I asked, my voice all sweetness and light like I can do.

'I want to go to my house,' he said.

'No can do, Jackass Earl Mayhew. I hope you don't mind, I picked for you,' I said.

'You evil mud woman! You're dark as the night! You're evil like the hounds of hell!'

I looked at my skin. 'No, sir, now I see myself more of a mocha-chocolate than a dark-as-night. My husband, now he's paper-bag brown, used to get you in all sorts of nice places back in the day, being paper-bag brown. But now we people of color, we're proud. I like my mocha-chocolate shade.' I stuck my bare arm in front of his face. 'Kinda pretty, don't you think?'

He drew back from me. 'Get away! Don't you touch me!'

I couldn't help it. I put my fingers in his hair and went, 'Bogga-bogga!'

He screamed and tried to stand up. After that I had to cuff him and the fun just went out of it for me. I left him cuffed to the metal folding chair and went outside to find someplace to wash my hands. His hair was on the greasy side.

Milt Kovak – Saturday
A young woman, maybe in her mid- to late-teens, opened the door of the double-wide.

215

'Yes?' she said timidly.

'Are you a daughter or a wife?' I asked.

'I'm Brother Earl's wife, Nadia,' she said, and I noticed a slight accent. Russian? I wondered. Brother Earl getting so desperate for wives he was now shopping for 'em online? I would think the state department would frown on this kind of marriage.

'I need to come in and talk to you and the other wives,' I said.

She let me in without a word. Russian or some other Eastern Bloc nation, I thought. Otherwise she wouldn't have obeyed so readily.

The door opened directly into one very large room, a quarter of which was kitchen, another quarter taken up with two large picnic-style tables, and the rest was couches and chairs around a large-screen TV. Two women were standing in the kitchen; one woman was nursing a baby in one of the chairs, the baby's face and her breast covered with a kitchen towel; another woman sat at one of the picnic tables, a Bible spread out in front of her and a legal pad and pen beside her. Counting the one who opened the door, that made five wives. Four kids, from crawling age to about four, were playing with toys on the rug in front of the TV, which was on and blasting *Thomas the Train* as loud as could be.

One of the women in the kitchen was the older woman I'd seen the last time I'd come to interview Brother Earl. I directed my first comment to her. 'Could you turn the TV down a little?' I asked. 'We need to talk.'

The older woman looked at the woman at the picnic table and nodded. The woman at the picnic table got up and went to the TV, turning down the volume. None of the children seemed to notice.

I walked toward the kitchen and held out my hand to the older woman. She just looked at it. Finally she said, 'I don't touch men who are not my husband. Usually I don't talk to men who aren't my husband. Unfortunately you took my husband away, so I have no choice.'

'You're the first wife?' I asked.

'Yes,' she said.

'Would you tell me your name and introduce the others?' I asked.

'Lucy Mayhew,' she said, pointing at her chest. This was the same very short woman I'd met before, her graying hair falling long down her back, her disposition unpleasant. Pointing at the woman at the picnic table, she said, 'Margery Mayhew.' Margery nodded her head. She was a great deal younger, at least ten years, and had very dark hair hanging to her waist. She had dark eyes and olive skin and was several inches taller than Lucy.

Lucy pointed at the woman next to her in the kitchen, a doe-eyed blonde with very large breasts to match the rest of a full-figured body. 'Abigail,' Lucy said. Pointing at the nursing mother, another dark-haired and olive-skinned young woman, Lucy said, 'Charlene, Margery's sister. And you've already met Nadia.'

'Could we all sit down?' I asked.

Lucy nodded to the other women, then said, 'Nadia, please take the children to a bedroom.'

Nadia hustled the children out. The baby stayed latched to its mother's breast. The women sat down on the couches. Nadia came back and squeezed in with the other wives.

'So there are five wives. How many children?' I asked.

'We have been blessed with seventeen children,' Lucy Mayhew said.

I asked, 'Have there been other wives, or always just you five?'

'There was a wife before me,' Lucy said, 'but she died in childbirth. The son she bore is now in his thirties and is a fine young man with three wives and five children. He lives in Utah.'

'So how's it work, five women in one household?'

'I run this house with Abigail and our children. I only have two left at home. Abigail has three,' Lucy said.

'Whose daughter is Naomi Ruth?' I asked.

Lucy's face clouded over and her head went down. 'Mine,' she finally said.

'Has something happened between you and Naomi Ruth?' I asked.

Lucy straightened her shoulders and held up her head. I wasn't going to see her shame more than once, her body language seemed to say.

'My daughter married within the church, but soon became a heathen. Cut her hair, dresses in modern clothes, takes her children to public school, skips church at least twice a month!' Lucy shook her head. 'I've washed my hands of her.'

'You don't like her husband?' I asked.

'David is a fine man,' she said. 'He comes to church as often as he can, but he is weak and doesn't seem to be able to control his wives. They do whatever they want!'

I nodded my head. This whole lifestyle was so fascinating I had a hard time staying on track. 'Ma'am, the reason I'm here is because Brother Earl said one of y'all might have been friendly with Mary Hudson.' I looked around for one of them to confess to a friendship with the dead woman. None did.

'Did y'all know her at all?' I asked.

'Yes, of course,' Lucy said. 'But I'm not sure what my husband was referring to when he said we were friendly.'

'Did any of y'all talk to her?' I asked.

'Of course,' Lucy said. 'The women of the church meet together quite often. We sit together during service and have our women's meetings and cook and clean together at the church. So we all saw each other while doing our church chores and such.'

I looked pointedly at Abigail, the one who appeared closest in age to Mary Hudson. 'Abigail, how well did you know Mary?' I asked.

Abigail looked at Lucy, not answering me. Lucy said, 'Sister Abigail knew her as well as the rest of us.'

I wasn't going to get anywhere with this bunch and I knew it. I changed tactics. 'Whose son is Earl Jr?' I asked.

No one answered. 'Mrs Lucy,' I said. 'Is Earl Jr your son?'

'Yes, and please refer to me as Mrs Mayhew.'

'Sorry, Mrs Mayhew. Could you tell me where Earl Jr is at the moment?'

'No,' she said.

'Is he here in the compound?' I asked.

She was silent. Damn, I wish I had a search warrant, I thought. 'Is he in the other trailer?' I asked.

No one answered.

'Mrs Nadia Mayhew, please take me over to your trailer,' I said, going for the weak one. Hell, that's what you do.

Nadia stood up and headed for the back of the double-wide.

'Nadia, no!' Lucy said emphatically.

Nadia stopped in her tracts.

'Mrs Mayhew, are you trying to impede my investigation?' I asked.

'Where's your warrant, Sheriff? And, lest you forget, this is not your county.'

I shook my head. 'Y'all aren't being forth-coming with me. I feel like one of y'all knew this woman better than the others and y'all are stonewalling me. And I know you know where

Earl Jr is. I don't like that. Somebody killed that woman, and when people aren't forthcoming, when people try to stonewall me, well, it makes me think something hinky is going on. So tell me, Sister Lucy, since you seem to speak for this sisterhood, what kinda hinky are y'all up to?'

Sister Lucy stood up and pointed at the door. 'Sheriff, it's time you left,' she said.

I was getting pissed. 'Well, I ain't leaving alone!' I walked out the door and called the shop. When Holly answered, I said, 'Send someone over here to Tejas County with the van. I'm bringing in the lot of 'em!'

It's true. Sometimes I overreact. I had to leave one wife with the children or have children's services come pick 'em up, so I left the nursing one. But even so, I had me a crowd. To even try to comply with the county regs on separating the sexes in jail cells, I had to put all the women in one and Brother Earl in one by himself. Hardly seemed right. The women didn't have very much room. Holly and I carried in some straight-back chairs so there'd be enough seating for all. Least we could do. Least I could do. I'm the one who started this debacle. I called Bill Williams and told him what I'd done.

'Shit, Milt! Why'd you do that?' he said.

'Hell if I know, Bill. That Sister Lucy was getting on my last nerve, wouldn't tell me anything, and I couldn't find Junior.'

221

'Shit, Buddy? He's a piece of work,' Bill said.

'Could you find him for me and hold him? I'll let his mama and the rest of 'em go if I can get his ass in here.'

'You got the preacher?' he asked.

'Oh, yeah.' I laughed. 'My deputy Nita Skitteridge had a grand old time with him.'

'She the lady of color?' he asked.

'One and the same. Seems Brother Earl has a problem with what he calls "mud people."'

'Yeah, saw that once in town. Called one of our councilmen, Bennie Charleston, a mud person. Thought Bennie was going to take him down.'

'Anyway, call me when you find Buddy, OK?' I pleaded.

'Not going to be a priority, Milt. Got my own shit going on here. But if we find him, I'll call ya.'

I got off the phone and was sitting in my office wondering why I'd pulled such a dumb stunt when David Bollinger walked in, followed closely by Holly.

'Sheriff! I tried to stop him,' Holly said.

At the same time, Bollinger was saying, 'Milt, what in the Sam Hill are you doing?'

I stood up and waved Holly away. 'It's OK, Holly,' I said. 'I got this.'

She left and I pointed at a chair for Bollinger. 'Have a seat, David,' I said.

It took a second, but he finally sat. 'I mean, really,' he said.

'Don't start. I'm beating myself up enough about it. But your father-in-law is a real pain in the ass, David.'

He laughed. 'Um, true. But we must honor our fathers and mothers, Milt.'

'Not when they're dumb shits,' I countered.

He shook his head. 'Don't remember seeing that in my Bible. I think even dumb shits must be honored, if for no other reason than they brought us into this life.'

'You're a more generous man than me, Counselor.'

Bollinger stood up. 'You want to set bail or can I just take them all home?'

'You know where your brother-in-law is?' I asked.

'Buddy? Haven't seem him since last Sunday,' Bollinger said.

'If you see him, hold on to him, OK?'

'You want me to tie him up or what?' Bollinger asked, being sarcastic.

'That would be nice,' I said, standing up and heading for the door. It was time to end this. 'I had to use the police van to get 'em all here.'

'I've got my wife's minivan out there,' Bollinger said.

'Which one?' I asked.

'Which minivan?' he asked, frowning.

'No, son. Which wife?'

'Does it matter?' he asked.

I shrugged my shoulders. 'Probably not,' I replied.

I'd barely released the lot of 'em before Holly got a call and said, 'Sheriff, it's Sheriff Williams from Tejas County.'

Being still in the reception area, I took Holly's phone. 'Bill?' I said.

'Got him,' he said.

'Buddy? No shit?'

'No shit. He was disturbing the peace at a little place here we call Joe's.'

'I know the joint. You got him in lock-up?'

'Yes I do.'

'I'm sending someone to get him.'

'Over and out,' Bill said.

Jean McDonnell – Saturday

John and I went up to ICU the next morning to check on Rachael and Melissa, but they weren't there. My initial reaction was a racing pulse and rising blood pressure, until the nurse told me they'd been transferred to the general medical floor, two floors down, because Rachael was doing so much better. I asked for and got the room number, went down to the second floor and found room 210. Mother and daughter were both sitting up in bed and smiling. When we got totally into the room, I found out the reason for the smiles: Roy Donley was sitting in a recliner across from them.

'Hi, all,' I said as we entered.

'Hey, Doc,' Roy greeted, and the other two said hello. 'And who's this fine-looking fella with you?' he asked, holding out his hand to

John.

'John, this is Mr Donley who's helping your daddy,' I said.

John took Roy's hand and shook. 'Nice to meet you, sir,' he said.

'You're back?' I said to Roy.

'Yes'm. The McKinseys got out of jail around nine this morning. The chief told me they were going up before the judge around then, and I figured they'd get out, so I came on up here around eight to get set up and found them being moved down here. So everything's copasetic.'

I saw Melissa wave tentatively to John, who walked over to her bed. After whispering together for about a minute or two, John crawled into Melissa's hospital bed and Melissa turned the TV to Cartoon Network, the volume turned low while the grown-ups talked.

I couldn't help noticing the ease with which Roy Donley and Rachael conversed. They seemed like old friends rather than new acquaintances. Although friends might be a rather tame word for what might be going on there.

Fifteen minutes later, as John and I were saying goodbye, Carol Anne Hudson stuck her head in the room. 'Good morning,' she called out. We all greeted her back. 'Rachael, I want you to know this was a unanimous decision by your children and I had nothing to do with it. It was all their idea; I just carried it out to the best of my ability.'

'What in the world?' Rachael said, laughing.

Carol Anne stepped back and Rachael's four other children, June and Samantha and Matthew and Luke, came in the room. All four with shaved heads.

Rachael burst into tears, laughing and crying at the same time. Melissa jumped down from her bed, rubbing the heads of her siblings. 'Cool, huh?' she said.

Rachael pulled her youngest, Samantha, into her bed. 'Your beautiful blonde hair!'

'We all wanted to look just like you, Mama!' she said.

Rachael pulled June to her and kissed her dome. 'You have a beautifully shaped head, Junie,' she said. 'I noticed that when you were born.'

She pulled the kids to her one at a time, kissing their bald heads. 'You are the best children any mother ever had,' she said.

'You say that now, but wait till we don't clean our rooms – you'll be singing another tune!' Matthew said.

She swatted at his backside but he was too quick for her. 'You bet I will. Cleanliness is next to Godliness, you little heathen!'

'Mama!' Samantha said. 'You sound just like Miss Emily!'

Everyone stopped laughing and looked at the youngest child. Melissa spoke up. 'Mama just used Emily's favorite word to call us, that's all. But Emily's going to prison, huh, Mr Roy?'

'Oh, Roy!' Rachael said. 'I'm so sorry. In all this excitement I forgot to introduce you.'

'I think I figured out who everybody is,' Roy said with a big smile. 'And Miss Melissa, to answer your question, you betcha Emily and Mr McKinsey are both going to jail big time!'

So introductions started as Carol Anne and a few of her children came in and John and I slipped out. I felt embarrassed that I'd made such snap judgments about these people. I appeared to have been totally wrong about Jerry Hudson and his family, and now here were these wonderful children, having gone through an incredible ordeal, banding together in solidarity with their mother by shaving their heads! It was an incredibly touching display – and an incredible sight. All those glistening domes. I felt tears in my eyes as we took the elevator to the main floor.

As the elevator doors opened, my son looked up at me and said, 'Mama, can I shave my head too?'

Milt Kovak – Saturday
Jean called me to tell me about the kids at the hospital and their shaved heads and Johnny Mac's eagerness to shave his own head.

'Ah, no,' I said emphatically.

'My response also,' she said.

'And he's pissed, right?'

'Big time.'

'I have a suggestion,' I said.

'What's that?'

'Instead of taking him home where he'll mope about it, take Johnny Mac to Jewel Anne's house,' I said, mentioning the name of my sister. 'Her pool's heated. That'll take his mind off it. He's got a swimsuit there, and they've got all those noodles and air mattresses and crap. It'll take his mind totally off of shaving his head.'

'Excellent idea,' my wife said. 'That's what I'll do.'

'So I'll meet you back at my shop, if you want to go with me to see Brother Bob,' I said.

'Who?' she asked.

'Brother Bob Nathanson, pastor of the United Brethren of the Holy Church of Jesus Christ in His Almighty Goodness,' I said.

'Hum,' my wife said, 'the name itself seems to exclude women.'

An hour later Jean came in the back entrance to the shop and sat down in one of my two visitor chairs.

'So we're off to the whatever of the whatever?' she asked.

'United Brethren of the Holy Church of Jesus Christ in His Almighty Goodness,' I corrected.

'I repeat: whatever. Your car or mine?'

I guess somebody somewhere's making good money selling metal buildings as churches, 'cause the Brethren was also housed in one. This one was a mite smaller, maybe three-quarters the size of the New Saints Tabernacle, but it had a big sign out front with the name. Of course it would have to be a big sign to get that name up there big enough for anybody to read from the highway – which is where it's located. Right on Highway 5, on the other side of Longbranch from where my house is. It had a huge parking lot and an area blocked off for buses. A sign said so, although I'm not sure what buses would be parking there. Did they really think they were a tourist attraction? I thought I might ask Brother Bob that.

Since the parking lot was mostly empty now, except for what I recognized as Brother Bob's Chevy Half Ton pick-up, we parked up close and went in the door marked office. Brother Bob was leaning against a counter talking to a girl all of eighteen who was staring at him dewy-eyed, seemingly enraptured by all the crap coming out of Bob's mouth.

'Brother Bob!' I said loudly as we walked in. It had the desired effect. Bob startled and almost fell down. Now that would have been a sight, Bob being as big as he is.

'Sheriff,' he said, straightening himself out. 'Nice to see you.' He held out his hand and I shook it.

'Have you met my wife, Dr Jean McDonnell?' I asked.

'Never had the pleasure,' he said, extending his hand to Jean, who leaned forward on her crutches to shake.

'Can we have a moment of your time somewhere private?' I asked.

'Of course,' he said, smiling. 'Come on into my office.' Turning to the girl he had only just stopped fascinating, he said, 'Shirley Joy, why don't you bring us some sodas, please?'

'Yes, sir,' she said, jumping up.

His office was a sight. His desk was the biggest one I'd ever seen, but you hardly noticed it for the cross hanging on the wall behind it. It was surely the size of the original.

'Made of the same wood, too,' he said when I commented on it. 'Olive wood. From the Holy Lands. Me and my wife and about twenty of my flock took a tour four years ago and I had that commissioned and sent over here. Cost a pretty penny, too, but it's worth it. I *feel* Jesus ever' time I touch it!' He grabbed my arm and pulled me over to him, which, due to his size, I was unable to ignore. 'Feel it, Sheriff! See if it don't move you!'

I touched the cross. It felt like wood. Nevertheless, I nodded my head. 'Wonderful,' I said.

'Ma'am?' he said, holding out his hand for Jean.

'I'm good,' she said, sitting down in a visitor's chair and settling her crutches.

I took a seat next to my wife and waited for Brother Bob to sit down. Then I asked, 'When you came into my office earlier in the week, you seemed to know a little more than I did about the incident at the New Saints Tabernacle—'

230

'New Saints Tabernacle!' he said in a mocking tone. 'That's not a church! It's a brothel! Them people are going at it like cats and dogs! Men saying they're married to three or four or even more women! It's blasphemy plain and simple! You know how many children some of them men have sired? Dozens! Dozens of more blasphemous fornicatin' brats!'

'There are some perfectly decent people at that church—' Jean began but was drowned out by Brother Bob.

'Decent? How in the world can you call any of them people decent?' Then he stopped and looked hard at Jean. 'Oh, that's right,' he said. 'I heard you was Catholic.'

'Excuse me?' Jean said.

He looked away from her and shrugged. 'Well,' he said, 'you papists believe in praying to idols and saints and stuff, so I don't expect you to be as shocked by such goings-on as what's going on at the, excuse the expression, New Saints Tabernacle.'

'So how offended are you and your flock by the people at this other church?' I asked.

'Offended? It's not a matter of me or any of my flock being offended! It's God who's offended! These people are going to burn in the fiery depths of despair and deprivation!' Brother Bob closed his eyes and lifted his arms to the ceiling. 'Dear Lord our God, and Jesus Your Holy Son, take pity on this here Sheriff and his papist wife for they know not what they

231

do—'

'Brother Bob!' I said, always hating to bother a man when he's praying, but since he was praying for me and my wife, I figured it was OK.

'What?' he said, eyes open but his hands still in the air.

'I want to know if any one person in your flock was offended enough by the people of the New Saints Tabernacle to maybe have done something about it. Go talk to them, visit with them, anything like that.'

'Neither me nor my people consort with that type, Sheriff,' he said, lowering his arms.

'But if one of them was to, who would it be?' I asked.

'But nobody would,' he said.

'But, say, if one of your people, listening to you, was to get riled up, feel like you weren't getting enough respect from them or what they were doing was in some way harmful—'

'Oh, it's harmful all right—'

'To you or your flock,' I said, real loud to drown him out, 'who would that person be?'

'You mean hypo-whatever?' he asked.

'Hypothetically,' I volunteered, and looked to my wife for confirmation. She nodded. 'Exactly,' I said.

'Well, and I ain't saying it's so, but if anybody were to get extra upset like, it might be Kenneth Jessup.'

He was right about that. I had no idea Kenneth Jessup was a member of the Brethren. I'd had him as an overnight guest at the shop on many an occasion, but I got to admit not lately. Maybe he'd seen the light, but Kenneth had mostly been in my cells for getting drunk and losing his temper, which resulted in somebody else ending up in the hospital.

I stood up, having spent what I felt was way too much time in Brother Bob's company. 'Thank you, Brother Bob,' I said. 'I appreciate your time.'

I held out my hand and he shook it. 'I can tell you a lot more about that lot over in Tejas County,' he said. 'I barely got warmed up!'

'I believe you, Brother Bob. But I gotta eat eventually. Thanks.'

We left Brother Bob with a confused look on his face.

When we got back in my Jeep, Jean asked me, 'You think Brother Bob had anything concrete to add about the New Saints Tabernacle or just more conjecture?'

'More bullshit, you mean?' I said.

'Hum,' she said. 'Exactly.'

'Yeah, I believe that's all. We coulda stayed there till the cows came home and even if there was a nugget of real information in there, we'd both be fast asleep before we heard it.'

'So where to now?' she asked.

'You're having fun with this, huh?' I said.

Jean shrugged her shoulders then laughed. 'Yes, I think I am.'

'Then how 'bout meeting a real-life redneck?'

'Gee, I thought I married one,' she said.

'We'll do that right after Mary Hudson's funeral,' I said.

Jean looked at her watch. 'I'm not sure we're going to make it,' she said. 'The funeral's at two, it's twelve-thirty now, and it's at the church in Tejas, right?'

'So we'll make the graveside service,' I said.

Jean McDonnell – Saturday

We got to the church as the cars were pulling out after the hearse. We managed to get in the middle of them and headed to the graveside. It was only about a mile from the New Saints Tabernacle, and it looked like an old abandoned cemetery that the church had somehow taken over. Surrounded by pine trees, the cemetery was in a clearing bordered by an old black wrought-iron fence, the gate of which was larger than one would think necessary for such a small cemetery. The cast iron of the gate was intricately wrought, with curlicues and fleurs-de-lys. In an arch at the top of the gate, the name 'Wingate' was spelled out in elaborate cursive. On seeing that, I could only think that at one point this was a private family cemetery, and I wondered if the Wingate clan had died out, or if the church had gotten special permission from what was left of that family to bury their own here.

With my disability, I've never been one to

234

want to traipse through cemeteries doing rubbings or being amazed and amused at the pithy sayings people put on tombstones back in the nineteenth and even the early twentieth centuries. Walking through this one, though, I was struck by the number of small stones, with days of birth and death the same, or just a few days, weeks, or months apart. Having children, even less than a hundred years ago, was often an iffy proposition. Seeing those stones made me want to leave this service and find my son and hold him tight.

As we walked to the graveside, I noticed there were no canopies or chairs, but there was a green outdoor carpet over the ground next to the open grave. Jerry Hudson and his family stood in front with the McKinsey kids, domes glistening, directly behind them. Other members of the church, the Bollingers, the Whitmans, and several families I hadn't met, were scattered behind them.

It looked like Milt had let Brother Earl out in the nick of time. He was dressed formally, but his hair was a little wild and he looked nervous when he saw us standing there together. I was a little nervous myself. The green carpet had been set directly upon the ground, and one crutch was digging deeper and deeper into the ground as I stood there. I pulled it out and placed the tip in another area, but still it began to sink. I was afraid I might fall into the open grave if I wasn't careful. Luckily Milt was on that side of me, so

I hooked my arm through his just in case.

'Brothers and sisters, little children,' Brother Earl intoned, 'we are here today to say goodbye to our beloved Sister Mary Hudson. She has gone to sit at the feet of our Lord God Almighty. We know God didn't call our good sister; she was taken before her time. This decision should be left to God only, never to man.

'But MAN made this decision, brothers and sisters! He didn't ASK God if it was Sister Mary's time! NO! He, this FILTHY BEAST, took our good Mary from us in a brutal fashion!

'But in our teachings here at the New Saints Tabernacle, we believe in more than one mother for each child, so Sister Mary's children are NOT left motherless! NO, good God they are not! Sister Mary's children still have two other mothers, Sister Carol Anne and Sister Rene. THANK YOU, JESUS! Bless You, Jesus, for letting us know the true way to lead our lives, the true way to protect our children, and the true way to further our existence in this world You made, dear God!'

I tuned him out, watching the crowd instead, thinking Milt might want my impressions after this. Thomas and Sarie Whitman and Sarie's two girls, Margaret and Melinda, were there. I noticed Jane Marie was also there, but further back in the crowd, standing with three other women – I would imagine the 'unmarriables' that lived in the dorm near the church.

The only one in that family I could ever imagine hurting anyone would be Jane Marie. She seemed like a bitter and lonely woman. But why would she hurt Mary Hudson? According to Sarie, Mary Hudson was trying to get Thomas to let the girls go to Sunday school, but would that be a reason for Jane Marie to kill her? I had no reason to think she would, but then again, I'm not a police professional. Their professional criteria are different from mine.

The Bollingers were there, a large contingent. I couldn't help noticing that David Bollinger was a good-looking man. I wondered how much flack he got from the church for 'allowing' his family to dress casually and for 'allowing his women' to cut their hair. As much as I respected Carol Anne Hudson, and in many ways her husband Jerry, there were still parts of their belief system I couldn't get around – the gender issues the most prevalent in my mind.

I tuned back in to Brother Earl just as he intoned, 'Dear God Almighty, please have Your blessed hand on the shoulder of our good Sheriff Kovak so that You may lead him to the BEAST THAT WALKS LIKE A MAN! The BEAST who took our dear Sister Mary from us! Let us pray.'

I prayed that my husband didn't do anything too terrible to poor Brother Earl.

Milt Kovak – Saturday
I noticed Andrew Schmidt, the man who had been at Jerry Hudson's house the first time I'd

gone there to interview him. I'd forgotten I needed to interview old Andrew. I need to write this stuff down, I told myself. I figured right after the graveside service would be a good enough time to grab ol' Andy. While Brother Earl droned on, I studied Schmidt and his family.

Schmidt himself appeared to be in his late fifties or early sixties, broad across the middle with a big ass and narrow shoulders. He had most of his hair, all of it salt and pepper, and was wearing his Sunday best – an expensive-looking blue suit with a navy silk tie, and cuff links that looked like a month's salary to me.

On one side of him stood a young man who appeared to be in his mid-twenties, as well dressed as who I presumed to be his father. He was a good-looking kid with conservatively cut dark brown hair, and eyes green enough to notice across the graveside. Standing next to him was a pretty girl with her arm entwined with his. New wife or fiancée, I figured. She was wearing the standard issue baggy dress in a dark color – as were most of the women here – and her long red hair touched the top of her hips.

On the other side of Schmidt Sr stood a woman approximately Schmidt's age, with gray hair hanging halfway down her back. She had a stern look on her face and her hands were clasped in front of her, the knuckles white, I noticed. The woman was not happy about something,

238

that was for damn sure.

The something might have been the young woman standing next to her. Somehow I doubted this was a daughter. The daughter (a faint replica of her mother) stood further down, clutching the hand of a girl child. No, the something was about twenty-five or thereabouts, with jet black hair, pale white skin, and black eyes. She had a full mouth and breasts big enough to stand out in those awful dresses. Yes, I do believe this was the something the first Mrs Schmidt was not happy about. The girl child whose hand the daughter was holding looked way too much like what I assumed to be the second wife not to be hers. Beautiful child, and the daughter appeared to resent having to hold her hand. Reminded me of Jane Marie Whitman and her two little sisters.

Finally Brother Earl was finished, after intoning God's blessing on me – by name, mind you – and I told my wife I'd meet her at the car. I hightailed it after Andrew Schmidt, who obviously knew what I was about, because he was hurrying his family to where the cars were parked, on the winding dirt road through the cemetery.

'Mr Schmidt!' I called, rushing up behind him. He ignored me. 'Andrew Schmidt!'

This time he stopped and sighed and turned around. 'Sheriff,' he said.

I smiled. 'Introduce me to your family,' I said. His eyes got big. I hadn't told anybody that I had no desire to bust any of these polygamists during the duration of this case. And afterwards, well, if they didn't bother anybody, if I got no calls on any of 'em, I didn't see any reason to become assertive on the issue. But I had no intention of letting Andrew Schmidt know this. I have a thing about paranoids – I love to push their buttons. I know, it's mean, but a man needs a hobby.

Schmidt just stood there, unable to move. His son came to his rescue. 'Hi, Sheriff,' he said, thrusting out his hand to shake. 'I'm Max Schmidt, Andrew's son, and this is my wife Michelle.' I shook her hand too. 'My mother, Hannah.' She nodded her head and I nodded back. 'My sister, Maureen.' Again, with the nods. Now came the fun part. 'And this is my wife's sister, Cecile,' he said, indicating the young woman with the black hair and eyes, 'and her daughter LeeLee.' I nodded to Cecile and her daughter.

The possibility that this black-haired beauty was any kin whatsoever to Max's red-headed, freckle-faced wife were slim to none.

'So, Andrew,' I said, 'either of your wives know Mary Hudson?'

He stammered around a bit before Max took the lead again. 'My wife used to babysit for the Hudsons occasionally – when one of Jerry's other wives were busy – or if they all needed to go someplace where the children couldn't.'

Now here Max was, throwing poor old Jerry

Hudson to the wolves by mentioning how many wives he had. Take the pressure off good old dad. But OK, Michelle could be a witness to something.

'Hum,' I said, looking at cute little Michelle. 'Notice anybody ever bothering Mrs Hudson?' I asked her.

Michelle shook her head. 'No, sir,' she said. 'Sister Mary was a wonderful woman and a great mother. I can't imagine anyone wanting to hurt her. I wouldn't take any money for baby-sitting, so she made me a beautiful quilt. It's on our bed,' she said and blushed, turning her head into her husband's arm. He patted her head like a puppy.

'So, Andrew,' I said, turning back to Schmidt Sr. 'What about your wives? Did they talk to Mary Hudson much?'

The older woman, Hannah, spoke up. 'I knew Sister Mary, of course,' she said, hands still clutching each other in front of her, knuckles still showing white. 'We weren't close, though. Different generation.'

'So, Cecile, is it?' I said, talking directly to the beautiful black-haired woman with the pale skin and black eyes.

Hannah answered. 'Yes, her name is Cecile,' she said.

'Cecile, how well did you know Sister Mary? Y'all would be the same generation or there-abouts.'

Again, Hannah answered. 'Not well at all.

Sister Mary spent much of her time with the kindergarten children and Cecile spent a great deal of time in the nursery.'

'I'm sorry, ma'am,' I said, again speaking to and looking directly at Cecile. 'Are you mute?'

Cecile opened her mouth but Andrew grabbed her arm. Again, Hannah answered. 'Cecile is fairly newly married. And as a young woman she does not speak to men other than her husband.'

'Ya know, that's funny. Some of y'all do, and some of y'all don't. Speak to other men. Like I been told Sister Mary didn't talk to other men, yet her sister-wives Carol Anne and Rene both do. So how can that be, in one family like that?'

No one answered me. After a long minute, Max moved toward me with a big smile and put his hand on my shoulder. 'Sheriff, are you and Dr McDonnell going to be joining us at the church for fellowship and refreshments?' he asked.

'Afraid not,' I said. 'I still got people to see. I'm investigating a murder, ya know.'

I scanned the faces of the family. The only one to show anything other than a blank stare was old Andrew himself. He cringed at the word and grabbed the hand of wife number two. Made me want to interview him at the shop. All by his lonesome.

Jean McDonnell – Saturday
I caught Milt just as the Schmidt family walked

away from him. 'Anything?' I asked.

He sighed. 'Not so you'd notice,' he said. 'Hey, wanna see a real live Oklahoma redneck?' he asked me again.

I've been in Oklahoma for almost ten years, and I thought I'd met and married a real-live Oklahoma redneck, until Milt introduced me to Kenneth Jessup, the man Brother Bob of the Brethren had said might have gotten 'riled up' enough to have taken his anger out on someone from the New Saints Tabernacle.

Milt had me get the address for Kenneth Jessup off the computer in his Jeep (he still doesn't know how to work it) and I entered it in his GPS (or how to work that either). We ended up in the north part of the county, full of scrub oak and mesquite, rocks and prickly pear, a far cry from the quiet beauty of the cemetery in the piny woods. We turned off the Farm-to-Market road onto a dirt road with broken-down trailers and shacks on either side. Kenneth Jessup's trailer was in the middle of this, a single-wide with the roof caved in on one side. The dirt drive leading up to it was littered with rocks the size of small boulders, broken-down vehicles of all shapes and sizes, an old refrigerator with the door hanging on by one hinge, and two washing machines that had seen better days.

A toddler in nothing but a diaper sat on one of the aluminum steps of the trailer, its feet trailing in the dust on the ground. The baby was one shade of brown from head to foot, including the diaper. Darker smudges on its face revealed, I'm afraid, the tracts of its tears. When Milt stopped the Jeep, a mangy dog crawled out from under the trailer, followed by what appeared to be a little girl, maybe three to four years of age, almost as brown as her sibling.

Before the child could get totally out from under the trailer, the door opened, hitting the toddler in the head and knocking it down the steps. The baby wailed and the little girl ran for it, picking it up out of the dust, while the woman who opened the door said, 'Destiny, I told you to keep an eye on your brother, for fuck's sake! What the fuck you doin' lettin' him sit on the steps like that? I liked to cracked his head open with the damn door!'

As she came down the steps, she swatted the little girl in the back of the head. It was hard to tell the age of the woman – anywhere from nineteen to forty. She was probably five foot five inches, give or take, but I doubted she weighed much more than the little girl. She was wearing cut-offs and a tank top, and the body revealed by her clothing was so emaciated you could see the tendons and bones. Her elbows and knees appeared enlarged, as they do on skeletal remains.

As Milt helped me navigate over the rocks and junk, he whispered in my ear, 'Speed freak.'

I nodded: that made more sense than my first thought, which was anorexic or bulimic. This woman saw no need to hide her body; an anorexic always tries to hide.

We stood together on his side of the Jeep as he called out to the woman, 'We're here to see Kenneth.'

'He ain't here. He's at work. You the sheriff, right?'

'Yes, ma'am,' he answered.

'I'm Kenneth's wife,' she said, holding her head up high.

'Nice to meet you, Miz Jessup,' Milt said. 'Can you tell me where Kenneth's working now?'

'Over at the feed store on the county road, up about five miles that-a-way,' she said, pointing in a northerly direction.

'When does he get off?' Milt asked.

'Supper time,' she said. 'I always fix him a right good meal, 'cause he works hard at the feed store.'

'Well, that's good, Miz Jessup. You got a phone?'

'Yes, sir, but we ain't got no service. They turned it off couple of months ago.'

Nodding his head toward the two children sitting in the dirt, Milt asked the woman, 'Those Kenneth's kids?'

Head up high again, the woman said, 'They are now.'

'How long you and Kenneth been married?'

'We're getting married in a couple of weeks,' she said.

'So what's your name?' Milt asked.

'I like Miz Jessup just fine,' she said.

'You got a first name?'

She sighed and stuck out one hip, putting her weight on her right leg. A jutting hip bone was the only thing keeping the cut-offs from falling down. Fishing in the pocket of her cutoffs, she pulled out a crumpled packet of Virginia Slims and a pack of matches. 'Charlotta,' she said, then lit up, sucking the smoke in greedily.

'Charlotta what? I mean, before it becomes Jessup.'

'Charlotta Murray, but that's the last one's daddy's name,' she said, nodding at the children in the dirt. 'My name 'fore that was Charlotta Cameron, and that was her daddy's name. My daddy's name, if you're interested, was Brown. So that was the name I was born with. Charlotta Mackayla Brown.'

'Well, Charlotta Mackayla Brown Cameron Murray soon-to-be Jessup, reason I asked if you had a phone was so you could call Kenneth and let him know we're coming to talk to him. Just some questions. No big deal. But I guess you can't. So we'll just head on up that way. 'Bout five miles, you say?'

'Yeah, up the county road that-a-way,' she said.

'Well, thank you for your time, Charlotta. You take care now.'

Milt and I got back in the Jeep. He turned it around and we took the dirt road back to the farm-to-market. 'How soon can I call CPS?' I asked.

'Let's wait until we talk to Kenneth. I just can't see him being part of the Brethren *and* living with that,' he said.

'Those children are in dire need of intervention,' I said.

Milt patted my hand and said, 'Just wait, honey.'

I grabbed my hand back and sat in the passenger seat, fuming.

Milt Kovak – Saturday

I understood why Jean was riled up. Those kids did need somebody other than Charlotta whatever-whatever taking care of 'em. The woman obviously couldn't take care of herself, much less two little ones. But I needed to see if Kenneth was invested in these kids, and if so how much. If, that is, he didn't happen to kill Mary Hudson, which was the main reason I was going to see him, after all. Jean had her priorities and I had mine.

The feed store Charlotta spoke of was another metal building plopped down in the middle of nothing. There were bags of feed and fertilizer sitting out front, along with wheelbarrows, post-hole diggers, and shit shovels – the flat kind that pick up dog shit, chicken shit and horse shit better than just about anything. We went inside to find rows of more feed, more fertilizer, a whole row of vitamins and additives

247

and such and, behind the counter, big as life, was Kenneth Jessup. Kenneth was about five foot six inches, weighed about 150 pounds, but was feisty. Little as he was, I've seen him cold-cock a guy twice his size. He had a wolfish face with beady little eyes the color of a lump of coal. His hair hadn't changed since he was like in the fifth grade, back sometime in the eighties – still in a long, stringy mullet, he had only one eyebrow going straight across his face, and had pockmarks from teenage acne. Lord, he was a sight to see. Pure Oklahoma redneck, just like I'd promised.

'Hey, Kenneth,' I said.

'Hey, Sheriff,' he said back.

'This here is my wife, Dr Jean McDonnell,' I said, indicating Jean. She nodded at him and he nodded at her. 'Your bride-to-be told us where to find you.'

'My what?' he said.

'Bride-to-be,' I repeated. 'Charlotta.'

'She in my trailer again?' he said, his face taking on a mean look.

'She came out of it,' I said. 'Two little kids outside.'

He sighed. 'She's probably over there cooking me something. She thinks if she keeps cooking for me I'll marry her. Hell, I don't even want to bed her. You seen her, Sheriff? Be like fuckin' a corpse! Excuse me, ma'am,' he said to Jean.

'So you are in no way responsible for her

248

children?' Jean asked.

'Hell no!' he said. 'They ain't mine! Nasty little rug rats!'

Jean excused herself and walked toward the front of the store, cell phone in hand. I figured she was on the phone with children's services before I got my next words out.

'So, enough about Charlotta and her brood,' I said to Kenneth. 'I'm here for another reason.'

'Anything I can do to help, Sheriff. You know that.'

'Yeah, Kenneth, I know. You're a real helpful guy.' I was being sarcastic, but I don't think Kenneth was aware. 'I understand Brother Bob at the Brethren's been preaching some about the New Saints Tabernacle and congregants thereof.'

'Huh?'

'Brother Bob's been saying bad stuff about the people who go to the New Saints Tabernacle, right?'

'You mean them people who marry a bunch of women? Yeah! That ain't right, Sheriff.'

'Well, it is against the law,' I had to agree.

'You gonna arrest them?' he asked. ''Cause if you're looking for, like, a posse, or something like that, you need extra deputies, like, I'd be happy to join up and help you round them people up. They belong in jail, if not in hell and damnation, if you ask me.'

'Seriously, Kenneth, nobody's asking you. But thank you for volunteering.' I cleared my throat before I laughed out loud. 'No, reason I'm asking about them, and what Brother Bob's been saying is that one of the ladies in that group got herself killed earlier this week—'

'I heard about that! Now that's just awful. What they're doing is unlawful, but that's the men, right, Sheriff? No call to be killing the women, right, Sheriff?'

'No call to be killing anybody, Kenneth,' I said. 'Which brings up a point. What if somebody were to think that what those people were doing was against God's law, decided to take that into his own hands, go after one of these blaspheming men, and somehow ended up hurting one of the women instead? That would be kind of an accident, don't you think?'

Kenneth was nodding his head through my entire little speech. 'Yeah, like an accident,' he said.

'And you can't fault somebody for an accident, can you?' I said.

'Honest mistake,' Kenneth agreed.

'So, Kenneth, you ever go over to Tejas County, to their church, just to see what was going on?' I asked.

He drew back. 'Who, me? Oh, no way, Sheriff. That's just nasty, what those people do.'

'You ever go visit one of those nasty men at their home, Kenneth?'

His face wore a look of confusion when he said, 'No, sir, I don't even know where they live. Do they all live together?'

'No, they don't, Kenneth,' I said. I was getting nowhere fast. 'Did you ever meet Mary Hudson, the lady who got killed?'

He shook his head. 'No,' he said.

'You ever meet any of the wives of that church?' I asked.

He recoiled. 'God, no.'

I was beginning to believe Kenneth Jessup had nothing to do with the murder of Mary Hudson. Hell, it had been a long shot anyway.

Jean was waving at me from the front door. I thanked Kenneth for his time and headed toward my wife.

'What's up?' I asked.

'I called in an emergency removal. We need to meet CPS over at the trailer,' she said.

The part of the job I truly hated.

TEN

Jean McDonnell – Saturday

By the time we got back to the trailer, CPS was already there. When Milt stopped the Jeep behind the CPS sedan, Charlotta, the mother, came running at us, flailing her arms and ramming the driver's side window with her fists.

'Why you doing this to me?' she shouted through the closed window. 'I din' do nothin' to you! You can't take away my babies! You can't!'

A woman with CPS had already picked up the filthy toddler and had him wrapped in a light blanket; another employee, also a woman, had the little girl, Destiny, by the hand.

'Mama, 'bye,' Destiny called out. 'See ya later!'

Charlotta whirled around. 'You ain't taking them!' she screamed, running at the woman holding the toddler, and pulling at her son's arm. The baby began to cry and the woman holding him grabbed Charlotta's arm, trying to release her grip on the baby.

'Mama, don't!' Destiny cried. 'You gonna hurt Dustin!'

Milt jumped out of the car and managed to get Charlotta's hands behind her back.

'Are you gonna act right or am I gonna have to arrest you?' Milt asked her.

'They're taking my babies!' she screamed, tears and mucus covering her face.

I managed to get out of the car and get my crutches under my arms. I made my way to where Milt was holding Charlotta.

'Charlotta, listen to me,' I said, getting in her face to try to find eye contact. 'Your children are not being taken care of. They're undernourished, they're dirty, and you left them outside by themselves—'

'No I didn't! No I didn't!' Charlotta screamed. 'I was coming right out! You seen me! I came right out, didn't I? I didn't leave 'em for no time! You gotta believe me! Honest I didn't leave 'em for no time!'

'Charlotta, you're stoned. You need to get cleaned up and stay that way before you can get your children ba—'

'How long I gotta stay clean?' Charlotta asked as she pulled away from Milt. 'I can do it! I stayed clean for a month when I was knocked up with Dustin! Din' I, Destiny? Din' I stay clean for almost a month that time?'

'Yes, Mama,' Destiny sang out from inside the CPS sedan.

'No, Charlotta,' I said, taking her arm, turning her to look at me. 'You have to stay clean forever. You can't go back. Are you doing crystal or crack or—'

'Crystal, but just a smidge,' she said, indicating a tiny amount with her thumb and index finger.

'You can't do any, Charlotta,' I said. 'You've got to get clean and stay that way.'

Charlotta stood staring at me, her hands on her hips. A mean look appeared on her face. 'You got kids, crip?' she asked.

'We're not talking about me, Charlotta—'

'Oh, hell, no you don't, bitch! I asked you a civil question, gimp! You got kids?'

'That's enough...' Milt started, grabbing for Charlotta's arm.

She pulled away and I looked at Milt, shaking my head. Finally, I looked at Charlotta and said, 'Yes, I have a son.'

'And they let you keep him?' she yelled. 'Hell, you can barely walk! They let you keep your kid! Why can't I keep mine? At least I got my own two feet and they work!'

I looked at Milt. 'She's stoned. I can't talk to her this way. It's your call whether you take her in or not. As long as we get the kids out of here, I'm OK,' I told him.

'Oh no you ain't!' Charlotta yelled, and came at me, arms out, hands curled like talons. I raised one crutch and tripped her. She fell flat on her face in the dry Oklahoma dirt as the CPS sedan pulled out of the dusty driveway.

Milt reached down to help her up. Charlotta was crying, sobbing like her heart was breaking, and part of me felt for her. Unfortunately for her, the larger part of me felt only for her children. As bad as the system can be, foster care, in this case, had to be preferable to the birth mother.

I dug in my pocket and found one of my business cards. I handed it to Charlotta. 'Call me when you're sober,' I told her. 'You need to go to rehab before you can get your children back.'

She took the card, spat on it, and tossed it in the dirt. 'Fuck you, bitch!' she yelled, pulling away from Milt.

Milt and I got back in his Jeep and drove away in a cloud of Oklahoma dust.

Milt Kovak – Saturday

I dropped Jean off at the hospital and headed over to Tejas County to the sheriff's office and an interview with Earl Mayhew Jr, aka Buddy.

'You gonna take him back to Prophesy with you?' Bill asked me.

'We'll see,' I answered.

'Well, don't expect me to keep him here overnight. I ain't got the budget for it anymore. They cut my night guy out entirely and there's no overtime, so I can't keep him.'

'If he looks good for it, I'll take him with me. If not, he can go home.'

'You'll have to give him a ride,' Bill said. 'Nothin' in the budget for taxi service.'

'All right, all right,' I said, heading back to his

cells. One of the deputies gave me the keys, as they no longer have a jailer due to budget cuts. As we never did have a jailer, I didn't really feel all that sorry for Bill.

Buddy was sitting in a cell, on a mattress covered in dried blood and urine, his hands in his lap and his head down.

'Hey, Buddy,' I said.

He looked up. 'Oh. Hey, Sheriff,' he said.

'Sorry about the lock-up,' I said. 'I thought they were just gonna hold you in an interrogation room or something. Didn't know they were gonna lock you up.' Sometimes, to get on the good side of a perp, a police officer has to fudge the truth. But a cop's gotta do what a cop's gotta do.

Buddy shrugged.

I unlocked the cell door and went inside, closing the door behind me. I took a seat across from him, on another blood-and-urine-stained mattress.

'Buddy, look at me,' I said.

His head came up.

'We need to talk,' I said.

'Where's David?' he asked.

My turn to shrug. It's not like he actually *asked* for an attorney.

'Buddy,' I said, 'I need to ask you about Sister Mary Hudson. I know you liked her.'

Buddy shrugged again.

'You didn't like her?'

Again, the shrug.

I sighed. 'Buddy, you gotta say something. If you don't, then I gotta leave and go back to my county, and I guess just leave you here. Is that what you want?'

He shook his head.

'Buddy!'

'No, that ain't what I want,' he said, his voice low.

'Then talk to me. Did you or didn't you like Sister Mary Hudson?'

'I liked her, all right,' he said.

'Is that why you spied on her through the window of the kindergarten room?'

He shrugged again, thought better of it, and said, 'I wasn't spying.'

'Buddy, don't fib,' I said.

Again, he sighed. 'I was just looking,' he said, a whine to his voice. 'She was real pretty, and real nice. And real good with the little kids.'

'I hear she was a real nice lady. You talk to her much?' I asked.

'Sometimes,' he said. 'Sometimes she'd say hello to me and I'd say hello back, and once she said ain't it a pretty morning, and I said I reckon so.'

I smiled. 'Sounds like y'all were friends,' I said.

He smiled back. 'Yeah, reckon so.' And he laughed.

'Y'all ever talk off the church grounds?' I asked him.

He shook his head. Then he looked up at me

and said, 'Is the parking lot offa church grounds?'

'You talked to her in the parking lot?' I asked.

'Yeah.' He beamed at me. 'One Sunday I helped her bring in some stuff from her car. Her husband wasn't there that morning and she needed help and I helped her.'

'That's great, Buddy,' I said, beginning to realize that ol' Buddy was maybe a taco short of an enchilada special. 'You ever go over to Sister Mary's house?' I asked.

He thought about it for a moment and said, 'No, I don't think so.'

'What do you mean you don't think so, Buddy? Either you went over there or you didn't.'

'My daddy goes to visit lots of his parishioners and I go with him sometimes, but mostly I stay in the car.'

'So maybe you went with your daddy to visit Brother Jerry Hudson and his family, and maybe you saw Sister Mary while your daddy was in visiting with Brother Jerry?'

He shook his head. 'I don't think so.'

'And you remembered where Sister Mary lived, and you decided to go back and visit—'

'I don't think so, Sheriff. I'm like real sure I didn't do that, Sheriff,' he said.

'Buddy, did you hear that someone hurt Sister Mary?' I asked.

He nodded his head, looking down again at his hands. 'They was going to bury her today, but my daddy wouldn't let me come. He said you'd be looking for me.'

'It's too bad you didn't get to say goodbye,' I said.

'Oh, I did. I said goodbye to Sister Mary,' Buddy said.

I frowned. 'When was that, Buddy?'

'When was what?' he asked, frowning back.

Trying hard to keep my patience, I said, 'When you said goodbye to Sister Mary. When did you do that?'

'Last Sunday when she was leaving the nursery with her little boy,' Buddy said.

'Baby Mark?' I said.

'Um hum,' Buddy said, beaming. 'He likes me. He smiles at me.'

'That's good, Buddy.'

So much for my interview with Earl Mayhew Jr, aka Buddy.

It was getting dark when I dropped Buddy Mayhew off at the New Saints Tabernacle. Since the tabernacle was at the northeast end of Tejas County and the township of Bishop, wherein lay the overly fancy subdivision of The Branches, was at the northwest end of Prophesy County, it was but a hop, skip and jump from one to the other. I called Jean and told her I'd pick up Johnny Mac at my sister's house while I was there, and found out Jean had already done it. So I told her I'd probably miss dinner as I needed to talk to the security guard at The

Branches and, while I was there, maybe check in on the Hudsons.

'That's not a bad idea,' my wife said. 'It's been a rough day for them. Knowing you're still trying to find out who killed Mary might lessen the burden.'

Thinking my wife had higher hopes of me solving this mess than I did, I said 'bye and hung up.

Being a Saturday night and all, I had a feeling I was going to have a hard time finding Maynard Ritchie, head of security at The Branches, but I was in luck. Turns out his weekend guy didn't show up, and Maynard was manning the front entrance himself. I pulled up, saw it was him, told him we needed to talk, and he pointed beyond the guard shack to where another car was parked. I recognized it as the car Ritchie drove onto the cul-de-sac the day Mary Hudson was killed. I parked next to it, got out and headed to the guard shack.

'Hey, Sheriff,' Ritchie said. 'Have a seat,' he said, pointing to the only stool in the small space.

As I'd been driving around a bunch that day, I said, 'I'm fine standing, Mr Ritchie, but thank you.'

'Actually, Sheriff, it's Captain,' he said, turning a little red. 'Just one of them honorariums places like this like to give out instead of a decent salary. I'd rather you just called me Maynard.'

I held out my hand. 'Fine with me, Maynard. I go mostly by Milt.'

So we shook on it, and I got down to business.

'Here's the thing, Maynard,' I said. 'It's been like five days since Mrs Hudson was killed, and you know what it's like. You don't solve a whodunnit in twenty-four to forty-eight hours, you might as well give it up. But I don't wanna do that. I think the Hudson family deserves some closure, so I'm still working it.'

'Glad to hear that, Milt. Thing is, we want this solved too. Looks bad for my security team, and it looks bad for The Branches. We've had two buyers back out after the news came out, and I've been on the carpet twice with the bigwigs. Not to mention we got people threatening to quit the country club 'cause of this. So anything I can do to help, I'll do.'

'You heard anything this week that sounds interesting? Gossip, innuendo – hell, I'll take whatever I can get.'

'Well, people are talking about them being bigamists and all. Not that many people knew until Mrs Hudson got herself killed. Been talk at the schools – elementary anyway – about making the kids leave because these dumbass parents don't want to have to explain anything to their kids. Hell, they don't have a problem with "Jimmy's got two daddies" and "Mary only has a mother and a test tube," so what's the problem with "Jacob has one daddy and fourteen mamas?" Huh?'

'See your point,' I said.

'But, hell, I can't say anything to these people. Ain't my job. I just say "yes, ma'am" and "no, sir," and shut the fuck up. Excuse my French.'

'So there's some resistance to the plural family, huh?'

'Yeah. A few people don't mind, the liberals anyway. You know how they are, live and let live. Hell, they'd let a two-headed commie lesbo live here if it was up to them.'

'Don't see many of them,' I said.

'Liberals?'

'No, two-headed commie lesbos,' I said.

He laughed. 'I'm just saying,' he said.

'I hear ya,' I said. 'The day it happened, anybody come in The Branches that didn't belong?'

'Yeah, I got that sheet here. I pulled it, was gonna bring it over to you, but you know how it goes.'

'Oh, yeah,' I said, taking the sheet he handed me.

'As you can see, nothing but workmen mostly.' He pointed to each name. 'This guy went to the Murrays on Chase Point to fix the trash compactor. This one went to Mrs Greene's house, over on Stanton Circle, says plumbing. I know she's been having a lot of problems. Looks like a new plumber. Here's a flower delivery over at the Macabees on Delta Gardens for their daughter home from college, and this last one was the usual UPS guy. He had four deliveries: the Davises, the Washingtons, the Millers, and the Renterias. Need their street names?'

'Naw,' I said, already bored and hardly listening. 'Anything else you can think of?' I asked.

'Uh uh,' he said. 'You want a copy of this?'

I nodded and he uncovered a small copy machine and ran the sign-in sheet through, giving me the copy.

'Country club keeps its own sign-in. It's got members from all over the county, not just The Branches. Got its own entrance too.'

'Yeah? Where is the country club?'

'South end,' he said, pointing in a southerly direction. 'Straight down Elm Street, the main one here, till you get to Willow Lane, cross Willow and there's the road up to the club.'

'So somebody could come in to the country club and keep on going into the residential area, is that what you're saying?'

'Well, yeah. But, you know, only the people who live here know about that road offa Willow Lane that goes to the club. It's more like a maintenance road.'

'Well, let me sign in for today. I'm gonna drive by the Hudsons for a minute.'

He handed me the sign-in sheet and I signed and timed it, said goodbye and headed out to my Jeep.

So, I thought, there's another way to get into The Branches. How hard, I wondered, was it to get into the country club? Did they have a guarded entrance, like the residential side? Or was the driveway open and you only had to show ID at the entrance to the club? That's the way it had been the only time I'd ever been to a country club, one near Tulsa that a cousin on my daddy's side took me to back when I was married to my first wife. If so, this really opened up the field on who murdered Mary Hudson.

As it was just about dinnertime, the main Hudson house, Sister Mary's former home, was jumping. All the kids, Sister Mary's, Sister Carol Anne's, and Sister Rachael's, were all out front screaming and carrying on. The big yellow dog, Butch, was with them, having as much fun as the rest of 'em. I sat in my Jeep for a minute and just watched. It made me kinda sad to think of Johnny Mac not growing up like this – with lots of siblings and stuff. Hell, my kid didn't even have neighbor kids to hang out with, since we lived in the country. But the truth of it was, Johnny Mac spent most of his time either in school or at the daycare at the hospital, and he had a bucketful of friends at each place, so I guess he was OK. But it did give you pause for thought. The one thing I could do to remedy the situation, was find my boy his own big yellow dog.

I finally got out of the Jeep and headed up to the house, realizing for the first time since I'd pulled up that all the kids, not just Sister Rachael's children, but the Hudson children as well, were in normal clothes. OK, normal's probably not the right word, but you know what I mean. The girls weren't wearing those God-awful baggy dresses and the boys were mostly wearing T-shirts with logos.

Before I even got inside, I noticed a change to the house. The plain doormat that had been in place during Sister Mary's reign had been exchanged for one that said 'Welcome to our Home.' The double oak doors had large wreaths on both sides, real fall-looking, with pinecones and corn cobs and colored leaves and such. There was also a wooden bench sitting on the front walkway with a full-size scarecrow sitting there big as life.

I rang the doorbell and stood back, waiting. Carol Anne opened the door wearing blue jeans and a man's shirt.

'Hey, Ms Hudson,' I said.

'Hey back, Sheriff,' she said, smiling. 'Want to come in?'

'Thanks,' I said and stepped over the threshold into an entirely new house. 'I noticed you and the kids are wearing different kinds of clothes.'

'We decided to go back to the way things were in Oregon, instead of wearing the required clothing of our church here. We're not the first to be so bold,' she said.

'Looks good,' I said.

Looking around the house, I noticed the beige-on-beige of Sister Mary's house had been replaced with the bright colors of Sister Carol Anne's paintings and wall hangings. The walls were still beige, but they were covered with color. 'House looks nice,' I said.

'Thanks,' she said as she shut the door behind me. 'It was your wife's idea.'

'Smart lady,' I said.

'Jerry's back in the family room,' she said, leading the way.

Jerry was in a recliner with Mark bouncing on one of Jerry's outstretched legs. Seeing me, he said, 'Good for the quads,' and laughed as the baby bounced harder and harder, holding on to his daddy's index fingers.

Carol Anne rescued the baby, picking him up and nuzzling his neck. 'You two talk while I go change this fella. I could smell him from the doorway.'

'We guys gotta have a manly smell, honey,' Jerry said.

'Little too manly for me!' Carol Anne said, carrying the laughing baby like a football into another room.

'So, Sheriff, what's up?' Jerry asked.

'It's Milt, Jerry, if you don't mind.'

'Not a bit. What can I do for you?'

'Just wanted to check in, after the funeral and all, see how everybody's doing, see if there's anything new y'all can tell me,' I said.

Jerry shook his head. 'Wish there was,' he said. 'I still can't totally believe it. I know she's gone, but that someone killed her on purpose?'

266

He shook his head. 'No, I still can't believe that.'

'But you know it to be true, don't you, Jerry?' I asked.

He stared at his feet for a while, then looked up at me. 'I was with Mary longer than I wasn't. Maybe twice as long. We'd known each other since we were in nursery together at our church in Oregon. Were best friends until sophomore year in high school when we decided we were more than friends and wanted to marry. Our parents wouldn't let us, so we dated until graduation. Then we got married, with their blessings. She was like half my soul.' Again, he shook his head. 'I know someone did this to her, Milt,' he said, finally looking up at me, 'but it's hard to get my head around. Mary was ... almost perfect. She only raised her voice to me once – right after Lynnie, our oldest, was born. Doctor said it was post-partum depression.' He smiled. 'I didn't put the dishes away properly,' he said.

I laughed. 'That'll still get me in hot water,' I said.

'Dr McDonnell yells at you?' he asked, his eyes wide.

'Naw. Much worse. She corrects me. In this tone of voice like she's speaking to our six-year-old.'

Jerry nodded his head. 'Oh, yeah, Carol Anne uses that tone on me.'

I decided to try out a theory. 'Would Sister

Mary ever butt into somebody else's business?' I asked.

Jerry turned red. 'In what way?' he asked, avoiding eye contact.

'In any way,' I said.

'I can't imagine—'Jerry started, but Carol Anne came into the room.

'Jerry, get serious!' Looking at me, she said, 'Mary was a fixer, and she was almost always right. I'm not saying she butted into other people's lives, but if there was something glaringly wrong, she'd try to help. And yes, there were people who'd get mad at her about it, but the only ones I can think of thanked her later because her words helped them!'

'Can you give me some examples?' I asked.

'Like back home, in Oregon?' Carol Anne said. 'There was this girl who was going to marry this older man who already had two wives – both of whom looked pretty miserable – and Mary talked the younger of the two into telling this girl how bad it was. The older man had money and the girl thought it would be an easy marriage, but the second wife told her he married younger women to clean the house since he was too cheap to hire a maid.'

'Anything around here—' I started.

'So then she goes up to the old man and tells him he'd have a happier family if he just hired a maid for this big old house of his and let his wives tend to their children, and he did it! And last I heard the three of them, the old man and his two wives, are doing just fine!'

'But around here, Sister Carol Anne? Since y'all moved to Oklahoma?'

'Did she try fixing things?' she asked.

I nodded.

Carol Anne looked at her husband and stood up. By the time I looked at Jerry, there was nothing going on, but I could swear a message was sent between the two of them that I wasn't privy to.

'Dinner's almost ready, Sheriff. Won't you join us?' she asked as she headed for the kitchen.

There were many reasons why I answered that question the way I did. One, I wanted to see how the two of them would react; two, I wanted to see if I could get more information out of them; three, whatever she was cooking smelled damned good, and four, I was hungry.

So I said, 'Sure, ma'am, I'd love to.'

Whatever you want to say about the lifestyle, there was absolutely nothing wrong with Sister Carol Anne's cooking. Like her home decoration, it was colorful and happy and, probably unlike her home decoration, delicious. I'm not a man who's big on casseroles, but this one had lots of cheese, green chilies, big hunks of beef, onions, all sorts of good tasting stuff, and then there was a big salad to go with it. She'd made three casseroles to fill up her crowd, but there was plenty left for me to have seconds. She seemed pleased when I accepted her offer of another helping.

There wasn't much to learn at dinner, as the large dining-room table, now extended to fill up even more room, and with extra chairs from Carol Anne's old house, consisted of three adults and fifteen children. There was so much talking going on that I couldn't keep up, much less start a conversation of my own.

Afterwards, as the children cleared the table, we adults took to the living room, away from the kitchen, so we could talk.

'Sister Carol Anne—'

'Sheriff, please drop the "sister,"' she said. 'Carol Anne is fine.'

'I'm Milt,' I said. 'OK, anyway, before dinner, we were talking about how Mary liked to fix things. Did she keep up this practice when y'all moved here?' I'd asked the question before, but this time I watched Jerry Hudson to see what he did.

Carol Anne didn't answer. Jerry sat mute. Finally Carol Anne said to her husband, 'I'm not going to lie.'

Jerry sighed and sat forward in his chair, elbows on knees, hands clasped together, head bowed. His lips were moving and his eyes were closed and I coulda sworn he was praying. Probably was.

Before he could say anything though, Lynnie came running in from the kitchen, screaming. 'Daddy! Come quick! Mama Carol Anne!

270

Hurry!'

We all jumped up and ran into the kitchen. The big yellow dog was sitting on its haunches by the dog door, her tail wagging fit to beat the band, and in her mouth was a large metal meat tenderizer, some blood, blonde hair, and dirt still clinging to it.

ELEVEN

Milt Kovak – Saturday

There were fifteen kids and three adults all standing around staring at the dog. Finally I got a grip, and said, 'Carol Anne, would you please hand me one of them rubber gloves and a paper bag if you got it.'

'Uh huh,' she said then moved slowly to the sink, grabbed a blue rubber glove and handed it to me. Slowly, I guess so as not to spook the dog, she made her way to the pantry, her eyes still on Butch, opened the door quietly and reached in for a brown paper bag. Coming back slowly she handed it to me.

'Thank you,' I said. 'Would you open the bag?' I asked, handing it back to her.

She did so as I gingerly went up to Butch, rubbed her head, said, 'Good girl,' a couple of times, then, with the rubber glove in my hand, gingerly took hold of the meat tenderizer. Butch growled and I let go, turned, and looked at Jerry.

He was so pale I thought he might pass out. Carol Anne must have looked at him, too, because she said, 'Jerry, sit down. Lynnie, help

272

him.'

Lynnie grabbed a chair from the kitchen table and helped her dad sit down.

'Hey, girl,' Carol Anne said to the dog in a pleasant voice. 'Whatcha got, girl?' Carol Anne held her hand out and Butch dropped the tenderizer on the floor.

Carol Anne went for it, but I grabbed her hand. 'Prints,' I said, as I picked up the hitting end with the glove. Carol Anne held out the bag and I set it inside, took the bag from her, and rolled it closed.

'First, keep the dog in, and don't let any of the kids go out back until after I can get a crime tech out here to see if maybe we can find out where this came from,' I said, holding up the bag. I sighed real big. 'OK, y'all, I gotta get this out to my car and get it in an evidence bag, seal it and all that sh— stuff, so thank you for a wonderful meal and—' I looked at Jerry, his head in his hands, elbows on knees, what I could see of his face still awfully pale. 'Jerry – man, I'm sorry,' I said.

I nodded at Carol Anne who nodded back, but quickly returned her concentration to her husband.

I headed outside to my car, hardly noticing Dennis Rigsby, Carol Anne's brother, sneaking out of Sister Rene's house.

Milt Kovak – Sunday
It was real late when I got home. After I'd left

273

the Hudsons' house, I'd gone straight to the station, which was dark and quiet, and locked up the evidence in the safe in my office.

The next morning I sent Jean and Johnny Mac on to church and gave a call out to Charlie Smith. We don't have any forensic people on staff at the sheriff's department, but Charlie had found this kid, straight out of high school, who was a forensic wunderkind. He was going to college full-time at OU up the road in Norman – twice a week actually on the campus, the rest of the time on the computer – and working full-time, more or less, for Charlie. Charlie told me he'd let the kid work upside down like a bat if that's what he wanted to do.

Charlie and the kid, Dell Sherman-Baxter (until lately, the only kid I knew of in Prophesy County with two mamas – different situation though) met me at the police station around eight a.m. I'd gone by the sheriff's department first to pick up the evidence, and had it with me. This was my first time to meet Dell Sherman-Baxter, and of course I had my own idea of what he'd look like: skinny, wimpy, thick glasses, crooked teeth, zits, and bad breath. Won't be the last time I'm totally wrong.

Dell Sherman-Baxter was about six foot one inch, maybe 180 pounds, wide shoulders, slim hips, blonde hair, blue eyes, clear skin and a smile that would make a lot of women wet their panties. He shook my hand like a grown-up and said, 'Sheriff, it's a pleasure to meet you.'

'Dell, likewise. I hear you know a little something about forensics.'

The boy blushed. 'Yes, sir. It's like my passion.'

I held up the bag. 'What I have here, I do believe, is a murder weapon. We had a woman out in the county bludgeoned to death—'

'Mrs Hudson, the polygamy family,' he said.

'That's the one. One of my deputies found a meat tenderizer missing from Mrs Hudson's kitchen. The ME agreed that the wound could have been inflicted by such an instrument. The dog showed up with this last night.'

I pulled the meat tenderizer out of the bag with a gloved hand. The boy leaned closer to get a look, not touching it. 'Dirt,' he said.

'Yeah, that's what I'd say.'

'Was the kitchen dirty?' he asked.

'No way,' I said.

'The dog came in from outside with this?' he asked.

'Through the doggy door.'

'Do you know where he came from?'

'No idea,' I said.

'Set it down please, Sheriff.'

I did as he asked and then stood back. The boy donned gloves, looked around at us and said, 'Y'all can leave now.'

We did.

Sitting in Charlie's office, I asked, 'How long you think it's gonna take him?'

Charlie shrugged. 'An hour. Three days. It

275

varies.'

I got out my cell phone and called Nita Skitteridge and told her about finding the tenderizer.

'No kidding!' she said. 'I'm surprised. The dog had it, huh?'

'That's about the gist of it. Wonder if you'd go out there this morning and see if you can find where she dug it up from.'

'Ah, I was just getting ready to go to church,' she said.

'Better change your clothes,' I told her. 'You wouldn't wanna get your Sunday best all messed up.'

I hung up before she could respond. I'd heard the woman's responses before and didn't wanna hear 'em again now. Especially not aimed at me.

So I sat there in Charlie's office, my chair tipped back on two legs, my feet resting on the front of his desk, thinking. I had more business over at the Hudsons myself. One, Carol Anne was going to say something last night, right before Lynnie came running in. Had something to do with Sister Mary butting into other people's business, I was sure of that. And then there was that thing I really didn't think about that I saw as I was leaving: Dennis Rigsby sneaking out – OK, maybe just coming out of – Sister Rene's house. It was only about eight thirty in the evening, but still, a good Mormon wife wouldn't be having male visitors over without her husband present, even in the bright of day. OK, so maybe Dennis was like family, being Carol Anne's brother and all, but still.

And here it was Sunday. Would they all be in church? At the hospital with Rachael and her daughter? I set my chair upright and with my hands on my knees, pushed myself up out of the chair. 'I got things to do,' I told Charlie.

'Like I don't?' he said.

I shrugged. 'You gotta babysit this kid?'

He grimaced. 'Yeah,' he said. 'I promised his mama.'

'I gotta murderer to catch,' I told him and headed out the door.

I wasn't pleased to hear Charlie snort as I left.

Nita Skitteridge – Sunday
Barry, my husband, was straightening his tie in front of the dresser mirror as I hung up my cell phone.

'Shit,' I said.

'Such language and us on our way to church,' he teased.

'You may be on your way to church, but I'm not,' I told him.

'Was that the sheriff on the phone?'

'Yeah. He wants me to go check out a scene,' I said.

He came up behind me and put his arms around me. 'Want me to record the sermon?' he asked.

I laughed. 'So I can go to sleep in the living

room while I listen?'

He kissed my ear. 'Told you when you went to the academy instead of that dental hygienist school that the hours were gonna suck.'

I elbowed him somewhat gently in the midsection. 'If you want me to tell you that you were right, it ain't gonna happen,' I said, pulling away.

I went in our walk-in closet to put up my Sunday clothes and change into my uniform. Barry yelled goodbye from the front door. Ten minutes after he left, I was in my car headed for the station and a squad car. Five minutes after that, I was in the squad car and headed towards The Branches.

Barry and I had a nice house in Longbranch, half an acre, three bedrooms, two baths, two-car garage. Nice covered patio with a good size gas barbecue pit. The furniture was fairly new and almost paid for, and the walls were painted in designer colors. Of the two extra bedrooms, one was set up as an office, and the other was a junk room, until such time as it became the nursery. Wasn't sure when *that* was gonna happen. All this is to say that I was happy with my lot in life, but damn if The Branches didn't set my millionaire fantasies off.

The landscaping alone turned me green with envy. And I could barely look at the houses without breaking the commandment on coveting. There was that one all glass and cement, three stories with walkways between buildings that didn't get me all atwitter, but other than that, I'd take any one of 'em God chose to give me, if He so chose.

I got to the Hudsons' cul-de-sac without committing too many sins and parked the car. The big van was just leaving with Dennis driving. His weirdo mama and Rene Hudson and a bunch of the kids were in it.

I wasn't sure exactly what the sheriff wanted me to do – find out where the murder weapon came from, he'd said – or how I was supposed to go about doing it. So I just got out of the squad car and headed into the backyards, starting in the middle with the former home of the victim, Sister Mary Hudson. None of the backyards were fenced and just seemed to go easily from one to the other. Directly behind the center house was an above-ground pool, covered over now that it was getting on toward winter, and a large wooden playscape with slides and tunnels and swings and monkey bars. Going towards Carol Anne Hudson's house was another playscape set up for smaller children, and a covered sandbox further on. Beyond that was what looked like a mini-racetrack set up for bicycles, with ramps.

The whole backyard area was a children's paradise. Right outside the back door of Carol Anne's house was the dog house. Butch was asleep, her big body inside the house, her head sticking out. When she heard me coming she looked up, and I swear to God she smiled. I could hear her tail thumping the sides of the dog house in her happiness to see me.

That's when I heard a car pull into the cul-de-sac.

Milt Kovak – Sunday
When I pulled into the cul-de-sac, the large van that was usually in front of Sister Mary's house was gone, as was the smaller one that was usually in front of Sister Carol Anne's former house. I did notice, however, that Nita Skitteridge's car was smack dab in the center of the cul-de-sac, like it had been abandoned. I pulled up neatly next to Sister Mary's driveway (I guess I should start calling it Sister Carol Anne's driveway, but then what would I call her other driveway?), and got out, calling Nita's name.

I saw her come out from behind Sister Carol Anne's former house. She didn't look happy. 'You looking for me?' she said.

'Hey,' I said, trying out a smile. I didn't get one in response. 'How's it going?'

'You don't trust me to do my job, Sheriff?' she asked, hands on hips.

'Now nobody said anything like that, Deputy,' I said, letting the smile slip. 'I came out to interview the Hudsons. Anybody left around that you know about?'

She nodded her head toward the middle house, the two-story that had once been Sister Mary's. 'I believe Mr Hudson and Carol Anne

280

are still here. All the kids left for church with Mrs Rigsby and Dennis and the other Mrs Hudson.'

There'd been a bit of emphasis on the word 'church,' but I let it slide. 'I'll just go on up then,' I said and turned away from her. The woman scared me a little, and I'm a big enough man to admit it.

I rang the bell and hardly had my hand off it before it opened. Jerry stood there. 'Sheriff,' he said.

Hell, nobody seemed glad to see me this morning. 'Hey, Jerry. Sorry, but I got a few more questions.'

He opened the door wide and ushered me in. We went to the family room where Carol Anne was sitting with baby Mark in her arms, feeding him a bottle. The baby's eyes were half-closed, and she was rocking him gently.

Jerry put his finger to his lips with a 'shhhing' sound, and we both tiptoed in. The three of us sat there for a few minutes, watching as Mark's eyes finally closed all the way. Carol Anne took the bottle out of his mouth, but kept rocking her body back and forth for another couple of minutes, then stood and took the sleeping baby to the far corner of the room where a playpen sat, leaned down and nestled the baby in.

'I'm sorry I have to keep bothering y'all,' I said when Carol Anne came back. 'But I got questions only the two of you can answer.'

'We noticed your deputy wandering around

281

the backyards, Milt,' Jerry said. 'Could you tell us what that's about?'

'That's why I wanted y'all to keep the dog in last night. She's looking to find a spot where the dog might have found the murder weapon.'

Jerry flinched when I said the words 'murder weapon' and I was sorry I'd said it but what could I do? You gotta call a spade a spade, especially when it is – am I right?

I continued. 'Last night, before the dog interrupted us, y'all were going to tell me how Sister Mary might have butted into somebody else's business once you got here to Oklahoma.'

The couple looked at each other then back at me and neither of 'em said a word. I sighed real big. 'Come on, y'all,' I said. 'Carol Anne, you said you weren't gonna lie to me. So I'm asking a question: what did she butt into?'

Carol Anne took a deep breath and said, 'Lots of things.'

'Jerry? Come on, man,' I said.

Squaring his shoulders, Jerry said, 'Mary never butted into anything. She had concerns for other people, that's all. She felt a Christian's job was to help her fellows. She never did anything that I didn't agree with wholeheartedly.'

'And what are the things she did that you agreed with wholeheartedly?' I asked.

He shook his head. I looked at Carol Anne. She looked away.

I tried another tactic. 'Last night, as I was leaving here, I saw your brother, Carol Anne,

282

coming out of Sister Rene's house. What's up with that?'

The two of them looked at each other as I watched closely. Sister Carol Anne flapped her arms as she stared at her husband, while Jerry shook his head. Carol Anne stood up. Jerry stood up. I kept watching. Carol Anne sat back down. Still standing, Jerry shook his head again. Carol Anne folded her arms over her chest and looked away from her husband. Jerry sat back down. These two were having a doozy of an argument and I hadn't heard a peep out of either of 'em.

'So what's the conclusion?' I asked.

'What?' Jerry asked, finally looking at me.

'What have y'all finally decided to tell me? I hope some of it's true.'

'I'm not telling you any—' Jerry started.

'I am!' Carol Anne said with what seemed to be just a little bit of heat.

'Carol Anne...' Jerry started.

'Oh, hush, Jerry!' she said, standing, hands on hips. 'I'm sick and tired of this! It's been almost three years we've been covering for her, and now she's after my brother? I won't have it!'

OK, I thought. Now we're getting somewhere. But I hated the thought that Sister Rene with the cute little butt was gonna be the bad guy in this scenario.

Jerry fell back in his chair, put his elbow on the arm of the chair, his chin on his fist, and stared off into space, a space far away from his wife and me.

Carol Anne sat back down, arms across her chest. And I sat there staring at the two of 'em. This went on longer than it shoulda.

'OK, enough!' I said, standing up. 'Somebody start talking and I mean now!'

I was loud enough and it had been silent enough that they both jumped. Jerry let out a deep breath, like he'd been holding it for some time. 'All right,' he said, looking at Carol Anne. 'This is family business and I'd prefer you not let this out.'

'If it has nothing to do with the murder of Sister Mary, then it doesn't need to go anywhere. But if it does, I'm not making any promises.'

'It's got nothing to do with Mary—' Jerry started.

'And how do we know that?' Carol Anne demanded.

'Stop! Just tell me,' I said.

Jerry leaned forward, elbows on knees, hands clasped. 'About three years ago, when we were still in Oregon, one of our friends at church came to Mary with a problem. Her seventeen-year-old daughter found she was going to have a baby and she wasn't married. She wouldn't tell her parents who the father was and this friend needed her daughter married off quickly. We knew the girl, and Mary and Carol Anne and I had a family meeting about it, and it was decided unanimously,' he said, giving a pointed

284

look at Carol Anne, 'that we should bring the girl into our family. I'd marry her, but she didn't have to be a *real* wife if the two of us – the girl and I – didn't agree that's what we wanted.'

'I take it,' I said, 'this knocked-up girl was Rene?'

He grimaced at the use of the term, but went on. 'Yes. I ... well, it just wasn't something I was thrilled about, so we became man and wife in name only.'

So now I was confused. The two-year-old holding on to Rene I understood, but what about the baby that was always in her arms? 'So whose baby...?'

'That's what we'd like to know!' Carol Anne said with, again, a little heat.

Jerry shot her a look then back to me. 'Sister Rene has decided not to tell us that, which is her right. But...' He looked at Carol Anne with a sheepish look, then down at the floor. 'She told Mary.'

'What?' Carol Anne all but shouted. It was loud enough to wake up baby Mark. She went to the playpen and stuck a pacifier in his mouth and came back. He quieted down.

Carol Anne stood in front of Jerry with her hands on her hips. 'Who was it?' she demanded. 'Not Dennis!'

Jerry shook his head. 'Mary wouldn't tell me,' he said.

'Bull!' Carol Anne said. 'She told you everything!'

'No, Carol Anne, she didn't!' Jerry said with his own heat. He stood up to face her. 'Mary wasn't perfect! OK? You keep thinking that, and thinking you can't take her place and that's not true! Mary was wonderful, but she was a flesh and blood woman, not something handed down by God! And no, she didn't tell me who fathered Rene's new baby! Hell, it could be Dennis! I don't know who it is, but it could well be the person who killed Mary!'

Carol Anne turned to me. 'It wasn't Dennis! I don't know why he was over at Rene's last night, but he was probably borrowing something for Mama.' She thought about that for a moment and smiled. 'That's exactly what it was! He was borrowing something for Mama! He saw your car over here and he didn't want to disturb us, so he went to Rene's to borrow whatever it was Mama needed!'

Jerry stepped up to his wife and rubbed her arm. Looking at me, he said, 'That's probably it. I'm sure it is.' The two turned to each other and smiled.

'Be that as it may,' I said, 'there's still the question of who fathered Rene's baby.'

They both shook their heads. 'We don't know,' Jerry said.

'Y'all sit down,' I said, taking my seat back myself. When we were all settled back down, I asked, 'So who was around Rene? Who could it have been?'

'That's just it, Milt,' Jerry said. 'We let Rene

286

have her own house, her and her little girl, Cheyenne, and we don't monitor her every move. She has her own car – her parents send a generous allowance so I don't have to pay much for her upkeep – she could have gone anywhere, done anything, we just don't know. When she started showing back about – when was that, honey?' he asked, looking at Carol Anne.

She sighed. 'Long before you ever knew,' she said and patted him on the thigh. 'Mary and I kept the knowledge to ourselves for a while before we even approached Rene about it.' She looked down at her lap, her face turning red. Finally, she looked up at her husband. 'We thought it was yours at first, then Mary and I talked about it and both agreed that you would have told us if you decided to take Rene on as a real wife.'

'Well, I'm glad you two worked that out. I hope you know I never would have done anything like that without talking to the two of you.'

She nodded her head and squeezed his hand. He didn't let hers go.

'So,' I said, 'the new baby...'

'Michael,' Carol Anne said.

'How old is he?'

'Six months,' Carol Anne said.

'So,' I said, 'add six months to nine months and let's say approximately fifteen months ago, which would have been summer last year –

remember what was going on back then? Who was around? What y'all were doing?'

The two of them thought about it. 'Nothing out of the ordinary,' Carol Anne said. 'The kids were going to school, we were all going to church, Jerry was going to work. Rene was volunteering some at the church for the autumn carnival...' She looked at Jerry, her eyes big.

'Who else was working that carnival?' I asked.

Jerry's face hardened and he stood up. I stood up too. 'What?' I asked.

'Just the women of the church,' Carol Anne said. 'And Brother Earl.'

When I got in my Jeep, I noticed Deputy Skitteridge's car was gone. I hoped she planned on giving me a report. I put that thought aside and thought about what I'd learned this morning. The Hudsons were thinking Brother Earl might have something to do with Rene's new baby, but there was still the possibility of Dennis Rigsby, Carol Anne's brother, doing more than 'borrowing something for Mama.' I looked over at Carol Anne's former house, now occupied by Mrs Rigsby and her son Dennis, and all the boys – Mary's, Carol Anne's, and Rachael's. Nobody home yet. Both vans were still missing. I looked across the street at Rene's house. Way too big for a woman and two small children, but all the houses in The Branches were big. If the girl was seventeen when she married Jerry, and now had a two-year-old, she was just nineteen now. Brother Earl obviously liked them young, if you looked at his newest wife, the Russian mail-order bride, or whatever she was. I wonder how long he'd had Nadia as his wife. Less than fifteen months? Had he found out his fondness for sweet young things by messing with Rene?

Personally I was sick of talking to Brother Earl. I'd rather eat a dirt sandwich than spend any more quality time with that quack, but it looked like I was gonna have to. I was just thinking about heading back to Tejas County, when the big van pulled into the cul-de-sac.

I got out of my Jeep and walked up to the van. 'Mr Rigsby,' I said to Dennis. 'May I speak with you a moment?' Looking in the back seat, I said, 'And you, too, Mrs Hudson.'

Dennis frowned and turned to his mother. 'Mama, take the boys on in and start some dinner, OK? I'll be right in.'

'What's going on, Dennis?' his mama asked.

'Nothing, Mama. Go on in now.'

Rene walked up to Mrs Rigsby and handed her her two children. 'Take the babies, will you, Mama Rigsby?' she said.

'Like I don't have enough to do already!' the older woman said, although she took both the two-year-old and the six-month-old, cooing to the baby in her arms as she herded the boys into the house.

'Girls,' Rene said, 'y'all go on in to the main house, now. Lynnie, take 'em on in.'

'Come on, girls,' Lynnie said, pushing her sisters ahead of her.

Rene walked up to where I was standing with Dennis.

'Yeah, Sheriff?' Dennis asked when Rene joined us.

'Saw you going in to Rene's house last night, Dennis,' I said, looking him in the eye. 'Care to explain?'

Dennis looked at Rene and Rene looked at her toes. She was leaving it up to him. Maybe she did that a lot – leaving decisions up to her man of the moment.

'Ah, Mama wanted me to ask Rene something,' he said.

'She couldn't call?' I asked.

'Phone didn't work,' he said.

'If I asked your mama to verify this, you think she would?' I asked.

Dennis looked down at his toes. Finally he looked up at me. 'What is it you want to know, Sheriff?'

'You the father of Rene's youngest?' I asked.

'No!' Rene said.

Dennis chimed in with: 'Absolutely not.'

I looked at Miss Cute-Butt. 'Then who is, Mrs Hudson?'

'My husband, Jerry, of course. I hear my babies crying. I gotta go!' she said, and ran into the house now occupied by the Rigsbys – mother and son.

'You hooking up with Rene?' I asked Dennis.

290

He shrugged. 'Probably not,' he said, shaking his head. 'Thought so for a while, but I had to tell her last night I lost my job at Jack-in-the-Box.' He shook his head again. 'I don't have anything to offer her. No job, living in one of Jerry's houses. Hell, I don't have a pot to piss in that doesn't belong to somebody else.'

I looked at Dennis. 'Sorry, man,' I said. Changing the subject, I asked, 'Who's the father of Rene's new baby?'

Dennis looked me in the eye. 'Hell if I know. She won't tell.'

'According to Jerry, she told Mary.'

'Yeah?' Dennis said, raising an eyebrow. 'So who is it?'

'According to Jerry, Mary didn't tell him.'

'Yeah, according to Jerry. Everything is always about Jerry,' he said, bitterness creeping into his voice.

'What's that mean?' I asked.

Dennis tried to make eye contact and failed. 'Nothing,' he said.

'Naw, now you started it. Spit it out.'

Dennis sighed. 'It's just that, you know, my sister marries the guy and Mama's all "Jerry does this" and "Jerry said that" and Carol Anne can't complete a sentence if Jerry's name's not in it. And now Rene...'

His voice faded out as he stared at his toes. 'What about Rene?' I asked.

When he looked up, he had a resolute look on his face. 'You know Rene's Jerry's wife in name only? That they never did the deed?'

'That's what Jerry tells me,' I said.

'Yeah, but did he mention they did it before they got married? Did he mention he's the father of Rene's little girl?'

TWELVE

Jean McDonnell – Sunday
After church, my son John and I drove to the hospital to check on Rachael and Melissa.

Roy Donley, the long-haul trucker, was sitting in a chair by the door when we got there, regaling the two females with his tales of the road. He stood when John and I walked in the room. 'Hey, Dr McDonnell,' he said, holding out his hand. 'Ma'am,' Roy said, indicating the chair he'd just vacated. 'Please have a seat.'

As I sat, Roy took my crutches and placed them within reach. Quite a gallant fellow.

Rachael said, 'We're getting out of the hospital today.'

Melissa said, 'Yea! I can't wait. Sister Carol Anne's gotta cook better than this place!'

I laughed, but Rachael said, 'Melissa, that's rude! They've been very good to us here.' Looking around and seeing no one from the hospital staff, Rachael stage-whispered, 'But you're right – anything would be better than here!'

Melissa giggled.

'What time are you getting out?' I asked.

'They're working on the paperwork now. All we have to do is get dressed.'

'Will you need a ride?'

'I'll be takin' 'em over to the Hudsons in The Branches,' Roy Donley said. 'They'll be staying there for a couple of days.'

'That's wonderful,' I said, smiling big. 'Well, John and I should probably leave and let you two get dressed.'

Rachael held out her hand and, grabbing my crutches, I walked up to the bed and took it. She squeezed my fingers. 'Jean, thank you for all you've done for us. I'm calling you by your first name because you've gone beyond your call of duty as a doctor. You've performed as a friend, and I'll consider you one forever.' She leaned forward and hugged me and I hugged her back. She was right – I considered her more than a patient. I turned and kissed Melissa on the cheek.

'You be a good girl for your mom,' I said.

'Do I have to?' she said, then grinned.

John and I left, with me feeling a little misty-eyed.

Milt Kovak – Sunday
So I didn't get back in my Jeep, but headed instead back to what I'd come to consider the 'main' house of the Hudson compound, Sister Mary's former abode. And I didn't ring the bell this time – this time I slammed my fist against the door in an attempt at a knock.

Jerry answered the door. 'Milt! I thought you—'

I grabbed him by the arm. 'Get out here!' I said between gritted teeth, pulling him out of the house and onto the porch.

'What?' Jerry said.

I slammed the door behind him. 'You son-of-a-bitch!' I said.

Jerry turned red. 'Now, Milt, I can't have you—'

'Don't you get sanctimonious with me, you asshole!' I said. 'Lying to my face not ten minutes ago!'

'What are you talking about?' Jerry demanded.

'The name Cheyenne ring any bells?'

The red got redder. 'Ah, I'm not sure...'

'You're not sure if I know the truth? Well, I think I do. I've been led to understand that you *are* Rene's little girl's daddy, and that you knocked her up before marrying her and didn't mention it to either of your other wives.'

Jerry looked around him in fear. 'Now, hush!' he said in a whisper. 'Don't let anyone hear you!'

'Why not?' I asked in a normal, maybe a little louder than normal, speaking voice.

'You don't understand!' he wailed.

'You bet your ass I don't!' I agreed.

'Can we sit in your car and talk about this?' Jerry asked.

I had this overwhelming urge to smack him.

Right in the kisser. I'm not sure why, but I was madder than I'd been in a long time. Maybe it was because I'd come to like and respect this man, only to find out he was just as weak as the rest of us, and holier-than-thou to boot. We sat in my Jeep and I couldn't bear to look at him.

'Less than ten minutes ago you said how you wouldn't take Rene on as a "real" wife without talking to Mary and Carol Anne about it – but that didn't seem to faze you when you were fucking the teenaged babysitter, you asshole!'

'It wasn't like that!' Jerry protested. 'I swear to God it wasn't.' He took a deep breath and sighed. 'Besides, Mary knew. I told her right after it happened. When she found out Rene was pregnant, she's the one who went to Rene's parents and suggested the marriage in name only.' He sighed. 'Mary was a great woman, but she could be spiteful. I think she did that – brought Rene into our family – as a way of rubbing my nose in it, reminding me every day of my transgression.'

'Mean old Mary, making you take responsibility for your own frigging child!' I said.

Jerry shook his head. 'I'm not saying that...'

'You just did!' I reminded him.

'She would always do the right thing. Rene was part of our family – Cheyenne is my child. But in the end it had the effect Mary wanted. I wouldn't go near Rene, no matter how much she wanted it.'

'Rene wanted it?' I said, a little – OK a lot –

skeptical.

Jerry shrugged. 'I don't know why, Milt. I'm not saying I'm some great lover or anything. She's the one who started the whole thing to begin with...'

That got me hot. Gritting my teeth to keep from screaming at him or hitting him, I said, 'You know how many pedophiles I've heard say that? She was coming on to me! That little twelve-year-old! Hell, Rene was seventeen! Coming on to you?'

Jerry was shaking his head like he was trying to get it to fall off. 'It wasn't like that, Milt, I swear! She babysat for Mary when she had to be at the church for something and Carol Anne couldn't do it. And sometimes I'd be there. And she just kept at me. I swear to God she'd come in dressed all proper and when Mary left, clothes would start coming off! And touching me, all the time touching me! I'm not saying I'm not to blame, I am! Totally to blame. But she was after me for some reason, Milt. And,' he looked out the window then, not looking at me, and his voice was low, 'she wasn't a virgin.'

'And how would you know that?' I asked.

'A man can tell,' he said quietly to the window.

I'm not sure if I bought that old wives' tale, although I'd personally deflowered two of my own (married both of 'em too), but not knowing the science of it, I let it go.

'So you knocked her up the second time?' I asked.

He shook his head violently. 'Absolutely not! I haven't been alone with her since that one night we had together.'

'So you told Mary. How about Carol Anne?'

Again, the head shake. 'She doesn't know. And I don't want her to. Carol Anne's not as...' He seemed to search for a word. 'Understanding as Mary was.'

'Yeah, but you said Mary used it against you.'

He nodded. 'Yeah. She could be devious,' he said, then smiled slightly. 'Carol Anne would just knock my head off and spit in the hole.'

I couldn't help but agree. She was one straight-ahead woman. 'You know it's bound to come out,' I said.

I swear his head was gonna come off the way he kept shaking it. 'No, no way. No need for that, Milt! Why? Why does it need to come out? I could lose everything...'

I reached across him and opened the passenger-side door. 'Shoulda thought about that before you fucked a seventeen-year-old,' I said.

On my way out of the cul-de-sac, I thought about what I'd learned. Somehow I thought the father of the second baby was maybe more important than the father of the first. I now knew Cheyenne's daddy really was Jerry. But who was the daddy of the baby boy? Dennis claimed it wasn't his, and so did Rene. Jerry claimed he didn't know, and Carol Anne claimed the same. But Jerry said Mary had known. Did Rene tell Mary? And if so, why? And did that have something to do with Mary's death? Was it possible Brother Earl Bishop, the so-called leader of this flock of multi-marrying weirdoes, had had his way with cute little Rene? Why would she? If I was a woman, I'd run like the devil away from the likes of Brother Earl. Then again, he had four women who up and married him for reasons unknown.

I needed to have a long talk with little Rene, but from what my wife had said, she didn't seem to be swimming in the deep end of the pool. What you saw was what you got. But then again, she did run like the dickens when I was asking her and Dennis about the paternity of her son.

OK, now, I was coming up with a theory. Rene tells Mary the name of the father of her baby. He, of course, is married, and in case it was Brother Earl, multi-married. He can't let his wife or wives find out about this. Mary confronts him and wants him to take responsibility for this new baby, and he whacks her over the head with the meat tenderizer. A heat of the moment occurrence. A crime of passion.

A thought – if Brother Earl was the daddy, then what was the problem? What's one more wife when you already have four? Except Rene is legally married to Jerry. Well, not legally, really. I suppose Jerry was only legally married to Mary, since plural marriage is not legal in the United States. But as far as their sect went, would the fact that she was Jerry's 'wife' be a problem in Brother Earl taking her on as his 'wife'? Would they have to have a divorce? And if so, how did you go about a divorce when you weren't legally married? And did any of this mean I had to go talk to Brother Earl yet again?

I was getting a headache.

I had two lines of inquiry to follow up on. Since I was here in The Branches, I needed to go by the country club and see the check-in list for Monday, eight a.m. to three p.m., which was from the time the kids left for school until the time the kids came home from school, which was as close as we could get to an actual time of death. And then there was Andrew Schmidt, the paranoid. I couldn't really see his involvement in any of this, but he did seem to like 'em young, as in his lovely wife number two, and maybe he took a turn with Miss Rene. The only thing I could do was ask. But being as it was Sunday, I wanted to get home, so I might just put off Schmidt until tomorrow, find him at his place of business.

I got to the club, simply called The Club (this place had a thing about the word 'the' with a capital 'T'), and asked to see The Manager. When she showed up, I was happy. Happy because I have no problem looking at pretty women, especially when my wife's not around.

This one was about six feet tall, had great gobs of black hair cascading down her shoulders, had a fair complexion, lightly dotted with freckles, and the bluest eyes I'd ever seen. And she was built like a brick shithouse. She walked up to me with her right arm stretched out and I was hoping she meant to hug me, but it was just to shake my hand. She smiled and I thought my knees would buckle.

'Sheriff,' she said, smiling and shaking my hand. 'Lily Daye, manager of The Club. How may I help you?'

For a minute there I had no idea how she might help me, then I remembered why I was there. 'You know about the murder on Magnolia Way?'

'Yes, quite tragic. They're not members.'

'I was told there is a back road from The Branches to The Club, so there's the possibility that someone coming to the club could have gotten through to the residential area.'

'Yes, I can see why you might think that would be possible.'

To make everything perfect, she had an accent, and it wasn't an Oklahoma accent either. 'You don't think it would be possible?' I asked.

She looked up, and put a long, manicured index finger against a perfectly chiseled chin. She was thinking and it was lovely. 'Not impossible,' she finally said, looking down at me. 'But highly unlikely.'

'And why is that?' I asked, more to hear her talk than wanting an answer.

'We have very stringent rules here for security reasons. We have many important people coming to The Club from all over the world. We don't want just anyone walking on to our grounds. As you probably surmised by that woman who was murdered, The Branches will sell a house to anyone. The Club, on the other hand, has standards.'

It was too bad about the hairy mole that grew on her nose, the hunch on her back, and the way her boobs began to sag. No way a woman like that could be pretty.

'I need to see your sign-in sheets for last Monday, between eight a.m. and three p.m.,' I said.

'Our membership is confidential,' she said in that phony accent and with the cheesy smile.

'So you're gonna make me go bother a judge on a Sunday for a warrant? Hope he's not one of your members – might make him testy.'

'If he's a member, I doubt he'll give you a warrant,' she said.

Damn, that kinda thing always works on television.

'I just need to see the names of the people who came during those hours. I don't want to bother any of your members,' I said, trying for a nicer tone.

She smiled that cheesy smile. 'I understand that, Sheriff, I really do,' she said. 'But I'm afraid you'll have to have a warrant.' She held out her hand to me and I'd have been rude not to take it. She shook my hand firmly twice and said, 'Good day, Sheriff,' and turned around and left.

I'll give the woman this: she left real good, if you know what I mean.

I got back to my house around three o'clock and me and Johnny Mac got a baseball bat and some gloves and headed out front for an impromptu game of ball. This past summer he'd played T-ball and learned he was good at it. Jean and me decided to encourage that, and, besides, I liked it too. We did that until around five then headed in to see if Jean had any ideas for supper. Lo and behold, the woman had a roast on, which Johnny Mac and I totally approved of. We found something to watch on ESPN to kill an hour before supper, had roast beef with mashed potatoes and a salad, then had our leisurely Sunday night: checking homework due the next day (we never had homework in first grade, but things are all kinds of different nowadays), watching TV while playing a rousing game of Chutes and Ladders, then bath, teeth, story, talk, and bed. Which took us to nine o'clock.

When I came downstairs Jean was watching something on the PBS channel and I waited until it was over before I told her what I'd learned about Jerry Hudson.

'OK, he *is* the father of Rene's baby?' She

303

shook her head. 'I don't see why you're so angry, Milt. We thought all along he was the father of Rene's baby.'

'Yeah, but then he said he wasn't, and that's what Carol Anne believes, and now I come to find out he *is*, but they did the deed way before he married her, or whatever you want to call it.'

She shrugged. 'Let's just say married, like we mean it.' She thought for a moment, then said, 'OK, I understand your anger, to a degree. But surely Jerry's not the first guy—'

'Weren't you beginning to believe this guy was for real? That he was as good as Carol Anne claimed he was? That he was actually a righteous, God-fearing Christian man doing what we all want to think God wants us to do?'

Jean sighed. 'Yes, I guess I was. I think it must be the psychiatrist in me that's not surprised by this turn of events. No one's perfect, honey, certainly not Jerry Hudson. And obviously not Mary Hudson, either, as Carol Anne would have us believe. What she did – while on the outside very noble – was really devious and vengeful. Bringing the girl Jerry was unfaithful with into their home, raising his bastard child with her own children, basically never letting Jerry forget what he did. Not a loving thing to do.'

'So does this get me anywhere with who killed Mary?' I asked.

Jean gave me a look. 'Are you thinking Jerry now? He got sick and tired of her rubbing his

304

nose in it and decided to get rid of her?'

'Why wouldn't he get rid of Rene instead?' I asked.

'Good question. He gets rid of Mary, he still has Rene and Cheyenne sitting in their house being constant reminders of his great "sin."'

'Maybe Mary was going to tell Carol Anne?' I suggested.

I could see her mind working on that one. 'Hmm, that's a good one, honey! Of course. Carol Anne is the one woman in his life who still believes in his goodness. But if she finds out that Cheyenne is really his child, then that all falls apart, and she'll begin to look at him like the asshole he is, just like Mary and Rene. So maybe he and Mary have an argument, and it escalates, and Mary threatens to tell Carol Anne the truth, and Jerry just loses it. Crime of passion – which is what you've thought all along.'

I sighed. 'Yeah. Makes perfect sense. He even has access to the backyard to hide the meat tenderizer that Butch later finds. I'll check with that forensic kid of Charlie's tomorrow and see if he's got the fingerprints off that thing yet.'

'You sound disappointed,' my wife said.

I laid down on the couch, my head in her lap. 'I am,' I said. 'Asshole or not, I really got to like old Jerry.'

THIRTEEN

Jean McDonnell – Monday

It had been a week since Mary Hudson's murder, and Milt felt he was closing in on the culprit; that the culprit was her husband, Jerry Hudson, was a problem for him – a problem I understood. We had both gotten close to personal involvement with Jerry and Carol Anne Hudson, and Milt's disappointment in Jerry's feet of clay was understandable. But feet of clay was one thing – murder was decidedly another. Could Jerry have murdered Mary?

Certainly, in my professional opinion, anyone could commit murder, given a certain set of circumstances. Were those circumstances present? And did Milt even know if Jerry had an alibi for the time of the murder? Of course, there was no definite time – anywhere from eight a.m. to three p.m. Could Jerry account for every minute of that time? Of course not, no one could.

I was in my office at the hospital, no patients for another hour, but with plenty of paperwork to keep me busy. But I couldn't concentrate on the paperwork. This entire mess with the Hudson family was too much on my mind.

Jerry worked for Telecom International, which was out on Highway 5 on the other side of Longbranch. To get there, Jerry would have to go down Highway 17 from Bishop to Long-branch – approximately twenty miles – to the Highway 5 interchange, then turn right on Highway 5 to Telecom International, another ten miles. Thirty miles, and only about fifteen of it posted at sixty miles an hour or more. The other half was posted at anywhere from twenty-five miles an hour – around the courthouse – to fifty miles an hour. So, approximately forty-five minutes, with minimum traffic, from Jerry's office to his home. Did he go out to lunch that day? Did he get an hour for lunch? Was he late getting back? Forty-five minutes home, forty-five minutes back, and at least a half an hour to get angry enough to kill his wife. So let's say at least two hours out of his day.

I called my husband and ran my scenario by him.

'Two hours?' he repeated.

'At least,' I said. 'Probably more.'

Milt sighed. 'Never did check out his alibi. I guess I need to go by Telecom and find out if he has one.'

'Sorry, honey,' I said.

'Do you think he did this?' Milt asked me.

'I have no idea. All I can say is, it's possible.'

Another sigh. 'Thanks heaps,' he said, then gave a quick goodbye.

I felt for him, I really did. It couldn't be easy

to suspect a man you liked and respected – feet of clay or not.

I'd barely hung up when the phone rang. 'Jean McDonnell,' I said.

'Dr McDonnell, it's Carol Anne Hudson.'

'Carol Anne, hi, how are you?' I asked.

'Not that great. Would it be possible for you to come over? I need your advice. I'd come to you but I've got all the babies today. Rene's off doing ... something,' she said.

'I have back-to-back appointments starting in half an hour,' I said, checking my appointment book. 'I'll be free around two this afternoon. How about I drive by then?'

'Thank you!' Carol Anne said with some enthusiasm. 'I'll see you then.'

As I hung up, I gave a fervent hope to the universe that I could keep my mind on my patients and not on what was going on with the Hudsons. But I was afraid the universe could fail me on this one.

Milt Kovak – Monday

I'd never been to Telecom International before. I'd met their security chief, Lyle Manford, because he'd been on the Longbranch police department for a while back in the eighties. Then he went off to Oklahoma City, worked for them until he 'retired,' (never did find out what *that* meant) then got the job with Telecom when they moved in a few years back. He's an OK guy, but let's just say I wouldn't be surprised if

308

his 'retirement' from the Oklahoma City force had something to do with him skimming a little something off the top, if you know what I mean.

I called ahead and spoke with Lyle, letting him know I was coming to check out an alibi. I drove up Highway 5, found the turn and went down a long road simply marked 'Telecom' before I saw the eight-foot big-game fence that went around the whole place, with razor wire on top and a double gate with a checkpoint at both ends. At that point, I had to wonder what in the hell Telecom International actually did and why the need for all this security. I'd had Emmett check this place and their security staff out when they first set up shop, and he never mentioned any of this crap. I wasn't sure I was all that keen on a place with this kind of security in my county. I stopped my Jeep about a hundred yards from the first check point and called Emmett on my cell phone.

'Yeah, Milt?' he said on picking up.

'Hey. I'm over here at Telecom International. When you checked them out a while back, did you notice the eight-foot big-game fence with the razor wire and the two checkpoints at the gate?'

'What the fuck?' Emmett said. 'No! They didn't have any kind of fence or anything when I was there. Of course, they were still building on it, but Lyle never said anything about that kind of security.'

'Well, that's what they got now. I'll talk to

Lyle. See you when I get back.'

'Give him some shit,' Emmett suggested, having been Lyle's boss when he was on the Longbranch force.

'I intend to,' I said and hung up.

I put the Jeep back in gear and headed up to the gate. A guard let me through the first check-point, then I was stopped at the second. Lyle was in the guard shack. 'Hey, Milt,' he grinned. 'I'll ride up there with you,' he said, climbing in the shotgun side of the Jeep.

Once he was settled and we were on our way, I said, 'You know, you should have called me or Emmett when y'all installed all this security. What're y'all hiding out here?'

'We're not hiding anything, Milt!' Lyle said with gusto and a big grin. 'Industrial espionage is a bitch!'

'Been having problems? Sounds like the law needs to be involved. Y'all are in the county, Lyle, you should be calling the sheriff's office if you're getting break-ins and such.'

'Oh, it's more subtle than that, Milt,' Lyle said, slapping me on the back. 'We handle it all in-house. But if we get a break-in, we'll call you for sure.'

Ever get the feeling you're being patronized? I was getting that feeling big time. My first instinct was to elbow him in the gut, but luckily I have good impulse control.

'So about this alibi I need to check out,' I started, but Lyle was way ahead of me.

310

'Jerry Hudson, right? Man,' he said, shaking his head, 'nobody here knew a thing about his marital situation, I swear to God! Three fuckin' wives? What kind of idiot does that? I had one of those, and luckily I got rid of her!' he said and belly-laughed at his own humor. When he slapped my knee instead of his own, I was ready to forget about impulse control. I'd stopped the Jeep and he was already moving out of the car before my elbow could make impact. I'd try again later.

'His supervisor's name is Drew Cathcart. He's a foreigner, but he's OK. Come on in here and I'll introduce you.'

We walked into a building that was two buildings over from the main road. Lyle opened a door with a keypad and we entered an area with a men's bathroom on the left and a women's on the right. Straight ahead was a drinking fountain. A glass door to the right said, 'Systems Analysis,' while to the left said, 'Systems Control.' We went to the right.

It was a room the size of a warehouse filled with a warren of partitioned cubbyholes in the middle, and glassed-in offices lining the south and north sides, where there were windows. Some of the cubbyholes I saw as we passed had been personalized with plants, pictures of kids and animals, bumper stickers, pins with pithy sayings, and lots and lots of sticky notes stuck on metal cabinets, cloth cubicle sides, and computers. We walked down an aisle and went into an office, third one from the bathrooms.

Drew Cathcart stood as we entered. He was a very short man, not more than five-four or five, with flame-red hair rapidly receding, large freckles, black-framed glasses, and crooked teeth. And Lyle, being the dumbass he was, obviously couldn't tell the accent was British.

He shook my hand and asked me to sit down, then looked at Lyle. 'Is there anything more we can do for you, Lyle?' Cathcart asked.

Finally getting the hint, Lyle said, 'I was just leaving. Milt, call when you're ready to leave and I'll have one of my men escort you out.' He turned and walked out of the room, thumbs stuck in his belt loops.

Cathcart sat down. 'He's a total idiot,' he said. Looking up, he added, 'Do excuse me. I hope he's not a friend?'

I shook my head. 'Not so you'd notice.'

'Now you're here about Jerry's alibi, is that correct?' Cathcart asked.

'Yes. Can you tell me where he was between eight a.m. and three p.m.?'

'Well, here of course,' he said, settling back in his chair.

'What about lunchtime?' I asked.

'I remember quite distinctly because after we found out about his wife, which was just later that afternoon, I was very careful to try to account for his time. I know how the police can be when a wife is murdered – always look at the spouse!'

'And how would you know that, sir?' I asked.

'The telly of course!' he said, grinning. 'I love police dramas, don't you?'

'Not so much,' I said. 'About his lunch that day?'

'Well, it wasn't any different, really, than any other day, now was it? Jerry always brings a lunch in a very fancy divided carrier. He told me once it was leftovers from the meal the night before.' Getting a faraway look in his eye, he said, 'I wonder if different wives fixed the meals, and if he had three of those carriers instead of just one?'

'You didn't know about his family situation until recently?'

'Goodness no! And, unfortunately, he'll probably get let off. There's a morality clause in the engineers' contracts, and I do believe multiple marriage might be perceived as putting a damper on his morality, you see?'

'So, he was here the entire lunch hour?'

'Oh, yes. He didn't leave at all. In fact, he didn't take his entire lunch period, but rather helped me with a project I was working on. Jerry's a very good engineer. I shall hate to lose him.'

'You know of anybody around here who had it in for Jerry?' I asked.

'You mean someone else who might be the culprit?' Cathcart asked, a big smile on his face. He sat back in his chair, fingers steepled under his chin and thought about it. The smile was

313

replaced with a frown. 'Not that I can think of, I'm afraid to say. Jerry's a very popular fellow, but wasn't really chummy with anyone. I can see why now.'

'Sir?'

He leaned forward. 'The multiple wives thing! If you get chummy with people here, there's always the possibility they might invite your family over for a meal/barbecue here. I do quite enjoy that, don't you? And then he'd have to make the decision: which wife, don't you see? And then you'd be required to return the favor, ask people to your house, and, Bob's your uncle! That would be the end of that!'

'Right,' I said. 'Is Jerry here today?'

'Oh, yes. No one has spoken to me yet about letting him go. I really do hate to lose him but, beyond the entire morality issue, there's the talk.'

'People are talking?'

'Oh, yes. There are the awkward silences when Jerry walks into a room, and all that.'

'Don't you think that would blow over?' I asked.

Cathcart thought about it. 'Well, isn't what he's doing, the multiple wives, against the law here in the States?'

'Technically,' I said. OK, yeah, it was, but I wasn't ready to start arresting people on that yet. Had a murderer to catch first. Besides, I didn't have enough room in my jail for all the perpetrators of that particular crime.

'Technically? Oh, I see. I'm sure the murder takes priority?'

'Of course.'

'But you'll arrest him afterwards?' Cathcart insisted.

'We'll be looking into certain irregularities,' I hedged.

'Hum,' he said. Leaning forward rather eagerly, Cathcart asked, 'May I use this with the higher ups? You see, if they see the possibility of Jerry not being arrested, and the Telecom name not being dragged through the mud, as it were, they might be disinclined to let him go, especially with a good word from his supervisor – me, of course.'

'Sure, I don't see why not,' I said. I stood up. 'So you'll vouch for Jerry being here all day, especially during the critical lunch-hour period?'

Cathcart stood up. 'Yes, definitely.' He held out his hand and we shook.

'Thanks for your time, Mr Cathcart.'

'It was a pleasure meeting you, Sheriff,' he said and I left his office. Neither one of us bothered to call Lyle Manford.

Jean McDonnell – Monday
I arrived at Carol Anne Hudson's home in The Branches at 2:20 p.m., after being announced from the gate. I'd had to wait while the guard on duty called Carol Anne and got the OK to let me in. Carol Anne apologized profusely when I

got to her house.

'I'm so sorry! I'm so bad with the procedures here! If I'd called ahead and told them you were coming, you wouldn't have had to wait!'

'It's no problem, Carol Anne. Really. I didn't have to wait long.'

'Please come in,' she said, ushering me into her home.

She led me into the den where there were three playpens lined up, each with a sleeping baby inside.

'Got your hands full, I see,' I said quietly.

'Yes,' she said. I noted that she didn't smile when she said it.

'Something's bothering you,' I said.

'The sheriff probably already told you. You don't seem like a couple that keep secrets.' She sighed and tears came to her eyes. 'I thought Jerry and I were a couple like that, too.'

We were sitting next to each other on the sofa, and I reached out and touched her hand. When I did, the tears started flowing down her face. 'They both lied to me. He and Mary both. I thought we had a union of trust, but obviously neither of them trusted me!' Her head came up and she looked me in the eye. 'Jerry impregnated Rene before their marriage. I was led to believe that she'd been impregnated by someone else, and that her marriage to Jerry was in name only. He still claims that's true of the marriage, that he only slept with her that one time, but it's hard for me to believe anything he

316

says now. He and Mary didn't trust me with the truth. Now I can't trust him at all.'

'What are you going to do with this information?' I asked her.

She shook her head. 'I'm not sure. For the moment, I've asked Jerry to leave this house. I told him to go stay with Rene, but he refused. He opted instead to go stay with my mother and the boys.' She laughed humorlessly. 'Heck of a way to atone for his sins.'

'I'm so sorry, Carol Anne,' I said, still holding her hand.

She took a deep breath. 'You know, I think the bigger of the two betrayals is Mary's. We were like sisters. Truly. I trusted her with my life, with my *children's* lives! And she kept this from me, lied to me. Said Rene wouldn't say who the father was; that we were taking her in as good Christians! How could she lie about that? About doing a Christian deed? That's like spitting in the face of everything we've done to help others!' Carol Anne shook her head. 'Not that I don't hate Jerry right now. Believe me, I do.' She pulled her hand back and crossed her arms over her body, holding herself as if she felt a sudden chill. 'I just feel so alone right now.'

And I knew she was. A little over a week ago, Carol Anne thought she had the perfect family. Happy children, a loving husband, two sister-wives, one of whom was her mentor and best friend. Now she knew that all three of these people, her husband and both sister-wives, had

317

been lying to her, betraying her trust. I could only imagine how alone she must feel.

'If it's any consolation, Jerry told Milt that he didn't want to tell you for fear you'd leave him.'

'I'm not surprised,' she said bitterly. 'Who else is going to take care of him now? Surely not Rene!'

The doorbell rang, jarring both of us. 'Are you expecting someone else?' I asked.

Just as I said that, one of the babies started to cry. I got my crutches and stood up. 'You get the baby and I'll get the door,' I said, smiling at Carol Anne as I went to the front door.

There was a man standing there who looked vaguely familiar. He was holding a chainsaw in one hand. 'Mrs Kovak, right?' he said, holding out a hand that didn't have a chainsaw in it. 'David Bollinger. We spoke briefly at Mary's funeral.'

'Right,' I said, smiling and taking his hand. 'Please come in. Carol Anne's in the den with the babies.'

He followed me into the den. Carol Anne was standing, holding Rene's youngest, Michael, the six-month-old boy. 'Sit,' she said to me, 'and take this one. I think he's wet.'

I put down my crutches and did as she said. 'Hi, David, sorry,' Carol Anne said. 'I didn't expect you.'

'I'm on my way to play golf. Thought I'd bring back Jerry's chainsaw. Got that old dead

318

tree taken care of.'

'Well, come on,' Carol Anne said, her voice sounding slightly miffed. 'I'll show you where it goes in the garage.'

'Carol Anne!' I called out as she was about to leave. 'Diaper and wipes, please. This one's not just wet.'

'Oh, I'm sorry—'

'Don't worry about it! Diaper!' I said, laughing. Carol Anne threw me a diaper, wipes, and a receiving blanket that I used to put under the baby while I changed him. I don't get to play with babies that much since my son is now practically a grown-up, and I was having a grand old time, tickling and cooing when Carol Anne and David Bollinger came back in the room.

'It was nice to see you again, Mrs Kovak,' Bollinger said.

I looked up, ready to acknowledge the niceness of it all, when it hit me. Bollinger had a cleft chin. Rene's baby lying on the couch had a cleft chin. Rene did *not* have a cleft chin. Quick mental fade-back to medical school: 'If the child inherits two cleft chin genes from his parents, he would develop cleft chin by being homozygous to the trait. If he inherits only one cleft gene from his parents, he would still develop cleft chin by being heterozygous to the trait.'

In other words, the only way baby Michael could end up with a cleft chin was if one or both of his parents had the gene. Rene obviously did not. David Bollinger, on the other hand, obviously did.

Collecting my thoughts and putting them aside, I said, 'It was nice seeing you, too, Mr Bollinger.'

To Carol Anne, he said, 'Tell Jerry thanks for the loan.'

'Why don't you call Jerry on his cell phone and thank him yourself?' she suggested.

Bollinger shot her a questioning look, but not getting an answer just said, 'Well, bye, then,' and headed out the door.

I struggled to my feet. 'Carol Anne, come get the baby,' I said as I maneuvered my way around the sofa. 'I'll be right back.' I headed out the front door with my cell phone in my hand as Bollinger started his car and turned around to leave the cul-de-sac. I had an urgent call to make, but before I could even hit the speed dial, I saw Bollinger pull around to the street side of Rene's house and sneak in the back door.

Milt Kovak – Monday

It took a minute before my wife's recitation of an old medical school book finally registered. 'You mean,' I said, 'that because Rene's mystery baby has a cleft chin, and David Bollinger has a cleft chin, that David has to be the father?'

'Exactly!' Jean declared.

I sighed. 'Honey, how many men do you think

320

there are in Longbranch alone with cleft chins?'

'Three,' she said automatically.

That surprised me. 'Three?'

'Just a ballpark figure. But by national norms and the population of Longbranch, one could conjecture—'

'OK,' I said. 'You got me. There are three. So who are the other two?'

'How in the hell would I know?' my wife answered with a touch of pissiness to her voice.

'Well, you said—'

'Whoever they are, *they* are not the ones I saw sneak into Rene's house less than five minutes ago.'

'Where are you?' I demanded.

'Standing in Mary Hudson's front yard,' Jean said.

'Jesus! Get in the goddamn house! Bollinger could very easily be the killer! Damn, Jean!'

'I'm going! I'm going!' she said and I could hear her open and close the front door.

'OK, good. Now stay there! Lock the doors! Both of you stay inside! I'll be there ASAP!'

'Don't hurt yourself,' my wife said.

I was heading out the door when Dalton stopped me. 'Hey, Milt, I think I got an ID on that dead body we found behind Vern's Auto Repair.'

'I can't now, Dalton, I gotta—'

'But, Milt, you need to look at this...'

'Damn it, Dalton! When I get back!' I shouted at him and hightailed it out of the shop.

321

Jean McDonnell – Monday

I came back inside Carol Anne's house. She was standing in the foyer. 'What's going on?' she demanded.

'Come sit down,' I started.

'No! You tell me now!'

I gave her a look. 'If you don't mind, I'd rather sit down. I may look terribly comfortable to you, standing her on these crutches, but the truth is they aren't as comfy as they look.'

Carol Anne turned red and her hands flew to her mouth. 'Oh, dear Lord! Jean, I'm so sorry! Please come in the den!'

Baby Michael, he of the cleft chin, was in his baby swing and seemed to be thoroughly enjoying himself batting at the toys hanging from the bar above the swing.

'That was so rude of me...'

I shook my head. 'It was rude of me, too,' I said. I touched her hand again. 'Carol Anne, I have something I have to tell you.'

Carol Anne closed her eyes, her lips moving slightly, I think in prayer. I waited. Finally, she opened her eyes and said, 'OK.'

'You know that dimple in baby Michael's chin?'

She nodded her head, a skeptical look on her face.

'He can only have that if one of his parents has one,' I said.

'But Rene doesn't...' Her eyes got huge.

'David Bollinger!' she said. 'He does, doesn't he? I didn't know! Oh my God! He's Michael's father?'

'It seems likely,' I said.

'Oh my God!' Carol Anne jumped up. 'Then he's the one who killed Mary!'

Carol Anne ran for the door. I was trying to get my crutches to rush after her when the other two babies woke up screaming.

Dalton Pettigrew – Monday

Dalton stood there staring after the closed door as Milt ran out.

Holly came up behind him. 'What's going on?' she asked.

Dalton turned around, a sheet of paper from the fax machine in his hand. 'I needed to show him this, but he wouldn't look,' Dalton said, a sad note to his voice. 'It's one of those missing persons' reports you asked for. I really think maybe Milt needs to see it. Like real bad.'

'What is it?' Holly asked.

Dalton handed Holly the paper. It was a missing person's report, with a picture of the man Dalton had found behind the dumpster at Vern's. 'Oh, you found him!' she said, smiling up at Dalton.

'Read that part,' he said, pointing at a paragraph under the picture.

Holly read aloud, 'Herman Nelson Walker, DOB 12/29/53, Caucasian, male, brown/brown, five foot five, 126 lbs. Reported missing by wife, Deborah Walker. Last seen leaving Brighton, Oregon, for Oklahoma (city un-known) to visit daughter, Rene Walker Hudson. Has not been heard from since 10/14/11.'

'Rene Walker Hudson?' Holly repeated. 'But that's the other Mrs Hudson, right? The youngest one?'

'Yeah, that's why I thought Milt should know, you know? Like there could be a connection?' Dalton surmised.

'Oh, Jesus!' Holly said, running for the radio. 'I think he's headed over there to the cul-de-sac now!' she said, as she grabbed the radio handset and began to call out.

Milt Kovak – Monday
'The DB's who?' I shouted into the radio.

'Rene Hudson's father!' Holly shouted back.

'You gotta be shitting me!'

'Radio protocol, Sheriff!' Holly shouted.

I threw down the radio and picked up my phone and called Jean.

'Y'all still behind locked doors?' I asked quickly.

'I am, but Carol Anne ran over to Rene's house after Bollinger! I couldn't stop her, Milt.'

'Ah, fuck!' I shouted. 'It's not Bollinger! It's Rene!'

Jean McDonnell – Monday
I was yelling, 'What? What?' into the phone, when the door opened and Lynnie, Mary's

oldest daughter, came in with her sisters. I could see the boys heading into Carol Anne's old house. No one, thank God, was going near Rene's.

'Lynnie's here! I'm going over there!' I yelled into the phone. As I hung up, I could hear Milt screaming, 'No!' but ignored it. Turning to the teenager, I said, 'Lynnie, all three babies are in the den. Please watch them. I'll be right back.'

'What's going on?' Lynnie asked, alarmed, no doubt, by what she'd heard me say on the phone. 'Where's Carol Anne?'

'Lock the door behind me! Don't let anyone in except me, Carol Anne, or the sheriff! Do you understand?'

'What—?'

'Do you understand?' I yelled.

'Yes, I understand!' she said, coming up behind me as I rushed, as best I could, out the door. I heard her throw home the dead bolt as I made my way into the street of the cul-de-sac.

I can make good time when I really need to. On a straight course I can go as fast as the average jogger, and it only took a few minutes to make it to the front door of Rene's house. It was the only one-story in the cul-de-sac. A red-brick house with a double front door of glass and hardwood. I tried the front door and it opened. Pushing it forward a crack, I stuck my ear to the door to listen. I could hear voices, but they weren't near the door. I'd never been in Rene's house and didn't know the layout, but I figured they weren't in the front of the house. I slipped through the front door and found myself in a fairly large foyer. In front of me was a rock wall, with openings on either side that led down a step to a living room. Peeking inside I could see that the rock wall was the back of a large fireplace. No one was in the living room.

Halls led off from the rock wall to the left and to the right. Glancing to my right, it looked like bedrooms; to the left was a kitchen on one side, with a formal dining room next to the sunken living room on the other. The voices were coming from the left, from beyond the kitchen and dining room.

I slowly made my way down the hall to the left, staying close to the living-room side, as I could see that the kitchen opened into a family room beyond, and I wanted to stay hidden until I could see what was going on.

As I moved closer, I began to make out the words.

Carol Anne's voice: 'I don't understand!'

Rene's voice: 'I told him! I told him twice – either marry me or I'm telling about Michael! But he kept saying he couldn't! That I was married to Jerry and he couldn't do that!'

Carol Anne's voice: 'But you shot him!'

Rene's voice: 'I didn't mean to! He pulled out this gun and he said, "Just shoot me." He said it would be easier than trying to work out him marrying me! He said he'd rather die than marry me!' I could hear Rene burst into tears.

Through her sobs, I heard her say, 'So I shot him! I didn't mean to! I just – I dunno – did it!'

I moved around the wall to take in the scene in the family room. Carol Anne was standing in front of Rene, who had a gun in her hand; however, the gun was pointed at the floor. Behind Rene lay David Bollinger, bleeding onto the hardwood floor from a wound in his groin. As it was still oozing blood, I knew he was still alive, but for how long I didn't know.

'Rene,' I said quietly, 'just put the gun down.'

Both women turned to look at me. The gun came up in Rene's hand, pointed not at Carol Anne but at me.

'Go away!' Rene shouted. 'Why are you here? Why is everybody ganging up on me?' she shouted, the gun now being pointed at Carol Anne, then at me, then back at Carol Anne. 'I'm just trying to do what's best for my babies! Can't you people see that? Everybody gets mad at me! I'm the one who should be mad! It's not my fault! None of it is! But everybody's gonna blame me! Just like Mary did! It just wasn't right saying it's all my fault! 'Cause it's not!'

'When did Mary blame you?' I asked, trying to cover the sound of the front door opening.

'Just shut up!' she yelled at me, pointing the gun once again exclusively at me. 'You don't have anything to do with this. You're not family!' She turned a pleading look to Carol Anne. 'We're family, Carol Anne, aren't we?'

Carol Anne replied with a tentative, 'Yes.'

'Then you know! Mary could be real bitchy, right? She'd get on your case and just hound you until she got what she wanted, huh?'

'No!' Carol Anne said which, had she asked me, I would have said was the worst possible answer. 'She wasn't like that at all! She knew that you slept with Jerry when you were baby-sitting and that he got you pregnant—'

Rene began to cry again. 'But he didn't. I just told him that. He's a man, so he was too ignorant to notice that I told him I was pregnant two weeks after we had sex.'

Carol Anne lowered herself into a chair, her mouth hanging open. 'So Cheyenne is not Jerry's daughter?'

Rene shook her head.

'She was your daddy's daughter, wasn't she, Rene?' Milt said as he walked into the foyer.

Milt Kovak – Monday

Rene's gun quickly turned on me so I raised my arms.

'Don't you ever say that!' Rene shouted. 'Never ever!'

'I'm trying to work it out in my head, Rene,' I said, hands still in the air. 'I'm thinking your daddy came here looking for you. Maybe to take you and Cheyenne back to Oregon with him?'

Rene didn't answer, just sniffed.

'That's what I think. But he approached Mary first, didn't he? He thought, and maybe rightly so, that when she found out Cheyenne was his child and not Jerry's, that she'd gladly send you and your children packing. Is that right?'

Still no answer, just a steady hand on the gun pointed at my chest.

'Now here's where I get a little fuzzy. How'd you get in Mary's kitchen? I figured your daddy got there sneaking in from the country club entrance and just rang Mary's bell. But did you just come over for a visit, or did Mary call you over after your daddy filled her in? Which was it, Rene?'

Rene took a deep breath and said, 'Mary called me.'

'So you're in the kitchen with your daddy and Mary. Where are your kids?'

'In the family room, in the playpen with Mark.'

'OK. So something happens. I'm not sure which happened first. But I think it was your daddy. He had to say something mean and stupid, right?'

Rene's voice broke on a sob, as she said, 'He said me and Cheyenne were coming home with him, but that my bastard boy should be put in a paper bag and thrown in a river, like a puppy.'

'I don't think I would have liked your daddy,' I said.

'Nobody did,' Rene answered.

'I bet him saying that surprised Mary,' I said.

She shrugged. 'I dunno. I wasn't paying much attention to her.'

I nodded. 'No, I guess not. All your attention must have been on your daddy. What did you do? Did you hit him with something first? There was a knot on his forehead.'

Rene nodded slightly. 'There was a grocery sack, a plastic one, on the counter and I just picked it up and swung it at him. There was a glass bottle in there, juice or something, and he fell down, but he was still talking, still saying ugly hateful things!'

'You had to stop him,' I said. 'What did you do?'

'I had the plastic bag in my hand after the juice bottle fell out. I just took it and covered his face with it and held it there. He kicked a lot. And Mary was screaming at me, pulling at me. But I held it there! I held it until he quit moving! I held it until he was good and dead!' Rene said, a slight sound of triumph in her voice.

'I bet Mary didn't like that,' I said.

Rene sighed and lifted up her arms, with gun in hand, in a sigh of resignation. 'She was going to call the police! She said I *murdered* him! That was justifiable homicide, right, Sheriff? 'Cause if he took me back to Brighton, it would be the same as killing me! And he threatened to kill my baby boy!'

'So you had to stop Mary from calling the police, right?' I said.

'I just grabbed the first thing I saw, which was the meat pounder she was using to fix dinner. I didn't mean to kill her – that was an accident. I just wanted to stop her long enough for us to talk about it. But I think maybe I just hit her in the wrong place,' Rene said, sitting down and dropping the gun on the floor. 'I really didn't mean to kill her.'

Nita Skitteridge, who'd come in behind me, hustled over to Rene and picked up the gun. I waved for her to back off when it looked like she was going to handcuff Rene.

'Did you have help getting your daddy out of Mary's house?' I asked Rene.

'Naw, Daddy's a little man, I weigh more'n him. I just ran and got my car and then dragged him out and put him in the trunk. I knew nobody'd see me, and there wasn't no blood. Kids were all in school, Jerry and Dennis were at work, it was Carol Anne's day to be parent helper at one of the kids' schools, and Mrs Rigsby, she never takes her eyes off the TV during the day. And I waited until late that night when the babies were asleep and I took them out to the car and buckled them in, then drove around looking for a dumpster. I found one and tried to lift Daddy into it, but I couldn't, and the place was a real mess, so I just kinda shoved him behind the dumpster, between it and the fence.'

'You took the children with you to dump your father's body?' Carol Anne said indignantly, standing up.

'Carol Anne...' I said, trying to shut her up.

331

'You killed your own father, you killed Mary, and you exposed your own children to your depravity—'

'Don't you get on your high horse!' Rene shouted back. 'Like you ever welcomed me into this family! You were jealous of me from day one! If you'd ever acted to me like a real sister-wife, maybe none of this woulda happened!'

'You're blaming this on *me*?' Carol Anne shouted then lunged at Rene. Rene lunged back, but Nita Skitteridge managed to get in between.

'Carol Anne!' Jerry shouted, coming in from the garage. 'Let go of her!' he shouted at Nita, grabbing at her left arm, while her right went for the gun riding her hip.

I figured it was time to intervene. So did my wife, who threw a crutch at Jerry before I could join the brouhaha. Jerry grunted and fell on his ass. Nita grabbed his arm and twisted it behind his back.

'Enough!' I shouted as I walked up to them. 'Nita, just stop it. He thought you were hurting Carol Anne—'

'She was!' Carol Anne said. 'When she should've been hurting this little tramp!'

'Who are you calling a tramp, scarecrow!' Rene said as she jumped up on the couch and grabbed a handful of Carol Anne's hair.

Holding his head, which was bleeding a little, Jerry looked at me. 'What's going on?'

'Well, you aren't Cheyenne's father after all,'

I said, speaking loudly to be heard over the screaming of the catfight going on in the center of the room.

'Milt!' my wife screamed. 'Stop them!'

'Sheriff?' Nita Skitteridge asked.

'Huh?' Jerry said.

'Cheyenne is the product of incest, poor darling,' I said. 'Rene's daddy did it. Rene killed her daddy. Unfortunately she did it in front of Mary, who of course was going to do something about it, so Rene killed her too.'

Jerry sat there for a long moment, then said, 'No shit?'

'No shit, Sherlock,' I said.

Jerry's two surviving wives were snatching each other bald-headed and screaming really mean stuff at each other. I sat down to watch, while Jerry watched from his position on the floor.

Jean moved into the room on one crutch, so I said to Jerry, 'Hey, hand my wife her crutch, OK?'

Jerry said, 'Oh, sure,' as he reached behind him at the crutch that had hit him on the head. Stretching, but not getting up, he handed it to Jean. She, in turn, glared at both of us.

Jean walked up to Nita, who was staring at the two combatants. 'Are we going to do something?' Jean asked Nita.

Nita yawned. 'Hell, ma'am, I don't feel like getting scratched. They'll settle down in a minute.'

And Nita was right – they did settle down, but it took more like fifteen minutes.

Milt Kovak – The Weeks Following
Rene pleaded guilty to killing her father and Mary Hudson. The judge, who must've liked cute butts too, gave her a year suspended for killing her daddy, saying the old bastard had it coming, and ten years for killing Mary Hudson, saying it was a crime of passion and mostly an accident. Neither Carol Anne nor myself thought that to be true, but both Jerry and my wife Jean thought it to be so. Chances were good that Rene could be out of jail in five years.

Meanwhile, David Bollinger refused to submit to a paternity test, although anybody with eyes and a smidgeon of scientific knowledge would know that about the whole cleft chin stuff. Carol Anne refused to take in Rene's children, even though all her own children felt they were kin – blood or not – and Jerry was up for it. So since the boys were back in Carol Anne's house, Rene's kids were staying with Dennis Rigsby and his mother. Dennis Rigsby asked Rene to marry him, which they had done by the same judge who sentenced Rene to prison, and Dennis started adoption proceedings for both of Rene's children. It should be final before Rene gets out of prison.

He and his mama are staying in The Branches, in Carol Anne's old house to be close to the prison where Rene will be; meanwhile,

334

Jerry and Carol Anne and all their kids are moving back west. No longer a plural family, they're moving to Salt Lake City and going to be real Mormons, according to Carol Anne. Which means, one of these days, we might see some of the boys riding bicycles and wearing white shirts with ties. It's possible.

It turns out there was never a marriage license filled out for Michael McKinsey and Rachael Owen, so there was no need for Rachael to divorce him. I had the county hire a forensic accountant, who went over the books I found on Michael McKinsey's desk and, sure enough, Rachael would be getting all her money back. Of course that, like Dennis adopting Rene's kids, would work out about the time Rene got out of prison. Meanwhile, Rachael and her kids are moving back to Tyler, Texas and, strangely enough, my good old buddy Roy Donley has decided to relocate his trucking business to east Texas. Go figure.

The two little kids Jean and I rescued from that trailer were placed in the same foster home – a new foster family, a young couple who can't have kids of their own – and the children seem to be thriving, according to CPS. I hear the couple would like to adopt them, but since Charlotta's in the wind, it could be hard to do.

Meanwhile, the VFW's Sadie Hawkins dance is coming up in about a week, and me and Jean are going. It's not that we dance all that much (although we can cut a rug on occasion). Mostly we're going to see how well Dalton does dancing with Holly Humphries. She finally asked him to the dance, once I explained what a Sadie Hawkins dance was. Dalton and Nita Skitteridge practiced at the shop during evening shifts. What I saw was pretty funny, but Nita said he's getting better. Jean and me want to see for ourselves.